JANET PYWELL

Stolen Script

Culture Crime Series - Book 3

First edition

ISBN: 978-1-9998537-1-6

This book was professionally typeset on Reedsy.
Find out more at reedsy.com

For Esther David

Grateful thanks to Salahouris Dimitris and Carmen Cohen,
Director – Jewish Community of Rhodes

Foreword

STOLEN SCRIPT - BOOK 3 - Culture Crime Series.

A deadly game...
**Book three in the Culture Crime Series features uncon-
ventional heroine Mikky dos Santos, a protagonist who is
brilliant, idiosyncratic and who does not always do the right
thing.**

Artist and photographer, Mikky dos Santos is brilliant but
rebellious. After a personal catastrophe in New York she insists
on going to Greece to authenticate a valuable parchment where
she makes a promise to return it to the Jewish museum in
Rhodes. But time is running out and Nikos Pavlides isn't giving
up the Torah easily. He's also hiding a deeper, darker secret
and, as he plays a deadly game, the stakes are raised. Faced
with drug dealers and human traffickers with no regard for life,
Mikky's survival instincts kick in as she uncovers the sordid
reality of the truth and its savage consequences.

Fighting for her life, how will Mikky fulfil her promise? This
enthralling, fast-paced thriller is an emotional roller coaster
of shocking twists and turns...

With a background in travel and a love of and fascination

for other cultures Janet Pywell creates a strong sense of time and place, taking the reader from New York (America), Izmir (Turkey) and Rhodes (Greece) this exciting novel will keep you turning the pages.

Expertly researched, each book in the series gives a harrowing glimpse into the hidden world of violence, greed and jealousy within the arts.

Chapter 1

'Man: a being in search of meaning.' - Plato, Philosopher of the 5th century.

H e watched her skip up the steps and into the marble lobby of the Turkish hotel. She was mid-forties, almost old enough to be his mother but she was still beautiful, long legs, dark hair and olive green eyes. He followed her into the air conditioned reception where she pulled a silk turquoise scarf from her neck and glanced nervously over her shoulder. It wasn't a hotel for tourists or for the numerous foreigners and pilgrims who came to visit the nearby ancient city of Ephesus, the House of the Virgin Mary and the Basilica said to have been built on the site of St. John the Apostle. This was a local hotel - for Turkish businessmen.

The lift doors opened and she stepped inside. Her bodyguard moved to stand behind the colonnade, nearer the reception. He didn't notice the stranger watching them.

Outside the September sun was fiercely intense, over thirty-five degrees, but inside the hotel sounds of Selçuk's busy town were hushed by thick glass doors. Deciding he couldn't take any more chances, the stranger tagged onto a group of departing men leaving the hotel and headed outside to wait.

He found shade under a ficus tree and within a few minutes he had plotted his only option.

He would have to kill them both.

Mariam walked briskly along the corridor, her heels clicking on the cool marble. She checked the room numbers counting in Greek, her native tongue. Her cotton blouse clung to her waist and the belt of her navy trousers felt tight and uncomfortable. She'd left Rhodes on the early boat to Marmaris and after a three hour car journey she was weary but the excitement of her task was far more important than tiredness. The air conditioning was a relief but the smell of olive oil and spices wafting up from the kitchen reminded her she hadn't yet eaten.

Later.

This was her destiny.

Room 2008.

Her hand was shaking and she knocked softly.

A tall slim man with narrow eyes opened the door. He looked behind her checking the empty corridor, then stood aside. His hunched shoulders and his protruding neck reminded her of a tortoise.

'Come in.'

A double bed with its simple cotton duvet took up most of the room. Two wooden chairs and a white table occupied the far corner and heavy green drapes hung at the wide balcony window. In the distance Mariam recognised the Ayasoluk Hill and the partially restored Grand Fortress, a tribute to the Byzantine, Seljuk and Ottoman times, standing proudly and resiliently in the midday heat.

He closed the door carefully behind her and they stood in close proximity and shook hands formally, slightly self-consciously. His hooded grey eyes were grave and solemn as they travelled over her face.

'I'm sorry about the room. It's probably not what you're used to - I hope you weren't followed?'

English was their common language and his apology with a Syrian accent was clipped and strange to her Greek ear.

'No. We were careful.'

'Water?'

He pointed to the minibar but she shook her head.

'Do you have it?' Her tone was brisk and she immediately regretted the impatience of her words but he seemed not to notice. Instead he pointed to the upright cylinder on the chair.

She took a pace forward but felt suddenly dizzy. She frowned and reached out to hold the table.

'It's just a tremor,' he spoke quietly. 'It happened earlier this morning.'

Disoriented she glanced down into the street. Everything was normal. Cars sped along the boulevard, people crossed the road and a dog scurried down the alleyway opposite. She couldn't see the car they had travelled in but she knew Ioannis was waiting for her in the reception.

The man handed her the package. It was heavier than she expected. Probably ten or eleven kilos. She lay it on the bed and pulled on a pair of purple powder-free nitrile gloves she'd bought on the Internet. She prized off the lid and carefully slid out the scroll. She knew that the nine-hundred-year-old Sefer Torah was originally used by Jews from the Iberian Peninsula and she held it reverently in her gloved fingers. It was just over sixty centimetres wide and she guessed it was over thirty metres long. She unfurled the script as far as possible holding her arms wide - enough to study the ancient Hebrew. The text was written on soft lamb or calf skin and carbon testing

3

would have to be carried out but Mariam was convinced that it would show that it dated back to the 11th century. It might be the oldest Torah in the world – older than the scroll recently discovered by Professor Mauro Perani and, like the one he discovered, this one also bore letters and symbols that were forbidden in later scripts.

Mariam was momentarily lost in the enormity of the task she had been given. Although she had studied archaeology this was way beyond her experience. She was humbled but also very excited.

'It has already been verified by a Sofer,' the Syrian whispered.

Mariam nodded. She knew Sofers were Rabbis, experts who evaluated the age and origins of ancient Hebrew scripts.

'It may still have to undergo Carbon-14 dating analysis at the Archaeological Museum in Athens,' she replied as she took her iPhone from her shoulder bag. 'May I?'

He nodded.

She snapped several photographs, making sure she captured the tear on the top right corner and the water mark in the shape of a fat serpent and the faded text beneath it.

The Syrian watched her silently, occasionally glancing down into the street and sometimes dabbing his forehead with a faded handkerchief. His shallow, nervous breathing filled the room.

Mariam attached the images to an email and pressed send. She made sure they were gone before she replaced the iPhone in her bag. Although she took great care, her actions felt clumsy and inept as she rolled up the ancient script and placed it back inside the cylinder. Her hands were shaking as she felt an urgent sense to keep the Torah safe. So many manuscripts had been destroyed. She knew that once a Torah became worn out it lost its holiness and could not be used for religious ceremonies but this one was in very good condition. She was determined to keep it safe. She replaced the lid just as the room shook.

'We must go,' he said, taking her elbow.

Her heart was beating so loudly she thought the Syrian might hear it.

'The donor still wants to remain anonymous?' she asked.

He nodded gravely.

'It's extremely generous.'

The Syrian's hooded eyes closed in agreement. 'But necessary. Too many artefacts from synagogues and churches have been looted. The Islamist organisation in Syria is associated with al-Qaeda and they've taken everything: scrolls, silverware, treasures...' He shook his head and spoke urgently. 'They exchange them for prisoners held by the Assad regime or they sell them for arms or drugs. They have no respect for any religion. I'm pleased that we can save something of value - something of our cultural heritage - that isn't being systematically destroyed. Soon there will be nothing left. What hasn't already been bombed has been vandalised or looted. You know yourself how bad the refugee crisis is in Europe. Greece is just one country that has helped families who have lost everything. The Syrian people have lost their security, their homes, their families. They have nothing. There is nothing left.'

'Tell your donor it will be greatly appreciated.' She took his hand and he gripped her fingers responding to the warm sympathy in her eyes. But just as suddenly he let her go.

'Come, we must move quickly. We both have a long journey

5

ahead of us.'

'You are going back to Syria?'

'I must. It's my home. Leave now. I will follow you down in a few minutes.'

'Take care and thank you.' She forced a smile that crinkled her dark eyes. Carrying the cylinder she slipped into the hotel corridor and walked quickly away knowing she wouldn't feel safe until she was back in Greece.

Downstairs she was reassured to see Ioannis. The young handsome boy in his early twenties with deep set serious eyes and a shaved head took the Torah from her arms just as the ground shook.

'Another earth tremor,' she mumbled. Her knees were shaking but she didn't slow her pace as she followed him outside.

The blinding sun and hot air hit her sharply and she gagged at the oppressive heat. Around her people walked quickly and the traffic flowed smoothly. All seemed relatively normal but she couldn't shake off the feeling of foreboding that encompassed her heart.

She opened the passenger door, climbed inside and Ioannis placed the Torah at her feet. He drove fast, concentrating on the traffic, negotiating the narrow backstreets, his darting blue eyes flicked from the wing mirror to his overhead mirror, constantly checking and monitoring the cars behind. He steered them through the unfamiliar streets and Mariam glanced up periodically from her iPhone keeping an eye on the road ahead.

There was a voicemail from Alexandros.

'I love you, my darling. Hurry home. We all miss you,' he said.

In the background her son Milos called out and although she couldn't decipher his words Mariam smiled. She was heading home, back to Rhodes.

Holding the cylindrical tube upright beside her legs she remembered how she'd met Alexandros on his thirtieth birthday. She was originally from Thessalonika but had been staying in Rhodes with a cousin and, as is the tradition of the island, she had been invited with the townsfolk to his birthday party.

He told her later that she had bewitched him that night. He had loved her at first sight but at nineteen Mariam had never expected to fall in love and certainly not with a man eleven years older. She wanted to go to university and then perhaps - if she had time - maybe one day - she might marry. That night she had wanted to push him away. She had wanted to say come back in six years time, but at that party - that night of his birthday - she knew for certain she would never love anyone else.

They married after she finished her archaeology degree at Athens University and it took eight years for Milos to come along. He was the son they craved and loved. Miraculously, two years later, her Dorika - God's little gift - had arrived. She was nine now, growing up quickly becoming more independent and Mariam felt she wasn't needed as much by her children. Working with Alexandros in his tourist shop didn't inspire her as archaeology once had, so when she was asked to do this job Mariam believed her luck had changed.

The car rattled along the narrow roads weaving away from the town centre and Mariam checked her gold watch. Milos and Dorika would be home from school soon. She imagined them sitting at the kitchen table and bending over their homework. At eleven Milos was already remarkably like his father, tall,

7

wiry, curly haired and easy-going. Dorika was more like her. She had sparkling green eyes and a happy contagious smile. She was affectionate, often climbing onto her lap and giving spontaneous hugs.

'I think there's someone following us,' Ioannis said. 'I'll lose him once we leave the town.' She was his first client. He'd even worn a suit to impress her. On the journey here she had been kind and interested but now he was disconcerted by her silence and the fear behind her eyes.

He glanced again in the mirror. The person following them wasn't even trying to be discreet but Ioannis knew he could look after himself. This is what he was paid to do. This was a much better job and far more lucrative than his normal backstreet work and the gang crime of his violent youth on the streets of Tirana. He'd been fortunate to escape the Mafia Shqiptare and, so far, the other Albanian criminal organisations in Turkey and Greece. He knew how to take care of himself - and her. He would protect her with his life.

Mariam turned in her seat.

'The white Hyundai?'

'Yes.'

She sighed aloud. Who could possibly know she had gone to collect the Torah?

The Syrian lawyer had contacted a well-know expert on scrolls, manuscripts and texts, asking him to help return the nine-hundred-year-old Sefer Torah to the Jewish Museum in Rhodes. After reassurance that the Sefer was the original and that the anonymous donor was authentic, the expert had contacted Mariam.

She had once been a student of Simon Fuller's and they had remained friends. She couldn't believe her luck when he asked her to collect the Torah from Turkey and take it to the Jewish Museum on the island. As a precaution the Syrian had provided her with a bodyguard and chauffeur.

Mariam had been excited but now she was scared. She glanced over her shoulder again and through the dusty back window it was impossible to identify the driver. She could only hope that once they were out of the town Ioannis would lose him.

The sound startled her. The rumbling was like a slow train, a tube train beneath the road, gathering momentum. Violent shuddering cracked one of the apartment buildings and a massive block of concrete slid off smashing onto the road, Ioannis swerved. Telegraph poles swayed dangerously as debris and glass crashed around them. The car in front braked.

Mariam shouted. 'Keep going!'

The ground shook, it was a sea of swells as buildings crumbled and bricks rained down from above. The noise was deafening. Their car rocked and shook and people surged into the street screaming and shouting, their faces filled with fear.

Ioannis negotiated the obstacles, weaving the car between bodies running frantically into the road. Buildings cracked and crumbled and people were hit and crushed by falling rubble.

Glancing in the rear view mirror he saw the Hyundai still following close behind. It struck a man, lifting him into the air and he bounced before rolling into the gutter.

Rocks smashed onto the bonnet and Mariam screamed. The car jolted and a screeching metal cacophony banged in time to the shuddering earth. The road shook violently, the land cracked open, and the tarmac ripped open to expose a lethal chasm. The car hung, mid air, before plunging forward, lurching into the growling, angry earth. Debris smashed around them, crunching the door, the roof and the bonnet. A slab of concrete smashed through the windscreen and flying glass and dust flew into Mariam's eyes.

She screamed as light exploded around her and the breath was thumped from her chest. Glass cut her hands, her legs and her feet as she was tossed like a rag doll coughing and choking. A metal bar from the electricity pole smacked her cheek and her head ricocheted. She was thrust forward, suspended, floating, flying and then came the terrifying explosion. The noise was deafening. Her world convulsing uncontrollably, the earth rattling at its core. Her piercing scream reverberated in her head and she reached out trying to grab anything solid but pain shot through her ribs. Her body collapsed in a dull, irrevocable thud and suddenly everything was still.

Only the earth creaked.

Mariam coughed.

Everything was silent. She thought of Dorika and Milos. She imagined their small hands hooked around her neck and Alexandros' strong arms holding her. Tears streamed down her face, dripping into her dry mouth caked with dusty cement, tasting thickly of iron. Death circled around her. She cried out. She pleaded and begged but the words never left her mouth. Then there were no more tears. Only silent rivulets of blood flowing freely from her face and neck onto the debris and squashed metal of the car, seeping onto the crushed cylinder that lay crumpled in the wreckage beside her.

Ioannis lay trapped. Blood spilled from a deep gash in his forehead. The weight of his body held rigid by an iron bar that had narrowly missed severing his head - the same iron bar that had killed his passenger. After the chaos and fear in the street a strange peacefulness filled his soul - was this death?

Ioannis was conscious of another man's body lying near him. A hand, a foot, the back of a man's head. He must have run from the crumbling building but fell with them into the cracked fissure that split open the road. The heat was unbearable in the trapped space and he was thirsty. He heard him before he felt the stranger's presence. Someone was tossing bricks and cement aside and a crack of light appeared above him causing him to blink at the sudden brightness. A surge of hope filled his senses and as the shadow leaned over him, Ioannis's voice was husky and dry.

'Help me, help the lady...'

The shadowy figure tossed aside broken bricks. He kicked away crushed glass, working silently and methodically, throwing the crumpled steering wheel and other bits of crooked metal to one side. The shadow grunted as he worked, coming closer, working with dedication and purpose. The dark silhouette was nearby when he gave a grunt of satisfaction.

'Help. Her name is Mariam...' Ioannis called.

The heat was suffocating and Ioannis watched through swollen bloodied eyes as the stranger lifted the Torah from the rubble. The stranger brushed dust from the cylinder and moved away, balancing, climbing over the crushed car toward daylight where he lifted himself up onto the broken tarmac and into the direct sunshine.

'Hey, help!' Ioannis called but the stranger was gone.

He had taken the script.

Chapter 2

'Since we cannot change reality, let us change the eyes which see reality.' - Nikos Kazantzakis, Writer of the 20th century.

April.

In the full mirror of the hotel bathroom I'm staring sullenly at St. John the Baptist's severed head across my naked breasts and Salomé's colourful veils wrapped around my waist. It's not the only ink work tattooed on my body but it is the goriest one. I'd insisted upon having it tattooed on my body during a dark period in my life when I was struggling to make sense of a cruel world. Now, although it would be a shame, I'm wondering how painful it would be to get the exquisite artwork removed when Eduardo calls out from the bedroom.

'Hurry up, Mikky. You don't want to be late for your own exhibition....'

I ignore him and turn sideways running my hand over my stomach. It's not as flat as it was a few months ago. Too much sitting around painting. I'm putting on weight. Salomé's dark, watchful, almond eyes are challenging me, daring me to have her removed.

'Mikky?' Eduardo peers around the bathroom door. 'Are you okay?'

'Fine.'

'Nervous?'

'Should I be?' I push past him and pause at the end of the kingsize bed where my cocktail dress is laid out. 'Do I really have to wear this?'

'It's beautiful. Josephine chose it especially. I thought you loved it.'

'At least it's black and the lace will cover some of The Scream.' I look down at my arm and the elongated face that for so many years has mimicked my confusion and turmoil.

'You'll look gorgeous, Mikky. You always do.'

'I need to exercise more. Get training again.' I pat my stomach.

'You've been working hard.'

'Painting is not work.'

Eduardo sighs. He wraps his arms around my waist but I move away from his grasp and he says. 'God, you're a pain, Mikky! If it wasn't for this damn exhibition of yours tonight, I wouldn't put up with you.'

'Yes, you would. You love me, remember?' I throw the dress over my head. 'Zip me up, angel.'

'Please.'

'Please.' I turn my back and he kisses my neck. It sends goose pimples across my shoulders and the tiny hairs on my arms stand tall on my skin. I shudder at his touch and lean back against him, enjoying the muscled hardness of his body. 'I'll be glad when it's all over.'

'Don't say that, Mikky. Enjoy the moment. Relax. Everyone is here for you. They've all come to support you.'

'Javier and Oscar haven't come.' I think of my last phone conversation with them and how apologetic Javier had been.

He had an important commission to finish in Buenos Aires but I'm still peeved that he won't be here - to be part of my success. 'I know, I know, I should feel happy to have all the support of my friends-'

'Yes, you should. Josephine and Simon have flown over from London, Glorietta has even taken a break from her tour of Japan.'

'I can't believe she would do that for me.'

'They love you. We all love you. Even Dolores and Maria have made the journey from Mallorca.'

'I hope they like it. I hope it's worth it.'

'Come on, Mikky. Have a little more faith in yourself. You're very talented and it won't do you any good now to start worrying. They're all here to support you.'

I know he's right. My closest friends and allies are here. My hotchpotch, makeshift family are all waiting downstairs for me but I'm terrified.

'What if it's crap. What if-'

'It won't be.'

'I wish I'd never agreed to this bloody exhibition. I wish Josephine had never talked me into it.'

'Don't be silly,' he says softly.

'I enjoy painting, Eduardo. I've enjoyed being here in New York. It's been good for me. I'm just not sure that I'm ready for, for all of this...' I cast my hand aside at the double aspect opulent bedroom. Our boutique hotel in New York's Soho is only a stroll away from the art gallery hosting the exhibition and a five minute walk from Little Italy and Washington Square Park.

I perch on the edge of the bed thinking of the last few days with everyone gathering in the city. It had been a whirlwind of lunches, dinners, and even a horse and carriage ride around Central Park. Now, tonight is my evening. The event they were all waiting for – the one they had come to see.

'I wish I didn't have to go,' I say. 'Can't they do it all without me?'

'Come on, cariño. Enjoy it. And then when it's all over, we can go back to Mallorca. I've missed you. I'll get you fit again. We can kite-surf, go running and take some time out, although I won't be able to take many more holidays... I've used up almost all my holiday allowance for this year and it's only April.' He frowns and scratches his cheek.

I sometimes forget that Eduardo is an intensive care nurse in Mallorca. He took holiday leave to be with me for two weeks while we arranged the exhibition and I doubt I could have done it without his love and support.

Feeling guilty I turn around and face him.

'I don't want to paint for a while, Eduardo. I need a break. I need to do something different.'

'I understand – and you can, Mikky. You can do whatever you like.' His smile lights up his face and I wonder if it's the thought of me finally moving to Mallorca and I turn away confused by my conflicting emotions. 'But Josephine doesn't understand. She keeps pushing me to do more paintings. She's talking about another exhibition in Vienna. I feel like a prostitute the way she's marketing me.'

'That's not true,' he laughs wrapping me in his arms. 'Josephine is proud of you. It's the art gallery that's promoting you and Miles Davenport believes in you. He agreed to exhibit your work and he has contacts in Austria. He's the PR man behind it all – not Josephine.'

I grunt. I know he's right. I lean against his chest.

'You're nervous and it's understandable–'

'Is it?' I push him away.

'Of course, when any creative person reveals their work to the public they're open to criticism, differences in personal taste, and they're also compared to what's expected in the current market. It's normal, whether you're a composer, a writer or in your case an artist–'

'I should stick to photography.' I pull on my shoes. 'It would be bloody easier than this.'

'You needed to paint, Mikky. After everything you went though in Malaga and losing Carmen. I think it's done you good.'

'Even though I was over here without you for four months?'

'I'm pleased I've been here with you for a few weeks. It's been a very special time in our lives. I love New York - with you.' Eduardo runs fingers through his tousled blond hair and I straighten his patterned tie as he continues. 'You know how much I missed you, Mikky. When you were here and I was in Mallorca, we were so far away from each other but we don't have to be apart again, Mikky. In fact–'

The house phone trills.

He sighs and walks over to the bedside table and lifts the receiver. He listens carefully and then says. 'We're on our way down. Yes, she's ready, we're coming now.'

In the bathroom my hands are shaking. Nausea is growing inside me. I add mascara, purple eyeshadow and pink lipstick. My dark hair has grown and is now curly around my ears. It hangs to my shoulders and I tie it up with a clip.

Eduardo appears in the doorway. 'Simon and Josephine are waiting downstairs. It's showtime Mikky and you must remember to smile.'

I look at his reflection. He's like Adonis personified and I have to block out the images of our earlier love-making and his strong, muscular body on top of mine.

'Do I have to go?'

'Yes.'

'What if they hate me?'

'How could anyone not love you?' he laughs. 'This is the Big Apple, Mikky. It's where dreams are made. Now your dream is about to come true.'

The exhibition is in one of Soho's most prestigious galleries and I'm listed as one of the Emerging Artists. There are three of us: an African-American, a French-Italian and me - Spanish-Irish.

Mohamed's work, Based on Sound, involves the release of paint across the canvas that represents noise, while Antonia's work, Lost, is darker and more intense. It is composed of the confusion of colour, abstract and cubism as if caught in a maze of mystification.

My sinister group of paintings, Ravished, hang on the pristine white walls at the far end of the enormous gallery. It's my first public exhibition and I drift nervously from group to group, smiling and shaking hands with the young and trendy, the Bohemian, old-folk and middle-aged suited types.

I mingle amongst them while also trying to distance myself and pretend they're not sneering at my work. Trying not to imagine overheard conversations as if I'm nothing to do with the paintings. I stand back and try to look at the work objectively, viewing them as a stranger might see them for the first time. But my paintings are dark and morbid. My bleak mood closes in around me covering me in a dark humourless shroud and even Eduardo's optimistic presence at my side, doesn't help.

I grip my glass and drink quickly. Everyone in America looks well-groomed, successful and confident and by comparison I feel drab and awkward. Buckets of iced beer and champagne are constantly refilled by penguin waiters who look like male models earning pocket money on the side from an acting career. I wish I had my camera to snap photographs of the bemused and complex frowns on the faces of the crowd. I wish I had my lens to hide behind.

Josephine links her arm through mine and I'm momentarily startled when she kisses my cheek and whispers. 'Come on, cheer up. This is your night, Mikky. You've worked so hard and I'm very proud of you.'

Not many people know that the once world famous opera singer is my birth mother. Sometimes I hardly believe it myself. I force a smile.

'It's so good to spend time with you again. Thanks for all your support, Josephine,' I say truthfully, hugging her arm.

I've never been able to call her Mama or Mum but she doesn't seem to mind. She has been supportive of me and tolerant of my changing moods as I've grudgingly accepted her into my life.

'It's good to be here with you too, Mikky. You know I love your work. You've grown as an artist and this is your time to shine. This is your night my darling and I can only see success ahead for you.'

Now that we are in America, Josephine's accent seems stronger. She was born here and she moved to New York before leaving at eighteen, venturing to Europe seeking a career as a soprano, never knowing that one day she would become world famous - more well-known than Maria Callas - her idol. And, never knowing that she would give birth to a daughter in London and have her child adopted.

The bristles of Simon's neatly clipped beard tickle my skin as he kisses me and he grins when I rub my cheek and grimace. Simon and I have been friends for over ten years and I'm pleased that he's now in a relationship with my birth mother. I'm delighted to see them both happy. They are well matched: intelligent, calm and dignified.

'You can be honest,' I whisper to him. 'You should be my harshest critic, Simon. You've known me almost longer than anyone else in this room - apart from Dolores.'

'I'm impressed. You've done well, Mikky. Some of them are darker than I thought they'd be but you have a skilful quality to your work that can only be admired.' He smiles but he appears distracted and looks quickly away.

'I love this one,' Dolores says huskily over my shoulder. 'You should be very excited, Mikky. In fact, I'm very proud of you. You were always an excellent student.'

Dolores was my Fine Arts teacher at University in Madrid. There's faint whiff of tobacco from her clothes and I squeeze her arm pleased to have stayed in touch. Happy we are still friends.

'Mikky, over here? There's someone who's dying to meet you...' I'm pulled away by the art gallery's director Miles Davenport to join a group of reporters.

Miles smells of expensive aftershave. He's well-dressed, smooth and confident and in contrast I'm awkward and tongue-tied as I shake the hands of a small group of reporters who have no idea of the emotion I put into my work. They have no concept of the anguish and energy that tore the sadness from my heart and how I painted with fire and vehemence on the canvases. Or, how difficult it was as I relived the horrors of my mind. How the ravaged images and the fragmented torsos reflect the part of my life that I hide and keep separate from my daily life. They're locked in a safe place at the back of my mind. They have no idea of the crimson blood that flows freely in the contours of my mind, mingling with the dust and dirt of back alleyways, the dirty used needles, the scattered white powder and the sordid reality of cheap lives.

For me Ravished is an exhibition of exhaustion, shame, fear and self-loathing. I have opened myself up like a stretching innocent baby, a young virgin or an innocent, pink lamb ready to be slaughtered.

But I'm not.

I'm terrified.

Several critics corner me and I recognise one from a prestigious art magazine and another from a national newspaper. I turn away. I will not interpret my paintings for critics or for art reviewers. I don't care about their magazines or their precious readers.

'Mikky, isn't this all a little dramatic?' asks one columnist with a yellow cravat covering his double chin. He catches my arm and stands in front of me. 'Isn't it a little, over the top, pretentious?'

'Over the top of what?'

'Reality?'

'Ravished isn't about reality.' I pull away.

'Is it supposed to be so dark? It reminds me of Caravaggio - the way you use the light and dark. Were you copying his technique?'

'Many artists use contrasts of light and darkness.' My sarcasm makes another journalist smile. 'You either get my work or you don't.'

'It's all very...staged.' His smile is insincere and it doesn't reach his small eyes. 'They make me quite unsettled – they're violent and dark but they seem...tarnished. The girl tied with a turquoise ribbon is injecting heroin...'

'They're supposed to unsettle you.' I remember witnessing a girl, so stoned she could barely find her vein. It was a split second, a frozen moment in time lodged permanently in the locked drawer of my mind. A snapshot with the lens of my eye.

'And this one? The women's head, she's bleeding, dripping blood onto the floor? Are you trying to shock? What would you say to the audience?'

This has been therapy for me, I've painted what I saw, now it's on record for life and it's not just etched on my brain.

'This is how some people die.'

'It's not just emotion though, is it?'

'It's anything you want it to mean.' I move a few paces away but he calls me back.

'Is that why you painted it – for effect?'

'I paint only for me.'

His laugh is nervously high. 'Is that arrogance or naivety?'

Anger bubbles in the base of my stomach. I want to grab his cravat and take him by the throat. I take a pace forward and he flinches. I stare into his challenging eyes, conscious of the wobbling fat under his chin that he's trying to hide with the yellow silk.

'Call it what you like, you're the critic,' I hiss.

Josephine links her arm through mine and pulls me gently away.

'Excuse me, gentlemen. Sorry to interrupt your debate but there are others waiting. Come on, Mikky, there's someone over here who wants to speak to you.' The once famous opera diva hasn't lost her grace and charisma. Her smile is captivating as she pulls me away and I catch a fleeting glance of the reporter scribbling quickly in his notebook. He has a satisfied smile on his wet lips.

Josephine is adept at handling the press. She has been through a rough time but now she is as revered as she was before her fall from grace in the opera world over five years ago.

Glorietta Bareldo, the world famous soprano who replaced my birth mother on the world stage has caused more heads to turn. I'm sure many of the critics would like to know why two very important and famous opera divas have cancelled their engagements to be with me on this special night.

A reporter is trying to interview her and she responds in perfect English with only the hint of an Italian accent.

'This evening is not about me, you need to speak to Mikky dos Santos. Her work here is truly amazing. I have purchased several of her pieces already and they look exceptional in my villa on Lake Como.'

'See? Watch and learn. You have to charm them, Mikky.' Josephine pulls me aside. 'It's not good to get tetchy and angry. I know you're tired but it's only for one night and remember it's part of the job.'

'He's an obnoxious git and I don't give a sh–'

Josephine squeezes my arm. 'Hello, Miles. I think it's going very well – don't you?'

'There's a good turnout,' he replies, rubbing his palms.

Miles Davenport talked me into this exhibition and he

beams confidently at us and around the room. His expensive beige tailored suit hangs perfectly on his trimmed body. His long trendy beard gives him an authoritative air and his grey inquisitive eyes never stop moving as they take in the important people in the gallery.

'I'm sure many will be sold,' she says.

'I think the reviews will be positive. Glorietta is a crowd-puller, as are you my darling.' He kisses her cheek theatrically. He has hovered around the opera stars all evening as if some of their glitz and glamour will rub off on him, hoping a photographer will snap his pose with the famous ladies.

'But this isn't about us, Miles. This is about Mikky and the other artists.'

'Of course, it is Josephine. It's marvellous. The artists' work compliment each other. Everyone is loving Mohamed's work. He's quite a hit and he's very eloquent with the critics. There's someone I'd like you to meet Josephine.' He waves at someone across the room and I take the opportunity to unhook my arm from hers and I walk away. Dodging small groups, I take refuge from the reporters on the far side of the room where to my surprise Simon Fuller is staring, deeply engrossed, at Bombed.

He is lost in thought and it gives me time to study his profile. He's six foot three and his brown eyes have an unfathomable expression. I wish I had my camera. Bombed shows the devastated body parts of a drinker - viewed by another alcoholic - confused, blurred vision. Blotchy, vague and unreliable.

He is suddenly aware of my presence and he blinks quickly.

'Are you alright, Simon?'

'Hi.'

'Are my gloomy paintings having an effect on you?'

In spite of our thirty year age-gap we are good friends. He's an expert on rare manuscripts and authoritative on just about any antiquities. He's always given me advice and as a lecturer linked to the Museum of London Archaeology - MOLA - he's simply the man I go to when I need answers.

Now as he stands looking vacantly at my painting Simon Fuller seems to be a man who has questions but no answers.

'What's wrong? Is it Josephine?' I ask.

'No.' He scratches his beard.

'Sorry, I had to ask. What is it? Are you worried about going to Ecuador tomorrow?'

'No, not at all.'

'How long will you be there?'

He shrugs. 'Maybe a month. They've found three rare manuscripts and I want to see them 'in situ' before they're removed from the cave in the hills.'

Over my shoulder a crowd moves nearer to us and so by unspoken agreement we move further away.

'Is there a problem?'

He sighs and shoves his hands into his jacket pockets.

'Tell me,' I urge.

'I had a phone call last night from a man who said he's got a nine hundred year-old Torah and he wants me to look at it.'

'Why you? Aren't they normally validated by a Sofer?'

'Usually, yes'

'How do you mean, got it? Is it stolen?' I smile ruefully. Simon knows about my illicit dealings in the past.

'He seems to think it's quite legitimate.'

'He has the provenance?'

'I assume so.'

'So, is that a problem?'

'I don't know but a nine hundred year-old Torah was recently donated to the Jewish Museum in Rhodes. Well, it was going to be a donation to the museum but then the earthquake in Turkey happened and it never got there...'

'The one last September that killed hundreds of people?'

I'd read about the devastation of the Turkish earthquake in the Izmir region and watched television as bodies were pulled from the rubble. It was the worst in hundreds of years. It had a severe effect on Selçuk and the surrounding area. The ancient city of Ephesus and the house where it claimed Mary the mother of Jesus had lived out her days in exile had been seriously damaged. Hundreds had been found dead and thousands made homeless as bridges, viaducts, roads and buildings had collapsed.

He nods.

'Could it be a coincidence? Perhaps it's the same one?' I ask.

'Not many ancient Torah's come to light that often so it's a difficult call.'

'So, what does he want you to do, sell it?'

'He wants me to negotiate a deal with the Archaeology Museum in Athens.'

'He wants to give it to them?'

'I don't think give is the right choice of word.' Simon's deprecating smile is gloomy and I know enough of the underworld, art theft and looting to understand the subtlety in his tone.

'If it's the same one that was in Turkey then wouldn't it belong to the Jewish Museum?'

'Therein lies the problem.' Simon's eyes narrow and he nods over my shoulder. 'I think Josephine is looking for you-'

'But if it is the same one that was lost in the earthquake then how did he get it? Is it his to sell?'

'It's in his possession.' Simon shrugs. 'Without going over there I don't know the entire story or the history of the scroll or even if it is the same one.'

I'm thinking of the provenance for such a document. 'Do you know how he acquired it?'

'He wouldn't say.'

Eduardo appears at my side. 'Cariño, Josephine and Miles are looking for you.' He passes a cold beer to Simon who takes the designer bottle gratefully.

'You'd better go, Mikky,' Simon says.

Eduardo kisses my cheek. 'It's going well, mi amor. Not long now then we can all go to dinner.'

I can't take my eyes from Simon's.

'There's more to this, isn't there?' I insist.

His eyes darken and he nods affirmatively.

'Let's talk later,' I whisper. I squeeze his hand and make my way with Eduardo back to Josephine and the savage reporters, all baring their teeth like greedy hyenas.

Chapter 3

'Nothing exists except atoms and empty space; everything else is just opinion.' - Democritus, Philosopher of the 5th century BC.

O ur round table at the family-run traditional restaurant in Little Italy is busy and noisy. The delicious aromas that fill the intimate dining room have taken away the earlier tension and sickness. Now I'm hungry and I am enticed by the enormous feast spread before us. Thinly sliced carpaccio, bruschetta topped with succulent tomato and sweet smelling basil, garlic and melted cheese, rich pastas and shellfish followed by an assortment of richly topped pizzas.

We drink wine with relish, all talking at once, buoyed up by the excitement of the exhibition. It's also our final night together. We talk over one another's conversations, laughing inappropriately, finishing each others sentences and assuming context. We tease and banter with familiarity and my shoulders relax and I giggle easily.

Our table is probably the noisiest and the most excited in the restaurant. Heads turn to watch us. It's not often that two famous sopranos dine together in public in New York. Surreptitiously, other diners take photos on their iPhones and occasionally Glorietta is approached for a photograph by a blushing fan.

Bruno leads the animated conversation with Dolores's teenage granddaughter Maria. It is her first time travelling outside of Spain and she's beside herself with enthusiasm for America, hanging onto everything she sees and hears. She's even developed a slight twang in her otherwise Spanish-English accent.

'More warder?' she asks lifting a jug.

'More water.' I emphasise the t and laugh. 'You're not American yet.'

'I wanna live here,' she replies.

'Perhaps when you're older,' Dolores interjects.

'It's been a great success,' declares Glorietta as we clink glasses. 'We're so pleased we came over here for it, aren't we Bruno?'

'I love your work. Salud, Mikky,' he says, winking at me.

'It was wonderful, I'm so proud of you,' Josephine adds.

'And I love you, Mikky.' Eduardo places his arm protectively around my shoulder and I lean against his cotton shirt enjoying its softness on my cheek and the warmth of his touch.

Glorietta and Josephine begin making plans for a summer holiday to the villa on Lake Como and Eduardo teases Maria about her accent.

Dolores, my ex art teacher in Madrid who now owns an art gallery in Mallorca brings us up to date with the latest news about Dino Scrugli our friend and philanthropist.

'It said in El Pais, he might be arrested for selling fake artefacts,' she says. 'He's under suspicion...'

'He doesn't seem to be the sort of man who would be involved in that kind of thing,' says Eduardo, although he's still grinning at Maria who can't take her eyes away from the bustle of the restaurant.

'He's not like that,' I agree. 'Josephine knows him very well. He wouldn't be involved in anything illegal.'

'But he didn't know they were fake,' argues Glorietta, cutting into our conversation. 'So, he can't be guilty, can he?'

'He has a duty, as a buyer, to check the paintings' provenance,' counters Dolores. 'We have to be careful of fakers. There are too many forgers who profit from this type of thing.'

Eduardo winks at me and I poke my tongue out at him. It's no secret between this intimate group that I once forged Vermeer's masterpiece The Concert.

'Dino is innocent,' Josephine insists biting into a slice of pizza.

'The problem is that he suspected they were fake and that's why he wanted to get rid of them,' adds Bruno. 'He tried to sell them off before he was implicated and now the Carabinieri are involved-'

'Carabinieri?' asks Maria.

'The Italian police who protect our cultural heritage,' explains Bruno. 'But it had the opposite effect. They swooped down on his place last week. They think he knows more than he is telling them and they want to find out who sold him the paintings.'

'Can't he just tell the police where he got them?' asks Maria.

'It's the most sensible thing to do but sometimes buyers protect their source especially if they suspect that it might have been gained illegally - or looted,' I reply.

'We don't know that's true,' interjects Glorietta.

'It's what the papers say,' Bruno adds.

'I don't believe the press at all,' says Josephine with good reason.

'Nor me,' I add. I'm trying to take my mind off the fact that the early morning papers are due out shortly and the reviews of the exhibition will be published in the art magazines and in particular the Art Review.

'Besides, they're only questioning him at the moment.' Josephine sips her wine. 'There's nothing official yet. It's not as if he's done anything wrong.'

'Do you know who he bought them from?' asks Simon.

'I didn't get a chance to speak to him but I will try and find out.' Josephine rests her hand on Simon's. 'Perhaps we can help him?'

'Let me know and I'll see if I can make some enquiries,' Simon adds.

If anyone knows the art world then it's Simon. He has contacts all over the world and a network of informants. Although he smiles reassuringly at Josephine I can see the worry in his eyes and I think back to our earlier, brief conversation. I assume the phone call about the missing Torah is definitely troubling him and the fact that he's due to fly to Ecuador in the morning is probably not helping.

Dolores says, 'Ever since Steven Drummond was arrested last year, collectors are looking at their own collections and realising that they may have purchased looted or fake paintings.' She glances at me and I smile back. 'I think you opened a can of worms in the art industry and a lot of them are scurrying away and hiding for their lives.'

I was responsible for getting Steven Drummond arrested. A Janus figure who paid local people to loot artefacts from around the world. He bought them for a nominal fee and sold them for a massive profit to the western market through his art galleries.

'Dino's friends are already distancing themselves from him,' Glorietta says. 'Many have turned down his invitation to sail on his yacht this summer.'

'It's a summer tradition and I have already accepted,' replies Josephine. Her dark eyes flash fiercely. 'He can't go to prison. I won't let him. He was the only one who was my friend when I had been abandoned by everyone else. He encouraged me to audition for Tosca when no-one else gave a damn. No-one believed I could make a come back, only Dino. And I don't believe he would deliberately sell anything that wasn't legal. I've known him for years. I've sung on his yacht and we've sailed around the Med many, many times. We must do something to help him.'

'I sailed with him last year but it was on the yacht belonging to an Asian. Who was that businessman, Josephine? I can't remember his name - the one who bought that Picasso last summer?'

Glorietta leans closer to Josephine and their conversation continues and I take the opportunity to sit back and think how lucky I am to have such good friends in my life. I lift my arm to help Bruno refill my wine glass. He is laughing with Eduardo and they are teasing Maria so I lean toward Simon and whisper, 'I've been thinking about what you said.'

He raises his eyebrows.

'And I'd like to help.'

His stares into my eyes.

'I could go to Rhodes for you.'

'And do what?'

I shrug and fold my cotton napkin in neat squares. 'Perhaps I could go over there on your behalf.'

'What would you do?'

31

'See if it's the same Torah. Find out more details...about the provenance. Visit the Jewish Museum. See who it really belongs to...' The thought of doing something other than painting has filled me with enthusiasm and I add. 'I'm ready for a change, Simon. I don't want to paint, not at the moment, and I don't want to photograph stuff for museums or galleries again. I want to do something different. You know me, I need a challenge.'

Simon shakes his head. 'There are people from the archaeological museum who will investigate it all.'

'Oh?' I slump back in my chair disappointed.

'I'm sorry, Mikky.'

'Why are you so sad?'

He barely hesitates before he speaks. 'A woman died. Her name was Mariam. She went to collect the Torah from Turkey. She is - was - my friend and I'm also godfather to their son Milos.'

'Oh no, I'm so sorry, that must be...awful...I don't know what to say.'

Simon's eyes cloud over and he looks away. 'It was my fault. I asked her to go to Turkey and collect it.'

I rest my hand on his and he stares back at me. The pain is so palpable in his eyes I think he might cry so I squeeze his fingers.

'What happened?'

'A Syrian lawyer contacted me last year. He said that a Torah had been found in Syria and it had been validated. His client had bought it and they wanted to donate it to the Museum. He asked me to recommend someone who could get it to the Jewish Museum in Rhodes and of course, I thought of Mariam. She lives - lived on the island. She had also been a student of mine. She studied archaeology but couldn't get a job. It was a coincidence but she had been in touch with me just a few weeks before about doing some work - something from home - something that involved her studies. She wanted to use her experience and this was a perfect opportunity. She was so excited about it. She felt she was finally doing something in the sphere she had trained in...'

'She was killed in the earthquake?'

'She went to the Izmir province to collect it but as they were leaving the town of Selçuk, the earthquake happened.'

'They?'

'The Syrian lawyer hired a bodyguard. They were travelling in the car and the road opened up and she was hit by falling debris.'

'And the Torah?'

He shakes his head. 'It disappeared.'

'And the driver?'

'As far as I can make out he was in hospital. Stuck in the wreck. Then I received this call last night from Elias Pavlides, a businessman on the island of Rhodes, to say he has this Torah.'

'Isn't that a coincidence?'

Simon shrugs so I ask.

'Why did he contact you?'

'Maybe through the museums - I am quite well-known...' His voice trails off and I acknowledge that Simon is the leader in his field. He has travelled and lectured the world over and is renowned for his experience with ancient texts. If anyone was to google an expert on the Internet then Simon's name would at the top.

'So, Mariam went to Izmir to collect the Torah from an unknown and anonymous donor who wanted to donate it to the

Jewish Museum? And now a Torah has turned up six months later. So, this one that Elias - the businessman in Rhodes - has, might or might not be the same Torah?'

'Yes.'

'But what about the benefactor? Surely the anonymous donor has been looking for it? They would want it to go to the Jewish Museum?'

'Yes. I would imagine so.'

'Do you know who the donor is?'

Simon shakes his head. 'I've no idea.'

'None at all?'

'The Syrian lawyer wouldn't reveal his client's name.'

'Who would spend that sort of money on a donation - what would it be worth?'

'Millions.' Simon strokes his beard.

'You wouldn't just let a Torah out of your sight and not investigate to see if it turns up after spending that amount of money, would you? I certainly wouldn't. Can't we look for the donor?'

'I've spent the past few months trying to find out but nothing has materialised. They've covered their tracks.'

'Maybe it's not the same Torah?'

'It can't be a coincidence that two Torahs dating over eight or nine-hundred years old have surfaced on the market within six months,' he replies. 'Both originating from Syria.'

'Both from Syria?' I repeat.

'That's what Elias said, when I pressed him for information. He thinks it came from Syria via Turkey.'

'But you wouldn't know if it's the same one? Unless you went back to the original source who authenticated it and provided the provenance for it.'

34

'We're trying to locate the Syrian lawyer who met Mariam and handed it over to her. We need to tell him that this one has emerged – that way he might reveal who the donor is. But it's very difficult with the war in Syria and all the refugees leaving the country. It's hard to get any information when people are fighting just to stay alive.'

'So what will you do? It's all a dead-end, isn't it? There's no verification or evidence.'

'Just before the earthquake Mariam emailed me photographs from the hotel. She had the Torah with her and she sent me a few images that she took on her iPhone. There are certain marks on the Torah that was donated–'

'Like what?' I can feel my excitement growing. It's like a trickling stream that's turning into a sudden torrent and I feel it creeping up my spine and I wiggle excitedly, closer to him, on my chair.

'There's a specific tear and a water mark in the shape of a–'

Eduardo touches my arm and taps his watch.

'Mikky, the first edition of the newspapers will be printed by now. I'll be back in a few minutes.' He pushes back his chair and the table falls silent. I glance around at the expectant and happy faces and nausea reaches into my soul like an angry fist and rips into my stomach. My excitement is suddenly replaced by cold fear that gushes and corrodes my confidence and the garlic bread I've eaten somersaults into the back of my throat and I choke.

'Champagne,' Bruno calls to the waiter. 'We'd like champagne, we're celebrating!'

I'm distracted by Maria who exclaims with the fake American accent she's adopted. 'Did you see the work of Antonia Latiffe? Her paintings were amazing. I simply love that one called

Finding. It is incredible.'

'I liked it too,' agrees Glorietta. 'It's created an indelible memory on my mind. Her paintings are like...'

But I'm not really listening.

I'm thinking about a woman travelling to Turkey to collect an ancient script and a little boy called Milos, on a Greek island, thousands of kilometres away missing his mummy and knowing she will never come home.

'And what about Milos's father?'

'My good friend Alexandros?'

'Does Alexandros know Elias?'

'He knows him by reputation but they're not friends.'

'Let me go over there, Simon. Give me a copy of the photographs and I can compare it with the one that Elias has. I can find out all the information you need and then pass it on to someone at the museum, anyone you chose in London or in Athens. And, I can visit Alexandros and Milos and make sure they're OK. What do you think?'

Simon is still staring at me as Eduardo dumps an armful of newspapers and magazines on the table. Eager hands reach out and grab them and although my quirky family are supportive and eager I'm suddenly filled with dread.

The headline reads: Han Dynasty Ceramics – Fakes.

I'm mildly aware that having been on loan from a Museum in Greece they are on show in the American Museum of Natural History in New York. But after only one week the American experts are declaring them as a fakes. The lawyers from both countries are in a legal tangle over their immediate return and slanderous accusations.

Josephine reaches for The Art Review and turns the pages quickly, her eyebrows furrow in concentration as she scans the headlines. Although she doesn't speak her lips move in sync with the words on the paper.

Simon leans forward. 'I suppose you could go but what would Eduardo say if you just disappeared?'

I'm watching my birth mother's face turn pale. Her optimistic smile of anticipation fades and it's replaced with a frozen look of complete disbelief and then horror. She looks up and her eyes meet mine. She closes the newspaper and rolls it up in disgust.

My heart seems to stop. I'm unable to move a muscle. Disappointment, resignation, anger - fear - are all bunched up inside me. Confused emotions roll over my body, flattening my happy mood, shattering my confidence and I want to sink to the floor. I'm hot, perspiring and nauseous. I'm weak and I sip water to keep me from fainting.

Rhodes would be the ideal place for me to go. It was calling me, loudly and stubbornly and nothing and nobody was going to stop me.

I had to get away from here.

But it wasn't as simple as that.

My evening didn't have the happy ending as I had thought, imagined or even hoped. Nothing ever works out how you plan or imagine it. No matter how many scenarios I dream up - there's always something, a hiccup, a surprise or subtle shift that makes me wonder why it's worth planning anything at all.

Nothing is ever simple.

Nothing is ever straightforward.

The critics panned my work.

I should have known.

After the furore of disbelief has washed over our table and cries of indignation and anger subside into complacent compliments by my cohorts I'm emotionally washed out. I just want to be on my own. I want to go to bed and bury my head in a pillow. But it's my friends' support and anger that keeps me rooted, stubbornly sitting at the table listing to their indignation and anger on my behalf.

I can't run. I haven't the strength. I listen with only half an ear as if it's happening to someone else.

Glorietta, who has unfurled the paper from Josephine's fingers vows she will never give the man with the yellow cravat another interview in her life. His critique is particularly severe calling my work 'immature and lacking in taste, depth and quality.'

'He's despicable,' she cries.

'He's unnecessary brutal,' Josephine agrees. 'I'll never speak to him again.'

'Inaccurate and illiterate little man,' adds Dolores.

Although I sit at the table, I distance myself from their disappointment and emotion. I float away, lost in the contours and random pathways in my head. I'm behind a cotton veil of softly padded gauze where I can gaze down upon my life as a spectator. I'm protected and unaffected.

This isn't happening to me.

I want to leave - run away but I'm too embarrassed and ashamed to move. I can't face the other diners in the restaurant or anyone at all.

It's Maria's disillusion I find the hardest to accept. Her childish sadness for me and her disenchantment with the reviews cause tears to well up in her eyes. Her previous excitement of New York is dissipated and she stares silently in disbelief at the harsh words, reading them again and again as if trying to make sense of them. Her mouth is moving whispering the words of my disgrace but I look away. When I try to stand my legs wobble. My knees have no strength so I lean against Eduardo. Fortunately he holds onto me but he too is staring at the papers in quiet disbelief.

I think I may be sick.

It's as if it is happening to someone else. They mumble aloud, re-reading the reviews looking for positive words of encouragement, ridiculing the critics and then they toss the papers aside with an air of determined pride protecting me from any more criticism.

More champagne is poured.

Inside my head I am alone.

I know the truth.

They hate my work.

I can't look at Josephine. It had been her idea. She had persuaded me. Along with Miles Davenport, they had insisted that I was good enough but I should have listened to my inner conscience. I had always painted for me and no-one else. It had always been therapeutic and this exhibition had been no exception. The sadness of losing Carmen last summer had been a shock. I had been duped into going to Malaga and deceived into thinking she wanted to renew our friendship and I hadn't been prepared for the events that had transpired.

The source of my creativity and the outpouring of my soul on canvas mixed with the torn emotions of my past life had not been for the public - or to be criticised - they were for me.

I had painted my soul.

The failure of this exhibition was mine.

It was my work.

It was my fault.

I put myself out there to be criticised and I had to take responsibility. I had placed my inner demons on canvas. My nightmares. I had painted Ravished which had not only reflected the trauma of what happened to those around me, it reflected my inner self and my most personal emotions.

I sit feeling stung and rejected. Hurt and torn inside. A part of me wants to crawl away and hide but there's a stubborn side to me that wants to stand on the table and roar with anger. I want to rant and swear. I want to fight and punch and pull the restaurant apart. I hate to be misunderstood and accused of something I haven't done but I know that no amount of shouting or venting my anger will take away these unkind reviews. No-one can take away the numbness spreading through my body. No-one can erase the hurt seeping though my heart and the cold shroud spreading over my body.

Eduardo places his arm around my shoulder and I'm brought back to reality by the softness of his touch and the gentle kiss he places on my temple. My lips quiver, tugging down at the corners and the burning stinging tears behind my eyes threaten to escape but my face remains rigid and impassive.

The waiter pours champagne and there is an awkward silence as Bruno meets Eduardo's gaze. He winks and nods, and Eduardo clears his throat, stands up and begins to speak.

'Tonight is a celebration for us all.' The table falls silent. 'Tonight is a very special occasion. We all know what the press are like. Josephine, you have experienced its negative side, as you have too, Glorietta and you too, Bruno. It is sometimes the price creative people pay to do the things they love the most...' He passes champagne flutes around the table and I am full of admiration at the way he commands attention. He is handsome and confident. He's been my guardian and my lover since he cared for me in the intensive care unit on the island of Mallorca two years ago.

He's simply my angel. I swallow hard, pleased that he is at my side and speaking for me because I cannot speak. My throat is blocked. I'm too frightened to move in case I crumble.

'I'm delighted you're all here tonight. Not just to support Mikky with her exhibition but because, quite simply, we're not just friends – we're all family. As different and as strange as we all are, we love each other and we care for one another.'

The table erupts into a frenzy of clapping, cheering and table thumping and I wipe a tear that escapes and rolls down my chin.

'But this is a special occasion – for another – very important reason.' Eduardo holds up his hand for silence and he turns to me. 'Tonight your family is with you, Mikky. We are all here. We understand the traumas you have suffered and we appreciate you. We understand your art and the work you've put into this exhibition but more importantly, we all love you because you are you. We are here to support you and to care for you – not just tonight – but forever.'

My eyes cloud with tears and I bow my head so that they won't fall in torrents.

He picks up my hand from where it lies listlessly on the table and he kisses my fingers. Then very slowly he moves back his chair and kneels on the floor beside me. His eyes are like violet pools and his smile wavers fleetingly as he pulls a small red, velvet box from his pocket.

'I love you, Mikky and I want us to spend the rest of our lives together. Will you marry me?'

41

Maria gasps.

Glorietta claps.

Bruno laughs.

Simon shouts something and the table erupts into spontaneous applause, cheers and laughter.

Eduardo opens the box and slides the glistening ring onto my finger. Or maybe it's the tears in my eyes that are shining brightly. My vision is blurred. This is not really happening to me. I am floating above them all and the excited commotion at the table is like thunder and I'm underwater where the sound is muffled in my ears and I fear my head may burst with the cacophony of chaos: laughter, applause and shouting. Happiness revolves around the table but inside my head is spinning and I am weakened by the knotted fear growing inside me.

'How delightful,' laughs Glorietta.

'Marvellous,' agrees Josephine.

'Say, yes Mikky,' Maria shouts.

Eduardo wipes away my tears then very gently he kisses me. His lips are soft, warm and comforting and I lean against his shoulder confused by the cascading emotions tumbling inside my head. I bury my face into his neck. I want to stay here forever. I want to lean against him and feel his skin on my cheek and his hand caressing the back of my neck. I don't want to move. I don't have the energy to even look at him.

I wipe my wet cheeks with the back of my hand until Eduardo reaches for a napkin and wipes them gently away for me.

'Speech,' Bruno shouts.

'Has she said yes?' Dolores asks.

'She's wearing his ring,' replies Josephine who circles the table and comes to embrace me. The warmth of her hug and the familiarity of her musky perfume is overpowering and I grip her hands unable to speak. She misinterprets my silence for happiness and she laughs.

Through my hazy tears it's only Simon who regards me silently. He has stayed out of the emotion and appears unmoved by the toasts, laughter and banter around the table.

'Where will you get married?' asks Maria. 'In Palma?'

'Maybe you could get married here in New York?' replies Dolores.

'Or at our villa - in Como in the summer?' suggests Glorietta. 'We can arrange it all, can't we Josephine?'

'STOP!' I shout and in the silence I'm aware that all the diners in the restaurant have fallen silent. Everyone has turned to watch the table with the two world class opera divas. I'm a guppy in a fish bowl. My mouth is moving but there's no sound. I glance around at the smiling expectant faces and suddenly a voice inside of me shouts.

'I can't! I can't do this!' I repeat.

Before Eduardo can reach out or anyone can stop me I run. I push past tables, knock into chairs and send a waiter flying with a silver tray in his hands. There's a cry of surprise and glasses shatter, smashing onto the floor.

I don't wait.

I don't turn around and I certainly don't stop.

The following morning Central Park is in flower. It's the end of April and Spring is on its way and in a few days it will be May. Ripening buds are on the tips of the trees, lilac bushes are flowering and the spring bulbs have been replaced by flowering red and lilac magnolias and beautiful ornamental cherry trees. It's a beautiful city and I love Manhattan but I can't help but feel angry that instead of my dream coming true here, it's been shattered into tiny fragments. Around the long rectangular park, skyscrapers reach into the the sky where fluffy clouds race across a brilliant blue sky. I sit on the bench contemplating their whiteness and silver edges and hug my jacket tighter to my chest, unsure if I am shaking with cold or with sadness.

'I'm not saying no, I'm saying I need more time,' I say.

Eduardo sits beside me. He's told me he's thinking things through and trying to make sense of my actions. His measured tone is calm and reassuring.

'I can't believe you just ran away, Mikky. I just wish you hadn't turned me down in such a humiliating fashion.'

'I'm sorry.'

'I thought it was what you wanted.'

'I was shocked. I never expected it. We've never even discussed marriage.' I try to make my voice sound normal but it comes out like I'm whiney and ungrateful.

'I thought you like spontaneity.' His mouth turns into a bitter smile.

I shiver and hug my arms tighter around my chest. 'Please Eduardo, give me time. I just need to think about it.'

He leans back against the bench and his long legs stretch out across the pathway. He crosses his feet at the ankles and at the same time he folds his arms and sighs heavily. 'How long do you need?'

'I don't know. Let me go to Rhodes...'

'You're running away.'

'I'm not. Simon's asked me to-'

He holds up the palm of his hands. 'I know all about the

Torah. You've talked to me about it through half the night. You seem more excited at the prospect of going to Greece for a few days than a lifetime with me.'

'I'm not, I'm really not.' And as the words spill from my lips I know I'm lying. Although I'm terrified of losing Eduardo, I'm just as frightened of spending my whole life with him. 'Can't we just continue the way we are?'

'I'm thirty-five, Mikky and you are only one year younger. I would like a family-'

'But you never mentioned that-'

'I thought you wanted children? After Josephine found you, you've often talked about what sort of life you would give your children and what you would do. How you would do things differently for your child.'

I gaze up at the sky looking for inspiration, conscious of the scent of lilac on the breeze, ruffling through my hair, colouring my thoughts and emotions.

He's right.

I have thought about it but not just now. Not at this moment in time. It was something in the future to be tackled when I was ready. Now his face is set with determined pride and I know that I've damaged his good intentions and his pride.

'Eduardo, please - give me time...'

'I don't know, Mikky. I don't think I can. It's not just about you. You seem to think it is all a game and nothing is serious.'

I reach out and take his hand. 'It's been so stressful. You know, the exhibition, everyone flying over, wanting it to be a success and then the bad reviews last night. I need time to digest it all. Please, my angel, give me time.'

'You're running away, Mikky.'

'I'm not. I just need some distance and some space. Then

I'll be able to move on–'

'From me?'

'From here–'

'I don't think you know what you do want.' He stands up abruptly and I drop his hand.

'I do,' I argue.

'I proposed to you last night because I want to spend my life with you. I thought it would make you happy but you look thoroughly miserable and so, I think that tells me everything I need to know.' He turns away.

'Please, wait. Eduardo...'

He pauses. 'I can't, Mikky. What's there to wait for? We keep going round in circles. What future could we possibly have together? You won't commit, will you?'

I can't answer him and he shakes his head.

'I just wish I hadn't been so stupid.'

'Where are you going?' I call.

'Home,' he shouts back but he doesn't turn around. 'Alone!'

I'm in London and waiting to board my flight to Rhodes when Simon phones me. He's already arrived in Ecuador and he sounds tired and the connection is poor. I press the phone to my ear, concentrating on his crackled and fading voice.

'I've emailed Stelios, he's my contact at the National Archaeological Museum in Athens. He'll meet you in Rhodes,' he says.

'I don't need a chaperone.'

'He will be in charge.'

'I thought I was doing this alone.'

'You can't do everything, Mikky. Alexandros replied to my

email and he's going to meet you when you arrive at the hotel. And check your emails, I've sent you the images Mariam took of the Torah. If you look carefully in the top right hand corner there's a watermark and a small tear. But it might be even more damaged by the earthquake. Stelios will take it back to the Archaeological Museum in Athens if necessary. If he thinks there's any chance it's legitimate, he will arrange for a Sofer to evaluate the Hebrew writing. If it's a fake then you can both walk away.'

'Mariam didn't tell Alexandros who the anonymous donor was?' I ask.

'She didn't know. Neither of us did. Only the Syrian lawyer was in touch with his client. We're trying to contact him. Look, it might be difficult for me to get Wifi here or any sort of phone connection. But stay in touch, Mikky. Don't look for any problems. Work with Stelios. Take a look at the Torah and see if you think it's the same one. You have a good eye for detail. If it is, then we can take things from there.'

Three hours later an announcement from the flight deck tells us we will soon be landing. I stow my table and check my seatbelt. Below us, the coastline of Turkey is hazy. As the plane makes a steep right turn over the coastline of Rhodes I catch a glimpse of the cruise ships in the harbour and the row of hotels along the shoreline. The blue sky and the glimmer of the shimmering sea below radiates warmth and a tingle of excitement ripples through my body. It's as far away as I can get from New York and I breathe a sigh of excited contentment.

Although I've been to a few Greek islands I've never been to Rhodes. While I was waiting for my flight I googled information about the island. It has a population of one hundred and twenty thousand people, sixty thousand of whom live in Rhodes town. As the plane descends I imagine the people below me leading their ordinary lives: shopping, working, laughing, worrying, and I wonder what the next few days will bring. Perhaps I'll have time for a little sightseeing. It's eighty-five kilometres in length and thirty-five kilometres wide so I could easily rent a car and as the plane touches down I am wondering what it would be like to live here.

Could I be happy in Greece?

Could I be happy anywhere?

Just thinking of my last night in New York fills me with unease and my stomach churns. I've been trying to block out Josephine's worried eyes and the feeling of nausea that has been with me since that awful night. Eduardo's words go around in my head. 'Are you happy with me? Do you really love me?'

I had avoided answering him but now, as the aircraft brakes the question continues to revolve in my head like a beacon, a flashlight in the dark, a lighthouse in a storm. I look down at the ring on my finger, a set of simple diamonds set in white gold that he insisted I keep.

Why didn't he mention it to me first instead of springing the surprise in front of everyone?

We'd never discussed marriage, children, family, the future - nothing. Nothing serious and nothing deep and meaningful. Perhaps maybe in passing, as couples do, in the hypothetical context when they talk about the future but nothing definite or defined.

There was no reason for him to think marriage was what I wanted - was there?

I hadn't replied to his question.

I was happy - so why do I feel like this?

The puzzling question still nags at me and occupies my mind as I disembark, collect my suitcase and find a taxi. In the back of the car I feel a little sick so I wind down the window and the rush of air and the sharp aroma of olives fills the small space. I'm lost in thought, absorbed in a maze of questions as I gaze out at rows of neat olive trees and sleepy villages, half-finished buildings, newly painted apartments and hotels set in tropical gardens.

Happy?

Eduardo loves me.

Eduardo proposed.

In theory, this should be one of the happiest times in my life. What's wrong with me?

Of course, I'm not happy. Can't he bloody see that? I'm angry. I'm very, very angry.

Chapter 4

'I don't need a friend who changes when I change and who nods when I nod; my shadow does that much better.' - Plutarch, Historian of the 1st century BC.

The Palace Hotel is situated on the north coast between the airport and Rhodes old town only twenty minutes from the airport. My first impression is that it looks like an Italian villa not too dissimilar from Glorietta's mansion on Lake Como. It's neo-classical and has three floors with closed wooden shutters, long windows and Juliet balconies. Wide stone steps lead to an imposing front door and interior glass doors open automatically as a bellboy in a brown uniform appears with a wide and welcoming smile.

Inside, the cool reception is filled with assorted colourful vases and fresh flowers. An eclectic mixture of paintings adorn the walls; landscapes of the island, local village people going about their daily tasks, fishing, farming and collecting olives. Lead and bronze sculptures of athletic bodies belonging to mythical Greek gods are poised on mahogany tables. To the right of the reception is a lounge area with white sofas and low coffee tables and against the far wall is a long bar. At the far end, an open glass door leads to a terrace balcony with deep-seated chairs where a few guests are already drinking mid-day cocktails. On the hazy horizon the panoramic view stretches across the sea to the shimmering Turkish hills.

It reminds me of a private house and then I'm distracted by a waiter offering me a warm towel and a welcome glass of freshly squeezed lemon.

Check-in is quick and I follow the smiling bellboy along the wide, opulent corridors. It appears there are two modern wings built on either side of the main building and I am shown to the one on the right. It's surrounded by a beautiful garden with colourful roses where birds sing and whistle from the trees in greeting and I feel the stress of the past few days beginning to leave my shoulders.

The large bedroom, on the first floor, has giant windows overlooking the sparkling sea. A bowl of fruit and an ice bucket with cold wine and water accompanied by a hand-written note from the management, presumably Arianna the Manager wishes me a pleasant stay.

I kick off my boots and pull my T-shirt over my head. I need a shower but I haven't even reached the bathroom when the phone beside the bed rings.

'Hello.'

'Mikky dos Santos? It's Elias Pavlides,' he growls in good English. 'Welcome to Rhodes and we wish you a pleasant stay here at the Hotel Palacio. I hope you find your room comfortable?'

'Thank you, yes.'

'Did you have a good flight? I'm so sorry I wasn't able to meet you in person but family commitments have made it impossible for me today.'

His charm throws me. 'That's fine, Elias. It's no problem.'

'I'm sure you will be jet-lagged. I normally sleep for a few days when I get back from America,' he chuckles and launches into an account of the places he's visited and the hotels he likes best.

I sit on the edge of the bed concentrating on his voice, blocking out my own memories of New York.

'Is this your first visit to Rhodes?' he says eventually.

'Yes.'

'I'd like to welcome you properly. We're having a party. It's my daughter's engagement party. We had to postpone it last year as unfortunately my wife's mother died last August. But today is the day. We're celebrating and the whole town is coming – I think.' His laugh is a deep rumble. 'Well, so Athena, my wife, has told me. It's our tradition here to invite everyone.'

I laugh with him and sit on the bed and wiggle my painted toes, listening to his deep melodic voice. It washes over me and my mood is suddenly lighter and the thought of a party fills me with pleasure.

'My nephew Nikos is here. He is the one who has the Torah so you can meet him and also a man from the National Archaeological Museum in Athens. I think you might know him?'

'Stelios?'

'That's right. He arrived earlier this morning. If you come to the reception when you are ready, someone will bring you along to the party.'

'Is it here in the hotel?'

'Of course, in the other wing to where you are staying. The music has already begun.'

'Thank you, Elias.'

When I hang up my mood has changed. The gloom is lifting. Elias is friendly and amiable. It's his nephew who has the

52

Torah and I think perhaps if I see it tomorrow, the job will be done. A few days sightseeing around the island will do me good. There may even be time for some kitesurfing and I'm beginning to wish I'd brought my own gear. Gazing out of the window, it dawns on me that I will have time to think about the future. I'll have time to reflect and find out what it is that I'm looking for. Why am I so afraid and not ecstatically happy and doodling his name on the hotel paper, entwining it with my own name with large red love hearts?

I pull on a robe and sit on the balcony with my feet on the glass table. I'm staring out to sea but I don't have the answer. It's too soon, I decide. Eventually I rally myself. Too much introspection isn't good for me. I take a quick shower, pull on a red print dress and slip my arms into my black leather jacket. I add purple lipstick, large gold earrings and I pull the bedroom door closed behind me.

Outside, near the reception, I pause long enough to gaze across the manicured gardens, the sea and the hazy outline of the Turkish coast. In the distance a gust of laughter and a blast of Greek music floats across the garden but I turn away from the gaiety and head to the bar where I'm meeting Alexandros, Simon Fuller's friend, Mariam's husband.

I glance down at my left hand.

It's bare.

My diamond engagement ring is locked firmly in the hotel safe.

Alexandros has craggy features, a large nose and wide mouth. He looks older than he probably is and I put this down to the recent trauma of losing his wife. He stands up and holds out his hand. His handshake is gentle and firm. There is an aura of vulnerability to him and his eyes are so dark and sad that I want to reach out and hug him.

I'm not used to children. I only know Maria – but she's a confident teenager and when I last saw her a few days ago, in New York, she still had the hint of an American accent.

So, I'm not prepared for Alexandros's son Milos. His eleven year-old frank appraisal makes me wish I could photograph his inquisitive gaze. He stands stoically at his father's side mimicking his father's good manners and firm handshake but he also has the same sad eyes, curly hair and hesitant smile.

What I'm not prepared for are the pretty almond green eyes of a beautiful little girl.

'This is Dorika,' Alexandros says, placing his hand on her shoulder and giving her a gentle nudge forward.

In my head I'm cursing Simon. He never mentioned Mariam had a daughter and I feel unprepared and inadequate. Seeing her so defenceless brings tears to my eyes and I bend down and hold out my hand.

'Dorika, that's a pretty name. What does it mean?'

I think of myself at her age in a bewildering world, confused, growing up, coping with life – also with sadness. Her hand is tiny and her fingers are loose in my hand. She could be me.

Her green eyes show a glimmer of a sparkle but it fades suddenly as she looks up at her father. When he nods and smiles encouragingly she whispers in English, 'God's little gift.'

'How lovely,' I reply.

I can't take my eyes from her anxious face and the dark rings around her eyes. She moves to stand beside her father and she grips his hand, appearing bemused and shy, and I have a sudden urge to photograph her lost expression and to capture the sadness showing on her face. My heart somersaults as I imagine how happy she once must have been. I want to allay her fears and comfort her. I want to protect her and to help them but I can't bring Mariam back. I can't revive their mother.

'You're very pretty,' I say.

'She's the image of Mariam – her mother.' Alexandros's voice is husky and he coughs to clear his throat. 'They're both like Mariam.'

Milos stands a little straighter and his father ruffles his curly hair.

'How old are you, Dorika?'

'Nine.'

I smile. 'That's a pretty dress you have on.'

'Red is mummy's favourite colour.'

'Really? I love red too.'

She smiles. Her eyes are trusting and thoughtful and she replies, 'I also like purple and green.'

'They're good colours too. I bet you like drawing, do you? I used to love painting at your age.'

'I like reading.'

'I like reading too.'

'And writing.'

'Me too.'

'I write to Mummy sometimes.' She glances up at her father. 'Papa says it's ok to write to her and we put them in a special box.'

'What a lovely idea.'

'Did you know her?'

'No, I didn't but perhaps you'd like to tell me about her?'

Dorika looks at her father again and he smiles and places his arm on her shoulder and says.

'Will we go and get a cold drink? Would you like a nice lemonade outside on the terrace?'

'That sounds fantastic,' I reply and as we walk outside to the terrace Dorika slips her small hand in mine and I squeeze it and wink down at her.

While we order our drinks Alexandros explains to the children that I'm a friend of Uncle Simon's so I show them photographs of him on my iPhone.

'They were taken in New York two days ago.' I'm pleased that it is beginning to seem a long time ago.

'He's grown a beard,' Milos says.

'Do you think it suits him?' I ask.

'It's okay.'

'You'll probably have one, one day,' I smile.

Milos rubs his chin and shakes his head seriously. 'No.'

He makes us laugh and I'm overwhelmed with a sense of family unity, their closeness and love, and the warmth between them saddens me.

Dorika wrinkles up her nose. 'Uncle Simon lives in Canterbury. Can we visit you when we come to England?' she asks.

'I don't live in England but you can come to Spain to visit me.'

'Is that where you live?'

I nod.

'Can I, Papa?' she asks.

'Perhaps you would all like to come one day?' I say.

Dorika wiggles to sit closer to me. 'Are you married? Have you got a family?'

Her feet don't reach the floor and the skin from her thigh is soft against my leg as she swings her feet back and forth.

I pause. 'No, I haven't.'

She strokes the back of my hand and traces the ragged scar. 'We're only half a family without mummy but it's better than no family at all. What about children? Have you got any?'

'No - no, not yet.'

'Why?' This time it's Milos who frowns at me and I stare at him.

'You shouldn't ask questions-'

'It's ok, Alexandros. It's fine.' I hold up my hand. 'Because, I'm not sure...perhaps because I haven't found the right man to be the father yet.'

'Why?'

'Daddy says everyone needs someone special and...'

Alexandros interrupts her. 'Children, enough questions! Do you want to look around the garden together? Finish your drinks and have a wander by the pool. Stay together and don't make any noise as other people are on holiday and are relaxing and want to be quiet.' Alexandros speaks to them sternly in Greek and I'm grateful to him. Their questions were rapid fire and I'm left reeling inside and confused.

Dorika concentrates on sucking her straw until the ice cubes rattle in the bottom of the glass, slurping until her drink is finished. I remember doing the same myself and I watch the intensity on her face. The concentration of sucking up the last drop from the glass. When she's finished she jumps up and Milos takes her hand and they go running down the steps.

'I've told them they can walk around the garden and go down to the sea but they must stay together,' Alexandros tells me.

We watch them for a few minutes until I say. 'Simon is very sorry he's not able to come over here himself. He feels so responsible for what happened. He blames himself.'

I let the silence lapse between us, waiting and wondering if he will reply. Eventually and with hesitation he says. 'I blamed him. I did at first. It was hard not to. He was the one that phoned up with this idea. He was the one who asked her to go to Turkey. I thought we were happy. I thought Mariam was happy but when Simon phoned...it was what she loved to do ...something involving the past, history, a legacy - archaeology. She loved it. She became a different person. During the two weeks it took for the arrangements to be made she came to life again. She was happy. She was somehow younger like she was when I met her. She was filled with vitality and purpose.'

'That was a good thing?' I ask gently.

He sighs. 'In some ways, yes. I was pleased for her but in another way I felt jealous, confused. I thought I'd somehow failed her-'

'You?'

'I am, was, eleven years older. She met me just before she enrolled at University and I guess a part of me secretly felt that I was holding her career back. She had plans to travel, work on excavations around the world, be involved in the discovery of history. Don't get me wrong, she loved us more than anything. The children were very special to her and we had a loving relationship but I always felt that she had never truly fulfilled her potential - working in our shop. It was such a different life to the one she had studied for-'

'She chose you.' I lean forward but I don't take my eyes from his face.

'I know.'

'She made her choice.'

He nods and bites his lower lip, so I continue speaking.

'Simon is so sorry. If he'd known, he would never have

suggested that she go-'

'I know that now.'

'He wanted to be here. He wanted to fly over and see you. You know, after the phone call he got last week about the Torah.'

Alexandros rubs his forehead. 'He flew over for her funeral last September but we were in a bad place. He tried to talk to me but I was angry. We didn't get a chance to speak properly and I was probably quite rude to him.'

'Simon doesn't think like that. He understands your hurt and your loss. If it wasn't for this project in Ecuador he would be here instead of me. It's all happened at the last moment.'

'I understand. I know how busy Simon's life can be. I met him over twenty years ago on one of those rare moments when he was on holiday. I was fishing off the rocks near where we live, near Lindos, and Mariam brought down a picnic to watch the sunset. I asked him to join us. It turned out that he had lectured at the University in Athens. By coincidence, Mariam had attended one of his lectures and he was enough of a gentleman to pretend he remembered her in class. We enjoyed each other's company and we ate with him most nights on that holiday. Afterwards we stayed in touch and then we visited him in England when he lived in Oxford and then Cambridge. We've also visited him after he moved to Canterbury. Milos loves going to England. He likes the London open bus tours and Dorika loves the shops - she loves clothes. She doesn't shop as much now as she used to of course, Mariam and Dorika used to disappear for hours in Canterbury,' he smiles.

'Then that's why they speak such good English.'

'They learn it in school too. They're clever children. Fortunately they take after their mother. Mariam was an exceptional person. She was devoted to the Jewish cause and when Simon asked her to collect the Torah, she was so...happy.'

'The Torah was a donation, wasn't it.'

'Presumably, there was a benefactor. It was all arranged through a Syrian lawyer.'

'Was Mariam a Jew?'

He shakes his head and reaches inside his jacket for an old leather wallet and he removes a photograph. Mariam has rich, dark hair and the same olive green colour is reflected in her daughter's eyes. Milos has an arm around his father's neck and his mouth is open wide in a captivating grin. It's a natural pose, a split moment in time: happiness and grief fill my heart.

How will they ever move on?

How do you heal a broken family?

Alexandros continues talking. 'Mariam was interested in all religions but she felt a special affinity for the Jews on the island. At the beginning of World War Two there were over one thousand eight hundred Jews living here. At first the Germans took no notice but then one day a German officer turned up and said that all the Jewish men over sixteen had to turn up with their identity and work permits. The Jews thought they had work for them but it was a trick. Once they got them all in one place, they told the men they had twenty-four hours for their wives and families to join them. They had to have all their belongings with them or they would be shot. There was terrible brutality... and plundering... and they were deported. Some died of thirst or hunger on the journey and the rest of them were killed in Auschwitz. Only a few survived after the war.'

He slides the family photograph back into his wallet. Silence hangs between us like a flimsy curtain drifting and floating, hanging memories between the past and the present.

'It's hard to imagine the suffering of so many people. It's a generation ago but no-one can forget the sheer horror and terror of what these people suffered. They were duped.' He spreads his big hands. 'And I'm afraid it might happen again.'

'What?'

'I'm afraid that we're being duped about this Torah.'

'In what way?'

'Simon told me that Elias Pavlides contacted the Archaeological Museum in Athens. He had heard about a Torah being donated to the Jewish Museum.' He puffs out his cheeks as he exhales. 'It's too much of a coincidence, don't you think? And I don't trust him. Well, it's not so much him as his nephew, Nikos. He's from Athens and by all accounts he's basking in the limelight of his uncle's business success.'

'Do you know them well?'

'Only by reputation.' He looks around the hotel. 'Elias has done well. He works hard. He has several hotels on the island and he is quite successful.'

'How did Elias acquire the Torah?'

Alexandros shrugs. 'That's the problem. I don't know.'

'Does he know that Mariam went to Turkey to get the Torah last September?'

He shrugs. 'I haven't spoken to Elias. It's Simon who told me that Elias had contacted him and wanted his help but I can't help thinking it's strange that there are two ancient Torahs in the space of six months turning up.'

'I agree.' Milos and Dorika wander across the lawn and down to the beach like two lost orphans. I remember my own upbringing and I have a sudden urge to protect the two children who stare out to sea, unspeaking and holding hands, looking toward the hazy Turkish hills and the country where their mother died.

It's then that I realise the extent of my determination. I will not let Mariam have died in vain or her death go unnoticed or unrewarded. She had a mission: to collect the Torah and bring it back to this island, and like a champion running the relay with the Olympic torch, I will pick up her challenge and finish the race.

Alexandros is staring at me as the children return to us. Milos sits beside his father while to my surprise and delight, Dorika snuggles up beside me. I put my arm around her shoulder and she wiggles closer to me, tracing the drawing of the anguished face and colourful Scream on my arm.

'This is pretty,' she mumbles, her breath is sweet against my skin.

'Thank you.'

'Can I have a tattoo, Papa?'

'Perhaps when you are older.' He smiles indulgently at his daughter then pulls Milos into a manly hug and the boy smiles up at him. For a split second I have a sudden image of what it might be like to be married and have children and I swallow hard.

'Did you and Papa finish your chat?' Milos asks.

'Are you going to help us?' Dorika's intense green eyes are inches away from mine and she frowns.

'I'm going to try my best,' I whisper

'Can you bring mummy back?'

'I'm sorry, sweetie. I can't do that. But I can take over the job that mummy was doing and I can finish it for her.' I don't add that I will do it in her name and for her children; for their sad faces. For the fragility of Milos who pretends to be a man and God's little gift, the green-eyed beauty, Dorika.

'Will anything happen to you?' Milos gives me a hard stare.

'I'll be fine.'

'You know that mummy was bringing a special scroll called a Torah to the museum,' Alexandros explains. 'Well, Mikky is going to see if the one that's turned up here on the island; the one I told you about; is the same one that mummy went to get in Turkey.'

'How?' asks Milos.

'I have the photographs that Mariam, your mummy, sent to Uncle Simon and when I compare them I should know if it's the same one or not.'

'That's clever,' says Milos looking up for reassurance from his father.

'And what if it is?' Dorika is unsmiling.

'I'll know more after I've seen it and if it is the same Torah then I will return it to the Jewish Museum.'

'Really?'

'I promise you.' This is the most solemn oath I have ever made.

'Can I come with you?' she asks. 'Can we get it together?'

I shake my head.

'Mummy was going to let us,' she adds.

I look questioningly at Alexandros and he explains.

'We were going to meet her off the ferry and take the Torah to the museum together - as a family.'

'But Mummy didn't come back.' Dorika pushes her way onto my lap and I put my arms around her. She smells of fresh air and sunshine. I can't speak. My throat is tight and my voice is a hoarse when I say:

'Well, perhaps when I get it back we could all take it to the museum together, would you like that?'

Her eyes are radiant and she hugs me tightly and nods her nose up and down against my neck.

'And what if it's not the same one?' Milos asks, distracting me from Dorika's affection.

'Then we will still have to establish it's authenticity anyway,' I reply with confidence.

'We?' asks Alexandros.

'The National Archaeological Museum in Athens is sending someone over. Simon is putting me in contact with him.'

He sighs and shakes his head. 'I doubt it will be that straight forward.'

'Why?'

'If by chance, it is the same one, I can't imagine Elias Pavlides or his nephew giving it up that easily.'

'He'll have to. I will have proof. I know what the one Mariam had looks like.'

Alexandros' laugh is hollow and mirthless. 'I doubt that will make any difference to them at all.'

It's mid-afternoon when I make my way to the discreet hotel wing on the far side of the building. Long tables with white linen cloths and a vast array of drinks and food are laid out under an awning of twisted vines. The shade is a welcome relief to the mid afternoon sun and a sweet aroma hangs in the air. A beautiful lawn, bordered with red and pink rose bushes, dumpy pineapple-looking palm trees and tall cypress tress line the garden and, a narrow wooden platform leads to a small and secluded shingle beach.

It's perfect.

I breathe in salty sea air and move into the sunshine, relishing the warmth on my face watching two dancing butterflies; cabbage whites. They flutter past me acting out their own wedding dance and I think of my own spontaneous and surprising engagement party last Friday night - only two days ago. My heart sinks.

Hotel staff in white shirts dodge between guests balancing silver trays and I take a glass of chilled wine. My emotions juggling with the disparity of locations: from a city that never sleeps to the warmth of a remote Greek island in the Mediterranean. It's like jumping from an icy bath into the arms of a warm lover and when the pianist at an electronic keyboard serenades guests with a medley of Elton John's classics and couples begin to sway in time to the music on the floor, I decide I will enjoy myself.

I will have fun.

A man with a handsome square face and long salt and pepper wavy hair that settles on the collar of his open-necked shirt, greets me and kisses me on both cheeks.

'Mikky? I'm Elias. Delighted to meet you.' His hand is warm and trusting on my arm.

'Thank you for inviting me.'

We spend a few minutes discussing my journey then he says. 'I want you to enjoy your visit with us. Please eat in the dining room and drink at the bar - don't worry about the bill - you are our guest. Just be happy here on our island.'

'Thank you, that's very generous...'

He waves away my words. 'Here's my wife - Athena.'

Athena is tall and like him, she is slim and dark. Her features are more angular and her cheekbones prominent making her eyes appear tired but she smiles happily.

'You're very welcome, Mikky. It's a pleasure to meet you.'

'This is your daughter's engagement party? It looks as if the whole island has turned up.'

She laughs with me and pretends to look pensive.

'Probably! It's the custom here in Greece. We invite everyone.' She waves a hand then sees someone she recognises and calls something back in Greek.

'That's my daughter over there, Arianna and her partner Michalis.' She points to a pretty girl in her late twenties hanging onto the arm of a tanned boy, equally as good-looking.

'They look like they're in love.'

'I hope they are,' she laughs. 'They are getting married later in the year.'

'Sorry, I didn't mean to say that aloud. Have they known each other long?'

She gives me a strange look and squeezes my arm affectionately. 'All their lives. They grew up together.'

'Wow. That's amazing.'

'Do you find that strange?'

'I was brought up in Spain. My parents were like nomads and we went from place to place-'

'So you never had the benefit of all of this?' She casts her arms wide and I laugh with her. 'All the crazy neighbours, family, cousins and villagers.'

'Unfortunately, no.'

'In the Greek language the word for stranger and guest is the same. But beware, although we ask you into our homes we will ask a lot of questions. So be prepared. Rhodes is a very special island. We still have many traditions from the old Greece that don't exist elsewhere on the other islands-'

Elias calls out and beckons to someone over my shoulder.

'Stelios, come, over here and meet our guest, Mikky dos Santos.'

Athena drifts away to speak to a couple behind me and a tall, lanky boy with red hair tied in a pony-tail and a long straggly beard detaches himself from a small group.

'Do you know each other?' Elias asks.

'Only by an introductory email from Simon Fuller,' he replies, shaking my hand. 'I'm Stelios, from the National Archaeological Museum in Athens. Good to meet you, Mikky.'

Looking closely at him I realise he is older than I initially thought. He's nearer my age, and his English is spoken with an American accent.

'Simon spoke very highly of you,' I reply and when he blushes I realise I'd like to take his photograph. His eyes are grey and his hair, in the sunlight is like rich copper. His beard makes him look like a beach bum, a hippy or an eccentric professor. 'Your English is very good.'

'I studied archaeology at Colombia University in New York for a year - specialising in historical documents.'

I gasp at the mention of the city that now haunts me and the exhibition that will forever be my nightmare but the attention is no longer focused on me as Elias slaps the back of a short, strong muscular man about my age whose eyes are like dark chestnuts.

'And this is Nikos, my nephew.'

Nikos greets me as if he's known me all my life. He pulls me into a hug and kisses my cheeks. His lips are firm and I feel the heat of his gaze as he pulls away. He's smiling and his eyes travel appreciatively over my body sending a shiver of warmth along the inside of my thighs.

67

'It's good to meet you, Mikky – and to have you and Stelios both here. Thanks for coming to Rhodes,' he says.

'I'm looking forward to seeing the Torah,' I reply. 'When can I see it?'

He smiles and then he's distracted and he disappears as quickly as he arrived, swept away in a Greek conversation, drawn away by other guests and I'm left alone standing beside Stelios. Although I'm tall, he's a head taller than me and when he speaks I have to twist my neck to look up at him.

'Have you been to Rhodes before?' he asks.

'Never. Do you know the island well?'

'I'm from Athens but we spent summers here as children. My Aunt had a house in Lindos in the south and I loved it – still do. I much prefer it to Athens but you have to go where there is work.'

'Archaeology?'

'That's right.'

'There must be lots of work here.'

He frowns. 'No, not really. Most of the islanders live off the land, growing olives or from tourists. You wouldn't believe the amount of Greeks who study for a professional career but then return to their native island and run a shop or restaurant or take over the family business. It happens all the time and not just archaeology. Most waiters, tour guides or airport workers are trained accountants or lawyers. There is not enough work on the island in these areas.'

'So why do they come back?'

Stelios stares down at me and says simply. 'It's their home. It's where their family lives.'

I'm distracted by the engaged couple entwined to the music. They dance as if they have been together all their lives. His hand cups hers and his other hand, in the middle of her back, guides her gracefully across the floor. I smile and imagine them still dancing like that in fifty years time.

'Elias and Athena's daughter never left the island though? It seems like they grew up together.'

'She might have studied in Athens or somewhere but they always come back. It happens on the islands. You'll probably find that Athena and Elias knew each other when they were young too. It's what happens here. Greeks like to stay near their families - it's what we do.'

I imagine a nation of Greeks who go to foreign cities to study and then want to return home. I can't imagine wanting to stay always in the same place but having spoken to Alexandros and meeting Milos and Dorika and now experiencing this warm welcome at the party I am beginning to understand it differently. I always wanted to know where I came from and where my roots belonged. How different my life might have been if I'd grown up here.

'Are all engagement parties like this?' I ask Stelios to take my mind off the unsettling questions stirring in my head about my own life.

'Mostly, they're all on different scales but normally it doesn't matter how poor you are, you invite the whole village to celebrate. These people know the families of both the future bride and groom. They've been neighbours and friends for years. Obviously this family is very wealthy and can afford to throw a big party but some are much smaller-'

'It's a beautiful hotel, Elias owns it, doesn't he?'

'Not any more.'

'Really? Why?'

'It's their daughter's dowry.'

'Her what?'

Stelios laughs at my reaction and replaces the empty glass in my hand with a fresh one from a passing waiter.

'Don't look so shocked, Mikky.'

'Is it an arranged marriage?'

Stelios laughs louder. 'Of course not, can't you see the couple are in love?' He nods across the room to where they stand laughing with a younger group of people. I have watched them circulate the room talking to everyone and I wish, not for the first time, that I had my camera with me. 'A dowry – is what they do here. It's an old tradition and is no longer upheld by the law but it still happens. Each family provides a dowry for their daughter. Have you not noticed the unfinished buildings on the island?'

I think of my drive from the airport. I had noticed many unfinished blocks and I was surprised at the number of buildings that were unpainted. Some were habitable on the ground floor but the floors above were an empty shell.

Stelios continues explaining. 'Apart from not paying taxes until the building is finished, they are left unfinished until the family has enough money for the dowry and then it's given to the daughter. She moves in with her husband and they look after the parents as they get older.'

I must look surprised for he laughs and continues speaking.

'Families look after their own so that grandparents, as they get older, have company and are cared for in their later years. I think there is only one small private care home on the island. Everyone looks after their parents as they get older that's why families are so close here and–'

'But what happens if you don't get on?' I ask thinking of my own family.

70

'They do.'

'But what happens if you can't afford a dowry?'

He shrugs. 'Everyone manages somehow. I've heard of some parents even moving out of their own house and renting another home near to the home they own. They then give the house they own to their daughter.'

'They give everything away just to be looked after.'

'That's a cynical way to look at life.'

'What if you have five daughters?' I ask.

'Then it's best to stop after two children or hope for a son,' he smiles.

'And the money goes to the daughter - not to the man she marries?'

'Exactly.'

'And what happens if they want a divorce? What happens if she wants to leave him?'

'Are you always this pessimistic?'

'I call it practical. Does it get signed over to the husband?'

'Not at all. It stays with the daughter. In Greece we are allowed three marriages by the church - although not all at the same time,' he laughs.

There's a gentleness to his character and this makes me feel safe and protected and I am happy to talk to him and let him explain life here.

'So the dowry for Elias and Athena's daughter is...'

'This hotel,' he finishes for me.

'Oh my goodness. But what will happen to it? Will she run it?'

'They have three hotels; one in Lindos, another larger one just along the coast, and this one. It's the smallest one and Arianna already runs it. She's been the manager for a few years.'

I remember the hand-written note in my room and I stare at the happy girl wondering how a person so young could manage such a big responsibility; a hotel with over one hundred rooms, the catering, the housekeeping, and the staff.

'Are you shocked?' Stelios smiles down at me.

'What about her husband?'

'Michalis runs a local garage. It's a family business too.'

'So in theory, the dowry happens throughout the island and not just amongst wealthy families.'

'On Rhodes yes. It's still a tradition but not law.'

I am lost in thought and I gaze out to sea thinking of Eduardo. What if we had both been born here. Would our destinies have been entwined? Would we be happy to accept a dowry from my birth mother?

I never knew my father and this family life is so far removed from my own that when Stelios begins a conversation with a couple beside us I move away to think.

My life wasn't simple. The couple who adopted me when I was a few hours old would never have been so conscientious as to provide for me. They could barely look after themselves as they dragged me around Spain each year looking for work.

Papa drank himself into unconsciousness and gambled what little money he earned doing meagre jobs and my mother had countless affairs and was possessed most of the time by jealous anger. I had never known security and comfort such as this.

Suddenly, feeling the warmth and kindness from strangers on this island I'm overwhelmed with a sharp pang of loss. I'd not experienced this whilst growing up and yet here it was in abundance.

I glance over at Stelios. His smile is warm and charming.

He's finished his conversation and he moves toward me handing me another glass of chilled wine and guides me toward the table. 'I don't know about you but I'm really hungry. Come, we'll sit here.'

Spicy aromas fill my senses and the stomach churning and nausea of the past few days begin to recede as my appetite returns. My shoulders relax and I sit down and sigh happily. This will do me good, I say to myself, this will heal me from all of the stress and disappointment in New York.

'Salud!' I say, raising my glass to touch his and when he smiles back at me I'm already feeling very much at home.

Chapter 5

'Small opportunities are often the beginning of great enterprises.' - Demosthenes, Orator of the 4th century BC.

I'm not sure if it's a late lunch or early dinner – all I know is that the food is exquisite. I sit under the shade beside Stelios eating an assortment of shellfish and then marinated roasted lamb with onions, rich tomatoes and thick juices. I've been introduced to so many people that I have lost track of their names and who they are.

The excellent food and jet-lag from New York has made me weary. The wine that had at first energised me is now making me a little sleepy and I rest my chin on my hand looking at Stelios. He hasn't left my side and I find him an interesting companion. He carries on the conversation with other people at the table. Some of them assume we are a couple and I'm too tired tell them the truth. He seems to think it funny.

Athena was right.

The Greeks are inquisitive. We don't tell them we are here to see the Torah. We both pretend we are on holiday, visiting the island and we are vague about our connection to the Pavlides family. As it's my first time here they list the places that I must visit on the island starting with Rhodes old town.

I'm disappointed not to have brought my camera down from my hotel room and so I idly snap images of the guests using my iPhone. Some of the faces are like road maps with deep tracks at the corner of their mouths or tramlines across their forehead. The traces of their lives etched fully upon their skin. Others are youthful and attractive. Probably friends of the engaged couple. In contrast they have their lives ahead of them and their eyes reflect the excitement and enthusiasm of youth. They're all fashionable and look quite similar. The girls have long hair, soft skin and legs that seem to go on forever and the boys are tanned, confident and tall.

I don't fit into either age group and I wonder how they see me or even if they see me at all. Feeling slightly tipsy I snap images of the guests until Stelios leans closer to me.

'So, how did you meet Simon Fuller?'

I toy with my iPhone as I answer. 'We've known each other for years. I met him when I was at University in Madrid - studying art. He's now the partner of a very good friend of mine, Josephine Lavelle.'

Stelios raises his eyebrows. 'The opera singer - the famous soprano?'

'Do you know her?' I put my iPhone away and make an effort to sit up straight.

'My parents were her greatest fans. She sang in Athens many times and although I was young they took me with them. In fact, I think Elias and Athena met her once.'

'It must have been years ago, she hasn't sung since her accident several years ago.'

'She was very popular in Greece. Perhaps more famous than Maria Callas. So, Simon and Josephine are together in a relationship?' he asks.

'Yes, since last year.'

'I'm pleased. I always thought Simon was a loner.'

'Me too but they seem to get on well. They're very happy. How well do you know this family? Have you known Elias long?' I deflect his interest. I don't want to discuss my birth mother or her relationship with Simon with a man I met only a few hours ago.

'I've met Elias a few times. He's very well respected on the island and he's a shrewd businessman but I only met Arianna and Michalis today.'

'And his nephew - Nikos?' I glance down the table to where Nikos is sitting with an attractive girl with long dark hair. She has pale skin and bright blue eyes and it strikes me that she's not Greek. I raise my iPhone and take several snapshots of them. She is laughing. Her head is thrown back and he pulls her to him. When he kisses her lips he is looking over her shoulder at me.

I turn away and focus on Stelios as he speaks.

'Nikos lives - or lived - in Athens but I don't know him at all. Presumably he's been here a few months. He's helping out in one of the hotels. It's probably something to do with Arianna going on her honeymoon. They delayed the engagement party last year because of a death in the family-'

'Athena's mother?'

'That's right, she died last year. Athena was very upset so they put everything on hold. But I think the wedding will be quite soon now, probably later in the year. Perhaps you will be invited back to it,' he laughs.

'Back? Who says I'm ever leaving, Stelios? I'm beginning to feel very happy here. They'll need a good lawyer to make me leave the island.'

After the meal tables and chairs are spontaneously rearranged as neighbours and friends gossip together. I don't feel excluded and I'm happy to watch. I'm a spectator. A little drunk but contented. I stand up to wander toward the sea but Elias pulls out a seat and calls me to his table.

'Have you settled into the hotel?'

'Thank you, yes. It's absolutely beautiful,' I answer truthfully.

'It's my favourite. I brought the building back in the 90s during the recession.'

'I love the Italian neo-classical style. It's very classy.'

The wine and champagne combined with my jet-lag have loosened my tongue but I'm conscious to try not to slur my words. Instead I sip water and sit straighter in my chair.

Elias's voice is deep and it reminds me of a growling lion.

'I'm very fortunate that Rhodes is such a beautiful island. Things haven't been easy in recent years but we've managed the recession quite well. It's been a rocky road and they say that we're still not out of it yet. But I can't complain. We're doing well and tourists keep coming back here.'

'I'm not surprised. I haven't seen much of it yet but Rhodes seems a beautiful island.'

'It is. Thank you.' He places his arm across the back of my chair and waves at a guest across the room. 'I was born here and I'm very proud of all this. This day is very special to us and all our friends are here to celebrate. Today, I'm a very happy man.'

I smile and he says, 'Mikky? That's an unusual name.'

'It's short for Michaela - it's Irish.'

'But you're not Irish?'

'I was born in London but I was brought up in Spain.' I

give him a brief synopsis of my life, conscious that Stelios has moved his chair closer to us. I don't tell Elias the details about my adoption or the sordid details of my past. I tell him I'm a photographer and artist but I don't mention my unsuccessful art exhibition only last Friday - two days ago. It's now beginning to feel like a distant memory. A hazy recollection. Neither do I mention my quirky family or even my own proposal from Eduardo two nights ago.

I'm lost in thought when Stelios says to him: 'Mikky knows Josephine Lavelle.'

'Really? The opera star? We met her once, years ago. Arianna was quite small and we were invited on a yacht by an Italian businessman-'

'Dino Scrugli?'

'Yes, I think that was his name. He was very nice, very hospitable and we met Josephine then. She sang on the yacht and we had a wonderful time.'

'She is Simon Fuller's partner,' Stelios says.

I bristle at Stelios, annoyed that he is telling Elias these intimate details about my life and the people I love as if they're from some popular soap opera on television.

'Really?' Elias's face lights up. 'I haven't met Simon yet but he was recommended to me when I made enquiries,' he lowers his voice. 'You know, when I needed information about the Torah. They said that he would be the man to verify it, although it's only since then, that I realise we'll need a Scribe who can interpret ancient Hebrew. Are you a specialist in scrolls and manuscripts?' he asks.

'Simon insisted that I come over and look at it,' I reply avoiding his question.

'I fear you've had a wasted journey, Mikky.' Elias must see

the surprise on my face but he continues speaking seriously. 'Stelios is here now. So there's really no point in you getting involved. He will sort it all out. I'm sorry you had a wasted journey.'

'Simon asked me specifically to see it. I have travelled all the way from New York.' My voice sounds whiney and I lean forward to sip water before I add. 'I must see it.'

'Well, maybe but it's not necessary now.'

I sip more water and think quickly.

'Perhaps I could have a look at it with Stelios? There aren't many Torah's that old in the world and I would value the opportunity to look at it.'

'I wouldn't like to waste any more of your time. You might as well take a holiday while you're here and relax and enjoy a break.'

'My time isn't wasted – but it would be if I didn't see it, now that I've come all this way.'

Elias shrugs. 'Of course. I'm sorry, I must apologise for my rudeness. You've come from America and I've been extremely inhospitable, forgive me. I will tell Nikos you want to see it.'

'Nikos?'

'Yes, he owns it. I'm just the gofer who's arranged for you to see it.'

Athena calls over to us. She is swaying to the music and wants to dance so Elias stands up and as he walks past us he pats Stelios' shoulder and smiles conspiratorially.

'Have fun, you two.'

After he leaves I turn to Stelios.

'What the bloody hell was all that about? I need to see the Torah too, Stelios,' I say angrily.

'Leave it to me, I'll speak to Nikos and arrange something.'

79

'Can I come with you?'

'Of course. Otherwise Simon wouldn't forgive me.'

After the strange conversation with Elias I'm feeling marginalised and slightly drunk. I venture inside the hotel to the toilet where I focus on my reflection in the bathroom mirror. The circles under my glazed eyes look worse under the light and I add purple lipstick giving colour to my pale face.

I'm not in a hurry to return to the party so I pause in the hotel bar. Though the panoramic window the sunset fills the sky with warm rich hues of lilacs, pinks and oranges. I think I might get my camera but I know that if I go to my room I will fall asleep immediately and not come back to the party.

I think of Alexandros and Milos and Dorika and how we sat drinking lemonade only a few hours ago and I'm suddenly filled with a reckless desire to enjoy myself. To relax where no-one knows me, where I'm not watched and no-one cares about my art exhibition or my engagement and more importantly no-one expects anything from me.

I want to live. I want to be free. I want some fun.

It's warm inside and I so remove my jacket and sit near the window relishing the peace and quiet and staring at the sunset. Several guests are outside on the terrace and I hear whispers of their conversations in German and snatches of Dutch and French.

I close my eyes allowing the flow of their soft languages to wash over me when a hand touches my knee. I jump, startled.

'Mikky dos Santos. Are you sleeping?'

'What?' I sit up straight.

'Please tell me you're not English. I don't believe you could be with your beautiful features - you must be European.' Nikos moves closer to me on the sofa. He doesn't remove his hand while I rearrange my dress and even then it's with reluctance. I'm surprised but not annoyed at his casual warmth.

His eyes rest on Edvard Munch's Scream wrapped around my arm. 'That's some tattoo.' He lifts my arm and leans forward to peer more closely at the drawing and then he kisses my hand. I pull away and drag my jacket over my shoulders.

'Don't get dressed for me,' he adds smiling.

When I don't reply he adds.

'So, where do you come from?'

'I was born in England but I was brought up in Spain.'

'I can see you're a woman who has travelled.'

'Really?'

'You have a certain confidence that you carry like an aura. You're intelligent and well-travelled. I like that in a woman...'

'Too much flattery.' I hold up my hand.

'I mean it. You're different.'

I shake my head and move to stand up but he takes my fingers and his grip is surprisingly gentle.

'You remind me of someone and I can't think who?'

'That's an old line.'

'I mean it.' He looks rejected. My photographer's eye takes in the details of his demeanour. He's younger than me by probably a few years. He's maybe thirty, short but broad shouldered with an aquiline nose and strong jaw. His dark eyes crinkle with devilish intensity as he sits close to me with his arm on the back of the sofa resting his fingers behind my neck. Even though he's not touching me it's surprisingly erotic.

'There's some interesting art work here.' I nod at the array of paintings on the walls and lean forward away from his aura.

'You want to see art? I'll show you, come with me.'

Before I can resist, Nikos takes my hand and lifts me to my feet. He guides me across the room and I'm ushered with practised ease toward a closed door near the reception. Nikos calls out to the receptionist: 'I'm going to show her our family jewels.'

She waves, laughs and carries on looking at her paperwork.

Nikos opens the door to what seems is an old colonial library. It is like stepping back in time. Walls are lined with bookcases stuffed with rows and rows of ancient books, there are glass display cases and cabinets and green deep-seated leather sofas. Like a private club.

Nikos closes the door behind us.

'This is the library for our Gold Members. Guests can come here and relax. There's an honesty bar. Have a look around and take your time. I'm not in a hurry. It's lovely to be with the prettiest girl at the party,' he sighs dramatically. 'What a bunch of old fossils they are - not in the display cases - I mean those old codgers out there dancing on the terrace. God! They wouldn't know how to have fun if it bit them on the arse-'

'They're not all old,' I protest.

'Have a look around at the art in here, Mikky. Tell me what you think.' He pours whiskey from a decanter and hands me a glass like it's a challenge. I match his stare and when his fingers linger against mine, it's fleeting but I know it's intentional.

I take the drink and move away wondering why he's so magnetic and why his powerful energy draws me to him. He's not thoughtful and calm like Stelios or powerful and strong like Elias. But there's something that is dangerously fascinating about him, a recklessness that he plays on. It's as if he's testing me. Teasing me.

Cautiously I walk slowly around the room admiring the displayed artefacts. There's nothing expensive, strange or startling. In fact it's a mediocre collection and not really that interesting but I feign surprise over a jade bowl with a Chinese design. I feel it has been placed there deliberately as the most valuable item in the room but surely this family couldn't be so naive to think these objects have much value?

'What do you think?' he insists standing beside me. 'See this old thing?' He lifts the lid of a display cabinet and picks up a golden pocket watch on a chain. 'This is what I like the most. I haven't time for all these grand paintings of the island they've put on the walls. I'm sure they're important but this watch was given to my great-grandfather by the reigning Ottoman Emperor and see this...' He walks over to the far side of the room and picks up a rich tapestry the size of a dinner plate. 'This was made by my great-grand Aunt. It's these things I treasure, Mikky. Does that make sense to you? It's the personal things, the family heirlooms that are important. I don't want expensive paintings by some crusty old artist-'

'But you do have a nine-hundred year-old Torah.'

He stares at me and then breaks into a wide grin. 'You certainly don't hold back, do you?'

'Where did you get it?'

'I bought it.'

'Who from?'

'Someone you wouldn't know.'

'How much?'

He laughs. 'That's tantamount to asking someone's wealth.'

'Why did you buy it?'

'It seemed the right thing to do.'

'So, who did you buy it from?'

He walks slowly toward me, deliberately focusing on my mouth and I think he will kiss me but he places his index finger gently on my lips.

'Too many questions,' he whispers.

The alcohol is sweet on his breath and there are black flecks in his chestnut eyes.

'Not enough answers,' I whisper back.

His tone changes and he turns away. 'Have you met anyone else since you've been here apart from that boring archaeologist?'

'Stelios isn't boring–'

'Come on, you can't be on your own the whole night. This is supposed to be an engagement party and it's been a long time coming, one delay after another. So we might as well enjoy it now.'

'I thought it was delayed because Athena's mother died.'

'She did. But for heaven's sake, you can't mourn forever, can you? That was last summer her mother died but Athena kept postponing the whole thing.'

'Maybe she was upset?'

'The old woman couldn't live for ever.'

'It's still her mother.'

'But then she found another excuse and another. It's not fair on the living.'

'Do you mean on Arianna?'

'Well, I don't particularly like the girl. She's spoilt. She's a jumped-up self-important brat but she didn't deserve to have it postponed like that. Elias overindulges her but he's a softie at heart and it sometimes makes me wonder how he's done so well in business.'

'He's giving the hotel away,' I say, referring to Arianna's dowry.

'So rumour has it.' He frowns, takes my arm and guides me to the door. 'Now let's get back to the party and have some fun. You need to get away from Stelios. That bean-pole hardly knows how to put one foot in front of the other let alone whip you around the dance floor.'

'I don't need whipping,' I giggle and as we reach the door Nikos spins me around and I'm suddenly in his arms. Although he is shorter than me I'm aware of his muscled body pressing against mine and I hold my breath and gaze into his dark intense eyes.

'You're a spirited woman, Mikky. I like that. Now, don't disappear too early. I want my dance with you,' he whispers.

Before I can push him away he places a brief kiss on my lips, squeezes my bottom and ushers me out of the room toward the music and excitement of the engagement party.

I'm tired, jet-lagged but I'm having fun. I'm dancing with anyone who asks me. I'm whisked from one dancing partner to another. I love rock music, Queens of the Stone Age, Led Zeppelin, Foo Fighters but tonight on this island - I feel different. The music is melodic and my mood is mellow and carefree. The stress from New York is dissipating and although I love the city I'm experiencing a new sense of freedom. For six months I've been painting, walking, dreaming, sleeping and living in my head. Living with the demons and the fragments of my tortured mind. Reliving the horrors of the past. Only the occasional visit from Josephine and a quick break at Christmas broke my self-imposed solitude and although I enjoyed the intensity of painting, my only regret is the exhibition.

Now as I whirl on the dance floor, my eye is my camera lens. Flashes and snatches of people, their expressions, actions, laughter and movements are all rapid images in my mind.

I flop down at our table and drink water, gasping for breath and giggling as a man plays the bouzouki. The Greek men stand and the music starts slowly and I have a vague recollection of a film.

'Zorba the Greek,' Athena whispers sliding into the seat beside me. 'Anthony Quinn?'

I giggle. 'How did you know what I was thinking?'

'I could see it in your eyes.'

The music gets faster and the men, bob and turn, each action seems regal and well measured. Nikos, Elias, Michalis and tall Stelios at the end.

Afterwards I applaud wildly, placing my fingers in my mouth and whistling. Beside me Athena and Arianna laugh and clap. The music changes and the pianist sings REM's Everybody Hurts.

Nikos is suddenly beside me and he pulls me into his arms and we are swaying together with the other couples. He's murmuring in my ear and my arms are around his neck.

'I've been waiting to dance with you all evening,' he whispers.

I sigh and say nothing. There's a distant hazy recollection of a promise to Eduardo and I make a mental note to phone him before I go to sleep.

Nikos's thumb travels slowly down my spine sending a tingling sensation between my thighs. 'Come with me tomorrow.'

'Where to?'

'I'll take you out on my boat. I'll show you the island. We

can swim in a beautiful bay and get to know each other.'

'I want to see the Torah.'

'Afterwards.'

Very slowly he spins me around, under his raised arm and back to his chest. In my head I'm singing the lyrics: Everybody hurts... Sometimes.

I want to cry.

'I'll pick you up at ten.'

'What about your girlfriend?'

'I don't have a girlfriend.'

'Who was the girl at the table nibbling your ear over the meal?'

'Just a friend.' He pulls gently on my wrists pulling me closer until his body is pushed hard against mine. He's not even trying to hide his erection and when I pull away he laughs. 'Come on, Mikky.' He holds me tightly. 'It's not as if you're a virgin, is it? So it's a bit late to start acting like one. Do you have any idea how sexy you are?'

He plants a kiss below the lobe of my ear and it sends a shiver of excitement through my entire body. I want to ask him about the Torah but for some reason my mind is blank. I'm just enjoying the moment.

I should go to bed but the party is in full swing. I dance with Elias, a few neighbours and cousins and then Michalis. Afterwards when he dances with Arianna my mood turns melancholy and I try not to think of Eduardo.

Suddenly I want to be alone. I've been drinking all afternoon and evening and now I'm tired but too wired to go to my room and sleep. I also want to live and breathe and enjoy this feeling of liberty. I drift away from the party, slip off my shoes and tiptoe unsteadily along the wooden walk-way past the illuminated shrubs toward the beach. The sea is calling me. The cool breeze is clearing my head and the half moon is sinking lazily over the water. I sit on the bottom step; in the shadows; that lead to the beach and I'm inhaling the salty air when a small, urgent voice comes from my left.

I tilt my head to listen. The voice is carried on the wind; a whisper, a cry?

I freeze, listening intently, remaining motionless as another muted wail follows.

'Hello?' I call.

I rise unsteadily from the step and shuffle toward the row of cane sun umbrellas planted in the sand. I tread on a sharp pebble, almost topple over and curse loudly.

Someone is slumped over a beach bed. Long hair covers her face and her dress is awry revealing long thighs and a round pert bottom. Her large breasts reveal a deep cleavage.

I collapse and kneel drunkenly in the sand beside her.

'Are you alright?' I ask, sweeping her long hair from her face. She groans so I hold her shoulders and try to lift her upright. 'Hey? Do you feel ok?'

Her chin is square and her cheeks bones prominent and when she opens her pale blue eyes I realise she's the girl who was with Nikos during the meal. She looks Eastern European. She's young. She looks lost. Abandoned. Bewildered. Stoned.

I want to take her photograph.

'Come on. I'll help you up.' I try to stand and pull her to her feet but she's a dead weight.

She flings an arm out to steady herself and that's when I see the punctures and bruises in the crook of her elbow. A scarf is tied around her bicep and there's a needle at her feet.

'Cristina?' A woman's voice from behind us calls out.

I don't know enough Greek to understand the rest of what she says but I hear the urgency in the woman's voice. 'Cristina?'

I reply in English. 'She's over here. I think we need some help.'

I move away from under the umbrella to stand in the moonlight so the stranger can see me. I smile gratefully and speak quickly as she draws closer.

'I think we might need an ambulance,' I say.

The girl who appears out of the shadows is angry. Her hair is scraped tightly into a bun and she wears thick glasses and has a big nose.

'Get out of my way.'

'She's ill.' I know I'm slurring my words.

'Go away. I'll look after her. Go back to the party.'

She lifts the girl's arm and places it over her shoulder then she bends her knees to lift the girl onto her back.

'Let me help.' I wobble forward and hold the foreigner's face in my hands. 'She's beautiful but she's very young. She's ill. I thinks she's injected herself...'

'Leave her alone!' The Greek girl hisses angrily. A volley of rapid Greek. It doesn't sound friendly or kind and I back away and stumble. Losing my balance I fall onto the sun-bed.

'Oops.'

'You're drunk,' she hisses. 'Get away from us.'

I am about to disagree with her and tell her that I'm not drunk just very tired and jet-lagged. I want to tell her I've flown over from New York and that I went via London and the journey took ages and I've been invited to this magnificent party on this beautiful island where everyone is so friendly and kind but when I look up she's gone.

I watch her dragging the sick girl along the beach and away from the party.

'That wasn't very friendly,' I say aloud and when I look down at the sand and the shingle between my painted toes I realise, even in my drunken state, that the needle has also disappeared.

Chapter 6

'He who steals a little steals with the same wish as he who steals much, but with less power.' - Plato, Philosopher of the 5th century BC.

I lay on the sun-bed in the dark and wait until my dizziness has passed, trying to make sense of what happened. A kaleidoscope of emotions washes through me and I close my eyes disturbed by the sight of the young girl. I've been around drugs and I know their awful power.

I block out past images and resolutely stand up. I wait until I have regained my balance then I make my way back toward the hotel. I'm near the edge of the terrace avoiding the dancers and heading to my room when Stelios calls out.

'Mikky? Are you OK?'

'I'm going to bed.'

He takes my arm. 'You look a little unsteady.'

'I'm fine.'

'You're a little drunk,' he smiles.

'Jet-lagged,' I giggle and shake my head not wanting to speak but needing to know. 'Did you speak to Nikos about the Torah?'

'He says we can see it tomorrow.'

'Great. What time? Did he say how he acquired it?'

'He said it was given to him.'

'Given? By who?'

'He wouldn't say.'

'So, someone just came up to him and gave him the ancient scroll? Hello Nikos, here's a rare and valuable Torah,' I mimic.

'You sound angry and a little drunk. I'm not the police, Mikky. I can't quiz him when I'm a guest here - it's not very polite.' His voice is teasing and reluctantly I smile. He has a point.

'You could have pinned him up against the wall by his throat and threaten to beat him if he didn't tell you the truth,' I grumble.

Stelios laughs and a few people turn around.

'Who do you think the anonymous donor is?' I ask.

He shrugs. 'It could be anyone. Lots of Greek Jews in America have donated artefacts to Jewish Museums around the world - it could be anyone in the world.'

'But why be anonymous?' I persist. 'What's the point? It doesn't make any bloody sense.'

'Simon warned me that you were opinionated.'

'Is that what he said?'

'And more...'

'So how are we going to find out?' I cross my arms and stare at him, trying to keep my balance and wishing he wouldn't keep swaying.

'Be patient. Let's see how things unfold tomorrow.'

'Where would Nikos get the money from to buy a Torah?'

'It's late and you are stubborn, Mikky. Go to bed.'

'What thirty year-old has the money at his disposal to buy a rare and expensive artefact,' I persist.

'Maybe he didn't buy it.' Stelios leans and whispers in my

ear.

I look around to make sure there is no-one near us. 'You think he stole it?'

Stelios takes my hand. 'No he didn't steal it. Come on, I'll escort you to your room. I think you've had enough for one night.'

I pull away from his grip. 'What do you mean, then?'

'Maybe he bought it with Elias. Maybe they brought it together.'

I stare at him wishing he wasn't so hazy around the edges and I reach up to touch his hair and push a loose strand behind his ear.

'Could Elias afford it?'

'What do you think? Come on, we'll talk tomorrow.'

He escorts me to my room and it takes all my effort to put one foot in front of the other. At the door I stand on tiptoe to kiss his cheek.

'Good night, Professor.'

He laughs. 'Good night, crazy lady.'

I don't tell him that Nikos has invited me on his boat in the morning and when I'm safely in my room I check my iPhone. There's an email from Simon.

Hi Mikky. The internet connection is terrible here. I'll try my best to keep in touch. We have a problem. Nikos is in negotiation with an Italian businessman to sell him the Torah. The Italian arrives in Rhodes on Friday. Get the Torah verified ASAP. SX

I reply to him tapping the words carefully on the keypad.

93

Okay. All under control. MX

I sigh and check my watch. It's one hour later here than in Spain and two hours later than England. I send a text message to Josephine.

Arrived ok. Chat soon. Hope you are ok. You're famous here still. X

Disappointed to hear nothing from Eduardo I text him and to my surprise he texts me straight back:

Me: Rhodes is a lovely island. Hope you had a good journey home? XXX
E: On night-shift and a break x
Me: I'm sorry about everything. XXX
E: Did you see the Torah?
Me: Not yet. Tomorrow. XXX
E: Buenos noches x
Me: I love y –
But then the room starts spinning. I close my eyes and fall backwards onto my pillow.

The following morning I wake feeling sick. I dress in my jogging gear and head outside to shake off my hangover and to wake up my jet-lagged body. I leave the hotel and follow the pavement through the village in a looping circle. I take a few detours and it gives me a sense of orientation as I puff and pant my way past half-finished buildings that I know will one day provide a dowry for some lucky girls in the village.

I trot past olive trees and fields overgrown with weeds to the base of a hill and then back along a dirt track to the hotel.

I shower and eat breakfast alone in the dining room. There's no sign of Stelios and I'm pleased to have my thoughts to myself. I'm thinking of the day ahead. I don't want to have to explain that Nikos wants to show me the island.

The thought of spending the day with Nikos fills me with excitement and a ripple of nervousness. I tell myself that I must get him on my side if I want to see the Torah. I haven't come all this way and made my promise to Mariam just to fall at the first hurdle. If I was truthful I'm secretly delighted that he wants to spend some time alone with me but I tell myself I will be one step closer to seeing the Torah.

At ten o'clock I'm standing in the reception gazing out of the panoramic window at the blue sky that stretches to infinity when a strong arm comes around my waist and spins me around.

'Mikky, you look beautiful.' Nikos kisses me on the cheek and I'm distracted by the fresh scent of his aftershave and surprised at the thrill that travels through my body sending a shiver to my toes.

'Lemon and spices?' I mumble.

'Pardon?'

'Nothing,' I smile.

'It's a beautiful day,' he says. 'Let's have some fun.' His eyes are deep chestnut and they crinkle in naughty anticipation. He wears magenta coloured shorts and a navy Polo shirt and I'm pleased that I have my camera with me. I bend down to pick up my bag when he says.

'Hey, my good friend Stelios, how are you?'

When I look up Stelios is standing with a beach bag slung

over his shoulder. He hugs Nikos in Greek fashion, slapping each other playfully on the back and he nods a shy greeting at me. He's over a head taller than Nikos and his beard seems longer than I remember from yesterday. Today copper chest hair springs out of the V of his white T-shirt.

'Are you both ready?' Nikos asks.

Stelios grins at me as if reading my mind or perhaps he sees the disappointment in my face but Nikos links his arm through both ours and leads us outside together like we're auditioning for a part in the Wizard of Oz.

'Come, come, it's a beautiful day and we must all enjoy it.'

Inside his battered black Mercedes there is another surprise. Two girls with long blond hair and captivating but reticent smiles are sitting in the back seat.

'This is Lily and Lisa. Come on, Stelios fold up those long legs of yours and climb in the back. Don't frighten the girls with that hairy beard of yours.' He opens the front passenger door for me. 'And you my princess, you get to sit in the front of the chariot with the handsome prince.' He laughs and winks and when I'm seated he closes the door for me.

He drives scarcely paying any attention to the road, swinging the car into the traffic. He waves his arm out of the window. Slowing down to call out or to point out a particular landmark.

'How's you head, Mikky? What a great engagement party. And you Stelios, how are you?' He sits upright to look in the rear view mirror to get a better view of Stelios crammed in the back. 'Steady, you stallion. Those girls are very innocent and they don't speak any Greek or English.'

Nikos laughs and makes eye contact with me until I turn away wishing he would concentrate on the road, the vans, and mopeds that weave perilously in and out of our path.

'I can't believe these unfinished buildings are dowries,' I say.

'They say the uglier the daughter the bigger the dowry but with my sister she'd need more than a dowry to marry someone. It would have to be bigger than the Acropolis. That's why us single men have to be careful don't we Stelios? We have to be careful that we don't get trapped with some ugly girl just for the money.' Nikos laughs and ignores Stelios' reply in Greek. 'Some of the buildings are for a dowry but obviously the recession like in the rest of Europe has damaged the economy. It's bad in Greece but we're lucky. We're a strong and independent country and we are happy people. We are richer than any of the other EU countries.'

'Richer, really?' I say.

'We have everything. Sunshine, olive oil and land and that's all we need,' he laughs.

'And tourists?' I add.

'The tourists come here between April and September. In a few days it will be May and the roads will be crazy with rented cars and it takes hours to get anywhere. That's why I have a boat. It means you can get away from everyone.'

We stop at a junction and he places his hand on my knees and when I move away he doesn't take any notice. He places his hand back on the steering wheel and continues speaking. 'Sometimes you need a bit of privacy - the island can get very crowded.'

'I'm surprised at the Italian influence on the island. The hotel is neo-classical like the buildings you'd find in Amalfi or Sorrento.'

'That's true. You have a good eye for detail, Mikky. The Turks ruled Rhodes and the Dodecanese islands until 1912.

Then the Italians came that same year. You'll see evidence of their architecture all around the island...'

'Hence all the neo-classical buildings?'

'Exactly. There's a big Italian influence here. At first they treated the islanders very well but then fascism was on the rise in Europe and the Italians wouldn't let Rhodes self-rule, and then the Germans came, and the Greek resistance was born.' He stabs his chest as if he was one of them.

'Are you from here?'

'Me? No.' He leans his arm out of the open window and steers lazily, overtaking a motorcyclist and narrowly missing an oncoming truck. 'My grandparents were from here but like a lot of Rhodians they left in the 50s. It was a very poor island and there was nothing left after the war. I was born just outside of Athens.'

'So why are you here now? Are you working or on holiday?' I'm thinking of Simon's email to me last night and Nikos's meeting with the Italian businessman on Friday.

'My father and Elias are brothers. My father sent me here to learn the hotel trade.'

'So, you're working - in the Palacio Hotel?'

'Elias has another hotel in Lindos in the south of the island and another one further up the coast on the far side of the old city but I'm building a boutique hotel in the Old City. You know the old town of Rhodes? It's all pedestrianised and very beautiful with lovely shops. You'll like it. It's a walled city built by the Knights of St John between the 14th and 16th century using local workers. They left Jerusalem and Cyprus and settled here, building the city walls, gates, churches and palaces - even hospitals. I think there is still St Johns Ambulance in England. It's all part of the same historical brotherhood.'

The car squeezes along the busy street and winds down narrow roads toward the port and the glistening sea.

'It's marvellous,' I say, reaching for my camera and when we stop at traffic lights I snap a few shots of the old walls.

Nikos watches me silently until the lights change then he drives into the parking area and we sit for a few moments watching the old fishing boats together as if Stelios and the two girls in the back of the car don't exist.

'Have you been here long?' I ask replacing the cover over the lens of the camera.

'Only a few months.'

'And you're already buying a hotel?'

He grins. 'I'm a businessman. I bought a very old building and I have to renovate it. It cost me over two hundred thousand euros for five hundred square metres.' He pats my thigh. 'Come on, princess. Yannis is waiting. Everybody out!'

It's Monday morning and we haven't yet seen the Torah and somehow Simon has been in touch with one of his contacts and found out that Nikos wants to do a deal with an Italian businessman arriving here on Friday. I stand gazing at the limestone walled city as the single mast yacht prepares to leave the harbour wondering how Nikos earns his money. If Nikos is planning to sell the Torah then why are Stelios and I here?

Yannis, the captain, is at the helm of the wheel. He's good looking, quiet and goes about his work diligently as he casts off and negotiates our way out of the harbour.

Nikos is acting the clown and making Lily and Lisa laugh as they help pull in the buoys and wind in the ropes. The girls are like twins. They are doll-like in appearance; tight mini shorts, big breasts and long hair. They remind me of the girl on the beach last night. The one who sat beside Nikos at the meal. Cristina - wasn't that her name?

I take out my camera and take random shots of them all then I turn my attention to Stelios who stands beside me gazing at the view of the walled city.

'The Jewish Museum is in the old town, isn't it?' I ask.

'See the main gate that leads to the Old City?' He points to the arched gateway. 'That's where they say the Colossus of Rhodes once stood, astride the entrance to the harbour, over thirty metres high. Legend has it that Helios - the sun God - rose out of the sea and bestowed fertility and perpetuity on the island. It was one of the Seven Wonders of the World... more probably, it was in the courtyard of the Temple of Helios which is near to the Palace of the Grand Masters in the medieval old city. You must see the old city, Mikky. It's a UNESCO World Heritage site.'

'What happened to the Colossus?'

'It was destroyed by an earthquake.'

'Are there lots of earthquakes here?'

'In 1992 we had the last one - it was 6.2 on the Richter Scale but there wasn't much damage done.'

'Unlike the one last September in Turkey,' I say. 'The one Mariam died in.'

'It was as bad as the one in Turkey in 1980 - it was very bad. Tragic.'

'So, why didn't they rebuild the Colossus?'

'Sadly in AD653 Arab pirates stole the bronze fragments and sold them to Jewish merchants. But for years afterwards they still referred to the people of Rhodes as Colossans.'

'Now they are called Rhodians?'

'They say Rhodes is named after all the wild roses - Rhodians - on the island but others believe Helios named it after his beloved wife Rhoda the daughter of Poseidon.'

'They say? You're a true archaeologist, you learn everything but believe nothing.' I snap more pictures of the harbour view.

'I need evidence to believe.' He gives me a grin then turns his attention back to the vast array of boats in the marina. 'I forget sometimes how beautiful it is here,' he says.

'Really?' I'm watching a bald-headed man climb out of his car. He raises binoculars to his eyes as if he's watching us sail away from the marina.

'Doesn't that ever happen to you? Don't you take the beauty of some places for granted?' he asks.

'I suppose I do...' I'm not really listening to Stelios. I snap several images of the young bald man who stands beside a red car leaning on the open door.

Why is he watching us?

I glance at Stelios to see if he's noticed him but his gaze is wistful and there's a softness in his eyes so I turn my camera to snap his profile, his scraggy beard and his tied up hair.

'You're like a hippy,' I say.

'Does that bother you?'

'Not at all.'

I focus my attention on the other occupants in the boat and make my way past the mast toward the big wheel where Yannis stands guiding us out of the harbour. The two foreign girls could be sisters and when I try talking to them in English they giggle and Nikos says to me.

'They're from Romania. They don't speak English and very little Greek.' He rattles something in his native tongue and the girls laugh but Stelios' face remains serious.

'What are they doing over here?' I ask.

'They're models,' Nikos replies. 'Take photos of them. Get them to pose. It will be good practice for them.'

I take pictures with my Nikon and the girls become shy. I'm used to people not keen on their photograph being taken and I encourage them, even though they don't understand what I am saying, and they laugh and drape themselves around Nikos.

I'm quickly bored so I turn the camera on Yannis and he waves from behind the wheel. Until Nikos flexes his tanned biceps, lifts his Polo shirt revealing an impressive and tanned six-pack and thumps his stomach hard. He screams like Tarzan and we all laugh and I snap a quick shot.

'Your turn bean-pole,' he calls. 'Show them how hairy you are. You big gorilla.'

Stelios lifts his shirt to reveal a mass of curly ginger chest and stomach hair. The girls find it funny and I snap their laughing, disbelieving faces and I wonder what they whisper to each other in Romanian.

While Nikos and the girls disappear downstairs into the galley I stand companionably with Yannis who has been busy navigating our way out of the port. Now we are at sea, the wind blows hard, billowing into the sails and he smiles confidently. I look up at the mast and snap a few shots of the sapphire sky.

'You certainly know what you're doing,' I say.

'Years of practice,' he replies in good English. 'I sail here with my father all the time.'

'You must know all the islands and the sea. Is this the Aegean?'

'The Aegean and the Mediterranean meet at the southern tip of the island. We will see the island of Symi shortly and over there is Turkey.'

'Is it difficult to get in and out of Turkey?' I ask.

Yannis replies. 'Boats go everyday for seventeen euros - one way - to Maramaris or Bodrum.' He waves his hand in the direction of the Turkish coastline. 'But why go there when you have so much to see here on our Greek islands?'

'Do you sail for Nikos very often?'

He gives me a strange smile. 'Sail for him?'

'It's his yacht, no?'

Still smiling Yannis shakes his head. 'It's mine. I run excursions from the port for the tourists.'

'It's nothing to do with Nikos?'

He shakes his head and continues to smile.

Minutes later Nikos and the girls begin transporting ice boxes onto the deck. They come up laughing and I find myself smiling, their giggling and good humour is infectious.

'Drinks!' Nikos calls. 'Here Mikky, take this cold beer or do you prefer wine? We have everything. We'll find a bay to have some lunch and a swim later.'

We sit at the back of the yacht where it's protected from the wind. I take a bottle and swallow chilled beer relishing the tangy flavours on my tongue. The sun is hot but the breeze is cool and my flimsy colourful cotton trousers flap around in the wind like excited untethered sails and I'm grateful to have my leather jacket over my shoulders.

The girls sit huddled in skimpy T-shirts giggling contentedly chatting, heads bent together.

Stelios appears happy, helping Yannis like a crew member, moving backwards and forwards checking knots and testing the canvas.

It's pleasurable sitting lost in my thoughts. New York seems a long time ago although it's barely been three days since I left and although I've only been on the island twenty-four hours, I am relaxed and happy. There would be plenty of time later to see the Torah and in the meantime I'm determined to enjoy myself.

I play around with my camera and focus on the details of the yacht, taking pictures of coiled ropes, the billowing sail until Nikos calls me.

'Mikky, come here.' He beckons and so I step over ropes and feel my way past the mast to the bow of the yacht to where he stands watching the yacht slicing though the deep water. He holds onto the taught ropes like a pirate, swinging and dancing on his toes, skipping easily, navigating and guiding me into his arms until I grip the rail.

'It's like Titanic, do you want me to put my arms around you?'

'No, that's fine.'

'I'll sing if you like?' he laughs.

'Don't bother. What happened to your girlfriend last night?' I ask.

He squints in the sunlight at the horizon and I wonder if he's heard me but then he replies. 'Too much wine.'

'I found her on the beach. She had marks on her arm, Nikos. Haven't you noticed? She's injecting drugs,' I shout above the wind in case he can't hear me.

He looks surprised. 'No!'

'You must have noticed.'

He shrugs in Greek fashion and then over my shoulder he points and shouts. 'Dolphins?'

He scurries to the back of the yacht and stands between the two girls who lean over the side scanning the sea. There's great excitement and we search the water with expectation but there's no shoal of dolphins. The sea is clear and in places turquoise and I take pictures of the colourful reflections and the sun's rays through the sporadic clouds chasing behind us in the sky.

It's almost one o'clock when we pull into a secluded bay.

'This is Symi,' says Yannis, lowering the anchor.

I gaze over at the seemingly deserted island.

'This is the quiet side. Very few people come to this bay during the week but tomorrow, on the first of May, it will start to get busier.'

Out of the wind it's much warmer. We settle on deck together and Nikos fills glasses of chilled wine and hands them around. He pulls boxes of food from bags and begins to unwrap: hummus, tzatziki, taramasalata, Symi shrimps and dolmades - small parcels of tight wrapped vine leaves stuffed with rice and meat.

I sit crosslegged peeling prawns and drinking wine and occasionally joining in with the conversation. The sun is hot on my back and I remove my jacket. No one mentions my tattoos. The girls eat quietly, rarely speaking to each other or looking up. It's only when Nikos says something to them that they giggle but I doubt they understand what he's saying by the quizzical expression in their eyes.

Nikos refills my glass and I lean back against the railing gazing. I imagine Mariam in Turkey meeting the Syrian lawyer and taking the Torah. I try to imagine how she must have felt: relief, excitement, pride.

Simon and Alexandros had said she was thrilled and hon-oured to bring the ancient testament back to this land - where it belonged.

'Mikky?' Nikos hands me a plate of cold chicken kebabs. 'You're lost in thought?'

I smile but don't reply instead I eat slowly, biting the tender chicken pieces soaked in spicy herbs, savouring the tamarind, mint and cumin flavours.

Stelios says. 'These are delicious, Nikos? Are they from the hotel?'

'Of course, you think I cooked them, bean-pole?' Nikos replies with his mouthful. 'I asked them to make a picnic for us.'

'What sort of hotel do you want?' I ask.

Nikos frowns before answering. 'It will be small, probably fifteen suites, upmarket and expensive. It's in the old part of town and there's five hundred square metres big enough for a small restaurant with traditional Greek cuisine.' He holds up the kebab. 'I need to get the architect to map it out.'

'Do you have the plans drawn up?' Stelios asks.

'In my head.' Nikos grins and taps his temple. 'I know what I want. Come on, skinny, eat some more.' He holds the plate out to Stelios. 'You want to be like me. Look at this muscle.' He punches his stomach and the girls giggle. He speaks a few words in Greek and the girls look shy and then he turns his attention again to Stelios. 'You need to exercise more. Get in the gym, do some workouts. Too much sitting behind a desk all day.' Nikos waves his half eaten kebab at Stelios.

'I know, I'm a skinny runt who needs some proper exercise.' He flexes his non-existent biceps playing up to Nikos's banter and the girls giggle. 'I'm also a hairy, red-head with a long wise beard.'

'Your hair is copper,' I say.

'You noticed?'

'I'm a photographer.'

'I'm flattered.' Stelios stretches and smiles lazily.

'He's like a monkey, girls, don't you think?' Nikos makes sounds like a chimpanzee and they all laugh. He nudges Stelios in the leg. 'They like you Stelios. They like you a lot.' He continues to speak in Greek and Stelios continues to smile and accepts more wine as Nikos holds out the bottle.

'Which one do you think is the prettiest?' Nikos asks him.

'That's not very polite,' I say.

'They can't understand,' he replies.

Stelios focuses on the girls. 'They both look the same to me. They could be twins.'

'They're cousins,' Nikos says.

They're speaking English for my benefit, so I ask. 'What sort of models are they? They look very young and innocent. How old are they? Twelve?'

'Jealous?' Nikos asks.

'I'd like them to be able to speak for themselves-'

'They're twenty-one.' Nikos smiles.

'I doubt that,' I reply, matching his stare.

'They're good girls.' Nikos nudges Stelios' arm and mutters something in Greek and I'm suddenly uncomfortable with his manner.

Yannis stands up and disappears into the galley. When he comes out he's changed from his jeans into shorts and he's holding a crackly radio. He fiddles with the dial and music fills the air. The girls sing tunelessly and wave their arms in rhythm as if they would like to dance and Nikos encourages them clapping along. 'Come on girls, dance. This is a party, come on...'

They are shy at first but he gives them more wine and they

stand up, moving their hips, swaying to the music and flicking long hair over their shoulders.

Nikos stares at me and I feel the heat of his gaze.

'Is your uncle a good man to work for?' I ask.

'Elias? Of course. He's shrewd and he's done well but I'll do better.' He leans back and rests his foot playfully against mine.

'How will you do better?'

'Well, he had a dowry from his marriage to Athena...she's from a very wealthy family.'

'A dowry?' I perk up and Nikos takes this as a sign that I need more wine and ankle stroking.

'Athena's parents gave her the land where Nikos built their first hotel then ten years later Elias built another hotel in Lindos - it's where he grew up and lived with his family. About five years ago they bought and renovated the Italian Palacio where you're staying now.

'Did they grow up together?'

'They grew up on different parts of the island. Elias is from Lindos and Athena is from the north near the old town.'

I know Alexandros lives in Lindos. He's older than Elias but it's probably how he knew of him.

'So, if everyone on the island knows each other then no-one can be naughty? You wouldn't be able to get away with much here. Everyone would know what you are up to...'

Nikos rubs his toes against the instep of my foot. It's not unpleasant and I'm too comfortable and relaxed to protest.

The two girls have stopped dancing and they sit at the edge of the yacht and dangle their legs over the side. They have slim shoulders and narrow waists and from behind they look like very young children.

'There's very little crime here,' Yannis calls over. 'It's usually the foreigners - people not from Rhodes - who bring us trouble.'

'That's true,' Nikos adds. 'They bring more police over here in the summer. Sometimes small gangs work together to rob the tourists.'

'What about the hotel you're building? Will it cost a lot of money?'

Nikos ignores me but leans forward to place his hand on my ankle. His fingers are strong and I imagine them caressing my body. I want to ask how he will fund the building of his new hotel. I want to ask him if it's with the profit, I assume he will make, if he sells the Torah to the Italian businessman on Friday but Nikos is contemplating the olive trees dotted along the hillside and he says:

'Many, many years ago the people from here became very greedy and selfish and when they stopped being kind and helping each other, the Gods decided they didn't like what they saw. So, they sent one of the Gods down disguised as a mortal. Anyone who treated him kindly or with goodness would be granted any wish he desired.' He strokes my foot and his fingers caress my toes. 'Dressed as a poor man the God went from village to village and from town to town. He was turned away with abuse and doors were slammed in his face. Then he came to a lonely farm house occupied by two old people. He expected to be shunned but instead they invited him inside. He was surprised - they were poorer than he had thought. They apologised for their humble home and offered to share their supper with him. Then they gave him their straw bed for the night - happy to share whatever they had. In the morning, when the God revealed his true identity, he said that in return for the kindness they had shown him he would grant them any wish.... Expecting they would ask for material gifts he was surprised when they said that when the time came they wanted to die together and to be buried in the same grave. They didn't want be alone. So, when the time came, God granted their wish and to mark their passing he created an olive tree that grew in the place where they were buried. That's how the trunks of the olive trees are like two entwined bodies. They are linked for all eternity...'

Stelios claps slowly and Yannis smiles and nods as if he's heard it all before.

The two girls not understanding the story speak in their own language, their voices growing louder with excitement and wine. They're singing to Beyoncé's I'm a Single Lady, not understanding the words, dancing like school children.

I sip my wine. Nikos removes his hand and my leg goes cold.

'You're a good story-teller,' Stelios says. He holds out his glass for a refill and I do the same. While I contemplate Nikos's story he and the girls clear the food away and stow it below in the galley.

'I like stories,' I say to no-one in particular.

While Nikos is gone, I lean closer to Stelios and whisper. 'We must find out about the Torah. He's going to do a deal-'

But Stelios's eyes are closed and he yawns.

Frustrated I walk to the front of the yacht where there's more of a breeze, I welcome it blowing on my neck and enjoy the solitude of the gently rocking yacht. I mustn't forget my promise to Alexandros and the children. We must see the Torah and arrange for it be be returned.

When I turn around Nikos sits crossed-legged on the floor rolling a thick joint. He kicks Stelios with his toe, waking him, and hands it to him first. Stelios protests but after Nikos takes a drag and inhales deeply, he holds it out and Stelios takes it. He puts it to his lips and inhales as if it's something he's done all his life.

The girls sit sharing another rolled joint, passing it between them, talking in Romanian and convulsing in sporadic bursts of laughter. There's something about them that is so innocent and I want to smile but I'm distracted by Nikos and Stelios.

There's some sort of macho competition going on and so I sit at the base of the mast and close my eyes enjoying the gentle rocking and swaying lulling me to sleep. The sun is warm, my stomach is full and I'm relaxed and happy. I think of the exhibition in New York but it's fleeting, I'm not so focused on my failure. None of it matters. It was an exhibition and although it was my work - I don't care if no-one likes it. I'll take some time out and decide what I want to do. Maybe I'll go travelling through Europe - I've never been to Romania so maybe I could communicate with the girls and see where they would recommend me to go.

I feel a shadowy presence at my side and when I open one eye Nikos lies beside me. We are hardly touching but I am aware of his strength and the scent of his salty skin as we lay on our backs with our faces pointing up at the sky.

'You were born for this life, Mikky,' he says turning on his side.

Without opening my eyes I ask. 'What do you want, Nikos? I'm sleeping.'

'Try some of this. It's really good stuff.'

'I'm fine.'

He trails his hand along my thigh and my skin turns to goose pimples. It feels soothing, erotic and exciting. I don't want to move. I don't want him to stop.

'You're a girl who knows what she wants. I can tell that about you. You know about life. You like the good things. You like to have fun...'

I open one eye and lean on one elbow to face him. Our faces are inches apart. I watch his lips and look at his strong jaw and slim nose. His skin is smooth and soft and I want to touch him. His voice is just a whisper.

'You're very sexy but you don't know it. You're a natural, Mikky. Some girls have it – some don't but you definitely have it. You're a girl who has everything; money, looks, charm...' He glances over his shoulder where the Romanians sit with Stelios smoking together. 'Those girls need to learn from you. You could teach them.'

'I can't teach anyone anything.' I lie on my back and yawn.

'You're a photographer. You know how to model,' he urges. 'You know what looks good, how to move and stretch your muscles. I've been watching you. You've a beautiful body; long limbs and a kissable mouth.'

'Go away. I'm going to sleep.'

He runs a finger down my arm. 'Try this.' He holds out a thick spliff. 'It's good stuff.'

'Where's it from?'

'I normally get my stuff from Morocco. They produce the most marijuana resin in the world – the most hash – but this stuff is from Afghanistan. Like most things, it comes through Turkey. Come on, princess. Try it.'

'It's been a long time, since I smoked...'

'God, don't end up like him. That boring archaeologist. They threw away the recipe after they made him. Look! He's hardly exciting, is he. He'll smoke the hash and fall asleep. He's got nothing, the poor guy, he's not sexy or macho - he's hairy with pale skin and he's probably still a virgin.'

I take a deep drag and giggle. It's good stuff and I pass it back to Nikos. 'It's not always about being sexy or macho.'

'What's it about then? What turns you on? Is there a man in your life or do you prefer women?'

'I like men.'

'I thought so.' He takes a drag and passes it back to me.

'Who are those girls, Nikos? Why are they here?'

'They're friends. I told you. I'm looking after them. They want to be models and I said I'd help them find work in Athens but they need to learn a bit first. Do you like them?' His smile is suggestive.

'Not in the way you think.'

'My dream is a threesome - well, foursome with you, princess. How about it?'

'Hardly romantic.' The buzzing in my head is travelling at great speed through my body and combined with the wine I am woozy and my body is floppy.

'But great fun - we can have some real hard, crazy sex. What turns you on?'

I ignore him. 'Where's your girlfriend from last night. Cristina - isn't that her name?'

'She not my girlfriend. Besides, she has a hangover.' He inhales deeply, holding the smoke in his lungs before exhaling slowly.

'She's a drug addict,' I slur.

He strokes my arm in slow spiral movements and his fingers travel toward my breast.

I sigh contentedly but move his hand away. 'There is a man in my life.'

'So?' He drops kisses onto my shoulder. 'It doesn't matter.'

'It does to me.'

'Do you love him?'

'I think so.'

'Is he good looking?'

'I think so.'

'Fit?'

'Yes.'

'Does he fuck you with enthusiasm?'

It's the hash that makes me giggle and he passes it to me again and suddenly we are like children. He leans closer to my ear and licks my earlobe.

'Once I start, princess,' he whispers, 'you won't want me to stop.'

I push his shoulder away and as I do I can't help but notice his erection. He looks down at it too and his eyes crinkle in a smile. 'It's all yours. You want to come below or do you want to do it out here?'

I shake my head. 'Tell me more about this girl - the one from last night - is she Romanian too?'

'I'm going to make love to you, princess but I need to clear my head first. Come on, let's swim. Come on, Mikky.' He grabs my hand and lifts me unsteadily to my feet as I struggle to keep my balance.

'Wait!' I say. Our faces are inches apart and there are green flecks in his deep brown eyes. 'When are we going to see the Torah, Nikos? We can't keep having fun like this, we're not on holiday. I've got to get back.'

'Get back to what?'

'To - to - my life?'

'What life? This is life - this is living. Why the hurry?' He holds me in his arms and pulls me close so that I can feel his hardness. 'Let's get to know each other and have some fun. You know that we're the same type of person. We're not like them, Mikky.' He nods at Stelios and the laughing girls and Yannis fiddling with the radio. 'We're special. We're different. We need to live without constraints and without anyone telling us what to do.'

'I'm here to work,' I say, wondering if my words have come out right. My head is fuzzy, my knees are weak and I'm thirsty.

'And work you shall, my princess. But there's no harm in us getting to know each other first and enjoying ourselves a little, is there?' He pulls me closer and our lips are inches apart. I duck away from his kiss and he laughs.

'I know you want me and I'm a patient man. Okay, so hang on here a second, I'm going to get something for the girls.' He disappears into the galley and reappears a few moments later with a small bag of pills.

'Do you want an E?'

I frown. 'No thanks.'

'You want coke?'

'No.'

'Girls, you want coke?' he translates in Greek and laughs with them and they disappear downstairs. When he returns a few minutes later he's bouncing with energy. He grabs me and whirls me around to the music. He's infuriating and deliberately trying to side-track me from asking about the Torah.

'Stop trying to change the subject, Nikos. Are you selling the Torah to the Italian?' I blurt out.

His chestnut eyes are inches away from mine and they sparkle. 'What do you know about the Italian?'

He pushes me back against the railing and leans his hardness against me, smiling.

'Come on, tell me. How do you know about the Italian?' His voice is soft and close to my ear. His chest pushes against my breasts and my senses are reeling with the closeness of his skin and the tangy scent of his aftershave. I want to push him away but another part of me wants to pull him closer.

His head bends toward mine and then he whispers:

'It doesn't matter. Let's swim, princess.' He's filled with excited energy and he takes my hand and leads me to the ladder at the back of the yacht and I'm left feeling that I missed out on an opportunity. When I look at the sea a sense of foreboding sets off an alarm in my head and I know I'm too stoned. I should definitely not go in the water.

Chapter 7

'Anybody can become angry - that is easy, but to be angry with the right person and to the right degree and at the right time and for the right purpose, and in the right way - that is not within everybody's power and is not easy.' - Aristotle, Philosopher of the 4th century BC.

I stumble away, stepping over Stelios who lies with his eyes closed and his mouth open.

'I can't swim now.'

'Come on, it will clear your head. We'll stay right beside the yacht. Let's just get wet. It'll be lovely in there – so warm...'

'I need to change,' I say.

'Down there.' He points to the cabin below. 'You want me to come with you?'

'No, stay away. You bad boy.' I tread gingerly down the steps in the galley. One of the girls is washing dishes the other is drying them and packing away the lunch boxes and the debris of our lunch. They are laughing and dancing and so I say slowly:

'Thank you for your help. Tell me, where are you from? Romania?' I pronounce it slowly.

They nod in unison.

'Do you like Greece?'

They shrug.

'Where is your friend? The girl with the-' I indicate the inside of my forearm and mimic injections myself. 'Cristina?'

The one with the greyest eyes looks suddenly alert and glances up the stairs. They say nothing, so I add. 'She went to the party with Nikos yesterday.' I mimic a dance but stumble in the cramped galley kitchen. 'Is she okay?'

One girl shrugs. 'We...'

The other holds her hands out with her palms upturned. 'She-'

Nikos hurls himself down the stairs and collides into my back giving him the excuse to hold me around the waist.

'How long are you going to be, princess?'

He rattles off some Greek to the girls then says:

'You haven't changed, Mikky? There's two bedrooms. Go in there.' He pushes me and my bag into a small cabin and closes the door so I'm alone and as I change into my costume I hear him whispering to the girls. They sound like urgent commands and when I come out they are all gone. Only Nikos is waiting on deck.

'Where are the girls?'

'They're changing in the cabin. Romanians can't hold their drink but they're fine.'

Stelios is woken by our voices and he leans on his elbow, watching us.

'Yannis where's the snorkel stuff?' Nikos calls.

Yannis appears from the engine hatch and throws masks and snorkels to where I sit at the back of the yacht at the top of the steps. I flinch when a flipper accidentally hits me on the arm and before I can say anything Nikos is kneeling beside me kissing my skin.

'Feeling better?'

'Umm.'

'I'll help you.' He pulls flippers onto my feet as if I am a princess and I place the snorkel in my mouth and pull the mask over my face.

'You know what to do?' Nikos asks.

'No idea,' I lie and I launch myself off the boat backwards and into the water. The icy sea grabs my body and clutches me in a cold embrace. The air is sucked from my lungs and I scream inside my mask, sucking air into the tube. When I surface I blow hard to clear the passage and removed it from my mouth.

'It's freezing!' I call.

Nikos plunges into the water beside me and swims to my side wrapping his arms around my waist and I kick playfully away from him.

'You know how to tease me,' he calls. 'But you're playing with the wrong guy. I can be very, very bad and the more you turn me away the more you turn me on.'

He dips his head in the water but stops suddenly and shouts.

'Wait a second!' He swims back to the yacht but I'm captivated with the world under the sea. Not sure if it's the hash or the alcohol that has intensified my sight. I float on the water, kicking slowly, following a shoal of fish, marvelling at their colours and the underwater contours of the seabed. The sun's rays illuminate the shallow rocks where small marble-like stones lay untouched in a sea-world village. It's a magical sight, caught in a timeless motion of the drifting and swaying currents.

Realising I am alone I tread water and look around for the yacht.

Yannis is standing on the deck. He is holding a compressed speargun. He inserts a spear into the barrel on top of the piston and using a special loading handle, he places it over the tip of the spear forcing it down the length of the barrel, compressing the air further. He leads over board and passes it to Nikos.

I have dived many times and I know the damage it can do.

Nikos kicks his way toward me.

'Come on, Mikky. Let's catch dinner.' He raises the speargun like he's a masked terrorist and a ripple of cold water rushes over me. Regardless of the sun beating down on my head, my body is iced.

Time has no meaning. Underwater is another world. A translucent and transient, ever changing ever moving, ebbing and flowing life. I'm content to listen to my own breathing, rattling and rasping in my snorkel as we pass shoals of silver fish with iridescent stripes. Other smaller and darker fish and their contrasting colours are reflected in the distorted sunlight making me wish I'd brought my underwater camera.

In the shallow depths the water is warm but encouraged by Nikos we venture further into the deeper part of the Aegean where it turns from turquoise to navy and the contrasting cold and dark makes me shiver.

I'm aware of Nikos beside me. Occasionally he dives deeper toward the rocks below us looking for octopus, squid or bigger fish. He makes hand signals to me and I respond by pointing and nodding. We pass shoals of sea small sea bream who turn and flick their tails in unison. Near a rock formation is a bright blue, green and turquoise fish. It's colours are stunning and I'm wrapped up in the imagery of the isolated world underneath my body. It's bewitching and captivating and the deeper we swim the bigger the fish become. The sea bream are larger, the size you'd find on a plate in a restaurant, but suddenly I see a lone fish with dark vertical stripes and a pale patch on its abdomen.

I kick hard and follow it trying to identify its type. It looks like a colourful perch. I swim above it and circle slowly. It's maybe six feet below me so I take a breath and make a vertical dive, jack-knifing at my waist, using the weight to streamline my body to push me deeper where it's darker and colder.

It's a lone fish. Like me. I follow it wishing I could film its beautiful colours and imagine I'm a fish swimming quietly and alone. Swishing my tail, flicking my flippers. This is my home. This is where I belong. I want it to swim toward me. I want to be friends. I hold out my fingers encouraging it toward me.

A flash.

A sudden glint.

A quick movement and a spear darts past my eyes between my fingers lancing the fish in the gut.

Instinctively I jerk upright and kick to the surface. I rip off my mask gasping for breath, choking and spitting sea water.

Nikos surfaces beside me looking triumphant.

'Got it!'

'You fecking idiot, you nearly speared my hand.'

'I got him. Look!' He holds the spear aloft.

The colourful fish is spiked on the end of the blade. Its eyes are open and glazed in shock. Its mouth is still twitching.

'You almost killed me,' I shout and kick away from him. 'You're a bloody nutcase. Stay away from me.'

Yannis' grip is strong. He hauls me up onto the deck. His

forehead creased in a frown.

'What happened?' He flutters around me like a nervous butterfly as I throw my mask, snorkel and flippers on the deck. I'm swearing and cursing and my body is shaking.

'He's a bloody idiot! Stelios?' I shout. 'Where is he, Yannis? Where's Stelios?'

He's nowhere in sight and neither are the girls.

Yannis nods at the steps to the galley. 'He's down below.'

I stomp toward the front of the yacht pulling a T-shirt over my head then fall onto my stomach, laying prostrate on the deck on a warm dry towel. I wipe my nose and my eyes and lay my head on my arms reliving those few minutes thinking of the beautiful fish swimming innocently, dipping and dodging the rocks, inquisitive and friendly.

My arm tastes salty on my lips and my stomach is heaving, retching and gasping. I wipe sea water from my face and snot from my nose hoping the nausea will subside. I try to control my breathing, managing the muscles in my chest and trying to control my anger.

'I thought you liked excitement.' I feel Nikos's shadow over me. He stands with his back to the sun casting me in the shade. I don't reply so he sits beside me and touches my back.

'Mikky?'

'Get off.' I wiggle away and he lies down beside me. He's so close I can feel the small hairs from his thighs on the back of my leg. He rubs my shoulder and although I'm wearing a T-shirt his touch is cold, tantalising and yet erotic. He massages the back of my neck and very slowly his hands travel around and under the front of my T-shirt and he touches my skin.

I gasp.

'Do you wonder what our children would look like?' he

whispers.

His fingers are firm. He massages my hips, my bottom and the back of my thigh. I'm mesmerised by his gentleness and by the strength of his caress and I lose myself to his touch unable to respond to his question. When he stops, my shoulders tense and very slowly he lowers his wet body on top of mine. He doesn't crush me but uses his elbows to hold his weight so he rests gently on my back. Using his knee he prizes my legs apart and slides his right hand under my waist to my crotch. His hardness is between my buttocks and his fingers move against me.

'Piss off!' I push him away and my sudden movement knocks him off balance. 'You almost killed me you bloody lunatic!'

He lies propped up on his elbow and laughs. 'I know what I'm doing.'

'That poor fish was beautiful.'

'It's only a fish - it's food. You eat fish.'

I scramble to my feet and he lies on his back with his hands behind his head and watches me. 'God, you're sexy when you're angry. I want you. Come here my beautiful princess.' He pats the deck beside him.

'Stelios!' I shout. 'Stelios where are you?' I step over the ropes to the back of the yacht where Yannis is watching but pretending he is busy fiddling with the radio.

'Let's go,' I say.

I meet Stelios at the top of the steps. He's pulling his T-shirt over his head, covering the matted golden hairs on his chest, rearranging his shorts.

'What are the hell are we doing?' I hiss. 'We're not on bloody holiday.'

Behind him the two girls follow up the steps, giggling

playfully. He says something in Greek which sends them into further hysterics so I turn my back on them.

'Let's go!' I shout at Yannis. 'Pull up the anchor. Take me back to Rhodes. NOW!'

In the hotel I have a thumping headache. I stand under the hot shower for a long time rinsing the salty sea from my skin, my costume, shorts and T-shirt. I hang them on the back of the terrace chair to dry and pull on a white robe then I check my iPhone.

Simon's sent a short message.

Any news? Have you seen it? S.

Feeling tired, angry and frustrated and slightly sick I lie on the bed, blaming jet-lag and fall asleep. When I wake it's almost dark. I throw on cotton trousers and a black shirt and head downstairs to the dining room where I find a discreet table in the corner. I order lentil soup and a rack of lamb, washing it down with a glass of red wine and sparkling water and contemplate my bad humour.

What did I achieve today?

What did I do?

Nothing!

I'm angry and Simon's simple message has made me feel ashamed.

After I've eaten I sit at the table and email Simon with an update on my meeting with Alexandros. I tell him that Milos and Dorika are gorgeous but I don't mention my silent promise: to fulfil Mariam's quest and return the Torah to the museum.

I've let everyone down.

I gaze out across the velvet sea and conclude that if we're not quick, Nikos will sell the Torah to the Italian on Friday. He's almost definitely going to use the profit he makes on the sale to fund his boutique hotel.

I finish my wine and periodically check my iPhone. There's no message from Eduardo. But why would he text me?

I've been cold and distant. I've even flirted with Nikos.

How could I?

I think of my disastrous art exhibition last week and how my family have supported me. Even though it was a disaster they had tried to make me feel better but I had wallowed in self-pity. I'd been aloof and dejected refusing their goodwill and support.

What is wrong with me?

I order coffee just as Stelios wanders into the restaurant. When he sees me he raises his hand and waves.

'I'm just leaving,' I say by way of greeting, pushing my chair back, hoping to escape before the waitress returns with my order.

'That's okay. I've already eaten. I've been waiting for you. I thought we could take a walk and have a chat?'

He leads me away from the restaurant and I follow him grudgingly past the busy bar, the lounge and terrace toward the main door of the hotel. We stand beside neatly potted cactus plants and giant candle holders that illuminate the path to the road.

'Want to walk with me?' he asks.

We walk in silence. The pavements are unfinished, the street is badly lit and I stumble.

'Careful,' he says taking my arm but I push him away. 'Are you angry?' he says.

'Only with myself.'

'Why?'

'We haven't achieved anything. Simon emailed me to say that Nikos is in negotiation with an Italian businessman. He's going to sell the Torah to him on Friday. That must be how he's funding his boutique hotel.'

'If he had the money to buy the Torah, which would have cost a lot more than that, then why not just spend that cash on the hotel?' Stelios asks. 'It doesn't make sense.'

'It depends on what he paid for it. If he got it on the black market and someone wants to get rid of it then he could make a very neat profit.'

'It would still have cost him.'

'And what if Elias is involved like you suggested? What if he's the front man but he's getting Nikos to pretend that he owns it?'

'Is that what you think?'

'It's a possibility,' I say.

'Elias is well-respected...'

There's a stench of cat wee in the nearby alleyway and we cross the road and head toward the shops and a taverna with soft yellow lights.

'Did you speak to Nikos about the Torah? When can we see it?'

'He's a tough nut to crack.'

'He's stalling us. He's playing for time. He deliberately distracted us today.'

'He's got an agenda alright. He's not as easygoing as he pretends to be-'

'I thought the two of you were friends. You looked like you were the best of buddies laughing and joking all the way back on the yacht.'

'I was trying to cover up for your bad manners.'

'My bad manners? You're joking? It wasn't me that spent the afternoon in the cabin with those girls. Stelios? See that man over there.' I point to a bald headed man with piercing blue eyes. 'The one standing near that taverna with the orange table cloths, he's taking photographs of us? Who the hell is he?'

I don't wait for an answer instead I step into the road, narrowly missing a noisy Vespa, causing the rider to swerve and shout out. He curses me and raises his hand in a crude gesture.

'Mikky, stop!' Stelios calls.

'It's the same man that I saw in the harbour this morning. The one who was watching us through binoculars and he's watching us now.' Then I call out. 'What do you want? Who are you?' I'm determined that for the first time today I would have the upper hand. 'Why are you taking photographs of us? Let me see, give it to me.'

I hold out my hand and I'm glaring at him ready to snatch the camera from his grasp. The stranger looks inside the taverna for support but the waiters have disappeared into the kitchen.

'Come on, give it to me,' I shout. 'Who are you?'

'Mikky?' Stelios arrives beside me and takes my elbow. 'What are you doing?'

'This man was taking photos of us - he was in the hotel when we came back this afternoon.'

The stranger is shaking his head. He is small but solid and strong. He looks as if he wants to escape and he begins to back away.

Stelios speaks to the stranger. 'I'm sorry, she had a shock

this morning-'

'Don't you dare apologise for me, Stelios.' I pull my arm away. 'He's got photographs of us. Why?'

Stelios stands between me and the man. He's facing me and he whispers harshly. 'Pull yourself together, Mikky. The poor man doesn't understand what you are talking about. He's not Greek and he obviously doesn't speak English.'

I'm breathing hard and when I look behind Stelios at the man, his cold eyes are locked on mine. He seems to smile but then he turns and walks away.

'He's swaggering,' I say. 'You let him get away with it.'

'Come on, Mikky. I'll take you back to the hotel. You're tired. I think what's happened today has affected you. Mikky?'

Stelios grabs my arm to distract me but the bald man has disappeared into the darkness. 'Mikky? What are you thinking? You can't just shout at a stranger in the street.'

I turn and face him angrily. 'There are too many unanswered questions. How are we going to find the answers?'

'What are you talking about?'

'How did Mariam get to Turkey? Was she going to tuck the Torah under her arm and carry it? Was she going to an airport? Was she followed? Who else knew about it?' I can't keep the annoyed sarcasm from my voice. 'And what about the mysterious donor? After paying millions for it, they're not just going to let Nikos keep the Torah, are they?'

Stelios scratches his beard.

'For heaven's sake, Stelios. We must do something.'

'I think you've forgotten that we're here to examine the Torah. That's all. We're not detectives, Mikky. You're not some female James Bond Superhero.'

'Has anyone contacted the anonymous donor? Has the

Jewish Museum been in touch with the Syrian lawyer? '

'No-one can find him.'

I squint and gaze up into his eyes. 'Why not?'

'He's disappeared.'

I'm asleep when my phone pings and I wake immediately surprised it's not fully light outside. It's a text from Simon:

Italian now arriving Thursday. private yacht. main harbour. 18:00 hours.

There's also a message from Eduardo that came through while I was sleeping:

E: Did you have a good day? x

Then another message:

E: Did you see the Torah? x

I text back:

Me: Only just seen your message. Not bad. Haven't see the Torah yet. XXX

Eduardo replies immediately.

E: Why?

Me: He's stalling me XXX

E: Maybe you just want to stay in Rhodes?

Me: I miss you XXX

He doesn't reply.

I go downstairs for breakfast and Nikos is in the reception. I wonder how long he's been waiting.

'I'm sorry, Mikky - about yesterday. I think I upset you and it really wasn't my intention. Please let me apologise and make it up to you.'

'Don't you do any work?'

'What do you mean?'

'You didn't work yesterday and now you're waiting for me in the lobby. It's Tuesday - don't you have to work?'

'I do, but I want to speak to you first. Have coffee with me?'

'Only if you stop evading my questions.'

'Evading? Who's evading. I'll tell you anything you like, please.' He spreads his arms wide and his chestnut eyes sparkle. 'Please give me a chance to make things up to you.'

'I want to see the Torah.'

'Fine. But let's have coffee first.'

Mollified I allow him to guide me through the reception to the lounge and we take a seat outside on the terrace overlooking the gardens and pool. Several tourists are sunbathing, reading, sleeping or rubbing in sun lotion. Gardeners in matching green uniforms are busy in the garden and trimming hedges. The electric whine from their cutters mingles with a gentle roar from above as a plane turns to approach the airport runway.

We sit at the same table where I sat with Alexandros, Milos and Dorika. I remember my promise and it makes me more determined and strengthens my resolve. After we order coffee and the waitress leaves, Nikos says:

'I must apologise. The last few months have been very difficult or me,' he sighs. 'I am not close to my father. He's... how would you say? A very driven man and to be honest, I don't really know him that well. He wasn't around when we were growing up. He travelled a lot. His business took him around the world - finance, you know, stocks and shares that sort of thing. He worked hard and although I admire him I'm not like him. I'm more like Elias. I love him more than my father and I believe I can build a boutique hotel that would be very beautiful and very successful. I've worked hard these past few months to learn everything about the hotel business. I can't let Elias down. I will show him that I can be successful.'

'And your mother?'

'My mother was kind but she was a busy woman. She played lots of golf and met her friends. She had a busy social life and very little time for me and Anna.'

'Anna?'

'My little sister.' He gives me a boyish grin that makes me smile. 'More recently, I've been helping my father and Elias find employment for immigrants. They are refugees and they arrive by the boat load. I help in redeploying families mostly Syrians, Eastern Europeans, Afghans who want to reach their families in other parts of Europe. We've learnt lessons and we've worked with the government and the International Charities but it's been difficult in recent years-'

'Recent years?'

'Yes, new legislation, the European Union, tighter border controls, new immigration laws...You name it, we've done it. And we've done better than most. We provide employment. We boost the economy and the Greek Government would be at a loss without us. Tourism and hotel revenue constitutes over sixty percent of the Greek economy. We bring in wealthy tourists who spend their money and the government loves us.' He claps his hands together in delight.

'And you do all this in Athens?'

The waitress delivers our coffee and he continues.

'I did yes, but now my dreams have changed. This island is very unique and I like the lifestyle here. I'm happy and I feel as though I can put down roots and make this my home. If I said that I am the son that Elias always wanted then perhaps you will understand. We are very close and he believes in me.'

'Did he finance you to buy the Torah?'

'No, not at all.'

'Then why did he tell Simon Fuller that it was his?'

'Mine, his. It's all the same. We're family and we look after each other.'

'So, you bought it on the black market?'

He smiles. 'You're very persistent and that's why I like you, Mikky. Rhodes is a beautiful place to live. So why don't you let me take you on a small excursion of our beautiful island?'

I smile. 'That's kind of you but why don't you show me the Torah first?'

His smile doesn't fade.

'Of course, that's why you're here, isn't it? Sorry, I'd forgotten. I get carried away by my feelings for you. I'm sorry. You see, I thought I was dealing with Stelios. Isn't he the expert, he's from the Archaeological Museum?'

'Yes, of course.'

'Is there a conflict of interest?' he smiles.

'Not on my part.'

'So you represent Simon Fuller - the English expert on rare manuscripts, scrolls and documents?'

'Yes.'

'But you are not him.'

'Obviously not.'

He remains silent so I say. 'Simon was under the impression

that Elias was the one we would be dealing with – so I feel – how shall we say, extremely misled.'

'It was always mine. Elias just made enquiries for me.'

'And that's why I'm here.'

'But what do I know about your credentials, Mikky?'

'The fact that Simon Fuller has sent me should answer that question.'

He nods his head in acceptance. 'You would like to see the Torah without Stelios, is that correct?'

'We are not joined at the hip,' I reply. 'Is it near here? When can I see it? Now?'

He scratches his chin. 'Soon.'

'How soon?'

'Maybe we should have lunch together?'

'How did the Torah come into your possession, Nikos?'

He looks at me and I am disconcerted by the coldness in his eyes but it dissipates quickly and he laughs. 'Do I have to reveal my sources?'

'The provenance of anything remotely valuable must be tested. I'm sure you will appreciate that. It's important to establish the credentials of the Torah and its journey in life to check its authenticity. It must stand up to scrutiny. It's the first thing that the Archaeological Museum in Athens will insist upon. They will want to verify that you have the authority and ownership to sell it to them, if that's your intention, is it?'

'I wanted to discuss this with Simon Fuller. I thought he might broker a deal – or help me with some sort of negotiation–'

'That's why I'm here.'

He looks at me and levels a penetrating stare into my eyes. 'Perhaps you could negotiate with the Italian?'

'You want to sell it to him?'

'You're a very sexy woman, Mikky dos Santos.'

'Thank you.'

'You're also not what you seem.' He leans his head to one side and regards me closely. 'I checked you out. You've been involved in some shady dealings in the past. A stolen Masterpiece?'

'If you're referring to Vermeer's The Concert then it's best not to believe all your read.'

'I like you, Mikky. I think we're the same type of person. I think we have a lot in common.'

'Really?' I smile. 'I'm an opportunist. What are you?'

'I'm the same.' He takes my hand and kisses my fingers. 'I take every opportunity that comes my way. I'd be lying if I told you otherwise. That's why I'm successful. I take risks. I live life and I don't care what anyone else thinks. So, tell me, are you interested in working with me?'

I barely pause. 'If that's what you want.'

'For a fee?'

'Of course.'

'I need to be able to trust you, Mikky.'

'And I you, Nikos.'

'How about we see the island?'

'And the Torah?'

'And the Torah,' he agrees.

'What about Stelios?'

'You're not joined at the hip are you?' he laughs. 'Your lovely body is far too beautiful to be attached to a moron like him.'

Chapter 8

'Good people do not need laws to tell them to act responsibly, while bad people will find a way around the laws.' - Plato, Philosopher of the 5th century BC.

He drives with the window of the Mercedes down, swerving in and out of the busy traffic. The leather seat is hot against the back of my legs and my hair flies in the wind. My hangover has disappeared and the feeling of sickness has evaporated and I begin to relax and enjoy the drive. We're going to see the Torah. He weaves in and out of the traffic with natural ease unfazed when a hooter blasts at him. He raises his hand and waves as if he knows them.

'Why aren't you married, Mikky?' he asks. 'A beautiful woman like you should have been snapped up by now.'

'I'm not ready.'

'Or perhaps you're not the marrying type.'

'Interesting – why do you say that?'

'You're wild at heart. You like adventure. You're like me. You love excitement. You're a risk taker and you like to have fun.'

I laugh. 'Well, this may surprise you Nikos but I'm engaged to be married.'

'That doesn't mean anything.'

'Doesn't it?'

'No. If you loved him, you would be with him and not here, flirting with me.'

'I'm not flirting.'

'I think you are.' His fingers reach for mine but I pull my hand away.

'I'm serious, Nikos. I got engaged last week in New York. Last Friday.'

'Ah? New York, what were you doing there?'

I tell him about my art exhibition and keep facts simple then I say. 'Have you heard of an opera singer called Josephine Lavelle?'

Nikos turns to regards me carefully taking his eyes from the road. 'Of course, who hasn't? She was like Maria Callas – better – she has the most beautiful voice...why?'

'She's my birth mother,' I reply.

He pulls the car over to the side of the road, parking raggedly on the grass verge and I realise I'm not breathing. His gaze is penetrating and my heart is racing.

'Your mother?' he repeats.

I pull my mobile from my pocket. 'Here, look!' I show him photographs of my exhibition and I'm surprised at the emotion in my voice when I tell him how the critics panned it. I wipe away a tear and he places his arm around my neck and massages me gently.

I show him images of Simon Fuller with Josephine and other photographs of Glorietta and Bruno.

'And who is this?' he asks taking his hand away.

'That's Eduardo,' I squint at the screen.

Eduardo's angelic smiling face stares back at me. His blond tousled hair is wet from the shower. We had just made love and I had to capture the special intensity in his eyes. 'He's my fiancé.'

Nikos nods and hands me back my mobile then starts the engine. He smiles at me but it doesn't reach his dark eyes and as he drives into the countryside I wonder if I've done and said enough for him to trust me.

Ten minutes later, after weaving through country lanes, I feel as though we've come full circle, and we pull up into a field in the middle of nowhere.

'What are we doing?' I ask.

'We're going to see the island.'

He climbs out of the Mercedes and slams the door. 'Come on.'

There's a small, shabby cottage, a large shed and an old blue rusty Fiat.

'Come on, don't you trust me?'

'What about the Torah? I'm not on holiday, Nikos. Simon has emailed me to find out what's happening and why you haven't shown it to me yet,' I call over the bonnet of his car.

'What if I decide to sell it? Aren't you interested in helping me? I thought we had an agreement.'

'You don't need me to negotiate a deal with Stelios or any of the Museums.'

'I thought we had a deal about the Italian?'

'Do you mean it?'

'It will be a little more – how should we say – lucrative.'

'Selling it on the black market?' I ask pretending to be surprised.

'Isn't that your area of expertise? '

'What makes you think that?'

'Just a hunch.'

He walks away and pulls back the doors of the shed.

'I'll have to see if the Torah is authentic first.' I run after him.

'How will you know?'

'I'll know alright – believe me.'

'Will it matter?'

'Of course, even if you sell it to the Italian he'll want some sort of assurance.'

'That's where Stelios comes in.'

'Stelios?'

'Once the Italian realises it's authentic – which he will – he'll jump at a deal.'

'How will he know?'

'Are you really so naive, princess? This is a very small island. All we'll need to do is to have a word with the right people to say it's authentic – and Stelios will do that for us. He won't even realise he's endorsing it. By the time he's reporting back to the Archaeology Museum the Italian will know all there is to know. He'll be satisfied.'

'The Italian knows someone at the museum?'

Nikos' face breaks out into a wide grin. 'What do you think? Come on, let's see how brave you really are.'

'I thought we were going to see the island.'

'We are.'

He stands aside and in the gloomy interior of the barn is a dust sheet. He pulls it off and tosses it to one side revealing a blue mini-looking helicopter.

'Do you know what this is?' he asks.

'A gyrocopter?'

'It's an RAF 2000. Have you ever been in one?'

'No.'

He begins to push it outside into the sunshine. It has three small wheels that remind me of a baby's tricycle. It's just over four metres in length and two and a half metres high. There are two bucket seats, side by side, in a flimsy cockpit.

I watch him, unable to move, my mouth turning dry. I lick my lips and swallow. I'm starting to feel sick. I can't tell him I have a fear of heights. My palms are clammy and a knot is stuck at the back of my throat.

He calls out over his shoulder.

'You're lucky this one has doors. The one I used to fly was open.'

I stand speechless, glaring at the shiny machine knowing I can't climb inside it, but Nikos is too engrossed checking the propellors and the rudder on the back to notice.

'You see, I have to know I can trust you, Mikky. I want to do business with you. It's either this or a threesome. You know what I'd prefer - and the choice is obviously yours.' He suddenly pulls me into his arms and my throat is locked in fear. 'You might enjoy a threesome, princess,' he smiles. 'Stelios did.'

'Stelios?' I stutter.

'On the boat with the two girls - what do you think they were doing down in the cabin while we were in the sea - playing chess?'

He releases my arms, looks over my shoulder and begins speaking rapidly in Greek. I turn around and coming toward us, from the old cottage, is a girl. She's not pretty like one of the Romanians but she has a round-face, thick glasses and a big nose.

I recognise her immediately. It's the girl on the beach on Sunday night. Not Cristina the sick girl, but the angry girl with the severe face who dragged her along the beach.

'This is Anna,' he says. 'My sister.'

'She helped Cristina at the party,' I say.

He nods. 'Probably. She's kind like that.'

Anna approaches us speaking Greek and gesticulating wildly. She barely acknowledges me but she helps Nikos wheel the gyrocopter further out of the shed and into the field.

I slip off my leather jacket and hold it casually over my shoulder. Beads of perspiration lay across my upper lip but I wipe them away with the back of my hand wishing I'd brought a bottle of water.

I glance across the field and the small hill we drove over to get here. Our journey from the hotel had taken only fifteen minutes yet this was a world away from the busy hotels, shops and restaurants. This was a field of biblical proportions, arid, dusty and hot.

'Come on, Mikky. What are you waiting for?' He beckons me to follow them.

'Don't you need to know how to fly one of these?' I call back staring at the gleaming machine, my heart thumping so loudly, I'm sure they can both hear it beating like a raging drum inside my chest.

'It's a good day for it – you'll love it.'

'I'm not that good with heights.'

'Trust me.'

I wipe my hands on my jeans.

'Where's your camera?' he asks. 'You'll need it.'

'Don't you need a licence for one of these?'

'Only a pilot's license – I used to fly commercial airlines –

didn't I tell you?'

He is standing very close to me and his garlic breath mingled with his spicy lemon aftershave and the pungent aroma of olives floats in the air. I think I might be sick. I am shaking, rattling like an old skeleton, but my legs are heavy and my arms lethargic. I want to sit down in the shade. I want to hide.

'Where did you get it?' I ask as he walks around the machine, checking it over.

Anna steps back and out of his way.

'I've had one for a few years. I brought it with me from Athens. It's my favourite toy. There isn't another one on the island.'

'How far can it go?'

'As far as you like - it's wind dependent - you know, if you've got a tail wind you'll get there twice as quickly and if it's a head wind it can take twice as long but I can stay up for about four hours.'

A wave of nausea engulfs me. I can barely take in the technical details that he rattles off and then he says.

'But don't worry. I normally cruise between one to two thousand feet and you won't fall out - it's got doors.'

He taps the perspex glass.

'You can't take off here.' I stare across the naked field with fear. 'Won't the grass catch in the wheels?'

'I've done it hundreds of times. I can land this thing on the beach especially on a day like today. There's only a light wind from the south so we'll get airborne quickly.'

My heart sinks.

'Is it safe?'

'She goes like a dream. I can probably do about one hundred and eighty to one hundred and ninety kilometres an hour. I'll cruise at about one hundred and thirty metres. The view will be amazing. You'll love it. Come on.'

'I can't,' I say. 'I just can't.'

'It's okay, Mikky. It's safe. I didn't make it.'

'Make it?' I'm horrified.

He laughs. 'It's factory built.'

There's a two-bladed rotor that's probably nine metres in diameter that hangs precariously over the small cabin and at the back the propellor is almost two metres in length.

Nikos climbs inside, calls me and holds out his hand.

'Come on, princess. You can take the controls if you like-'

'I'm not flying this bloody thing.'

'Only joking! You'll be okay. I haven't got an instructor's licence anyway. I'll fly. You take the photos. You won't believe how amazing it is up there.'

I glance at Anna for support but her face is impassive. She doesn't smile but then when she sees me staring at her for reassurance she nods seriously in encouragement. I remember that she speaks English, so I ask.

'Is he safe?'

She nods but turns quickly away as if she didn't hear me.

I take a deep breath and raise my camera case.

'Okay. I'll take the photos - you can drive.'

It's a small cabin and we sit close together, our shoulders almost touching. Nikos helps me with my harness and passes me headphones for my ears.

'Put these on,' he shouts, 'then we can talk normally.'

He holds the joy stick between his legs and his eyes gleam excitedly. He's itching to get airborne and we trundle down the field - the makeshift runway - at an alarming speed. The engine sounds loud and tinny then it whines, something flaps and the wind buffets us and knocks the cabin sideways. The gyrocopter sways and shudders and I think I might be sick so I close my eyes. My knees are shaking and my hands are gripping the seat and we are lifted into the sky.

Nikos speaks in my ear.

'Open your eyes. Look down there, isn't it beautiful.'

He points to the distant coastline where the sea looks aquamarine and calm. The view is magnificent. I fumble for my camera, recognising Turkey and Symi in the distance.

Nikos points below. 'The Palacio Hotel,' he whispers in my ear turning the aircraft so that we're at an angle, leaning over the coastline. He's a good pilot and he holds the craft steady. I begin to breathe easier and the shuddering in my knees starts to fade.

Below us sunbeds and beach umbrellas are dotted around swimming pools and laid out along the beach. I snap photographs quickly trying to recognise my morning jogging route. He makes several circles of the hotel and I get my bearings, identifying the streets, the hillside and the fields beyond. I activate the video as he points to a small cluster of houses below and says.

'That's where I live - in that villa.'

We follow the coast and I'm snapping images randomly, taking pictures of the countryside and the coast flying toward Rhodes town. It's a breathtaking sight and from the air the medieval citadel is impressive. I gasp at the aerial view over the ancient city.

'The Palace of the Grand Masters,' he says, pointing out the places of interest: mosques, churches, parks, medieval streets and Roman-styled avenues. We swoop low over the commercial harbour where Yannis' yacht is moored and onto the business harbour where rows of smaller boats and yachts are lined up against the quay.

'Mandrake Harbour,' he calls. 'The three windmills are the harbour landmark. They used to grind the grain that was unloaded from the merchant ships. Now tourists come here to eat in the restaurants and take boat trips.'

The modern harbour contrasts with the old town and the people walking along the quay turn to look up at us. Some point at us and suddenly I'm filled with confidence and I laugh aloud.

I'm flying.

I've used the Phantom 4 drone many times and now I know what it's like to skim over trees and swoop low seeing everything like an eagle. I take pictures and videos and see the beauty of the island below me.

Nikos flies us out over the sea past two cruise ships docked in the harbour and we leave the old city behind. We fly along the east coast where sandy beaches look resplendent in the morning sunshine. Some bathers look up and wave.

I sit back and smile enjoying the shuddering journey, lost in thought and marvelling at the beauty of nature and the world. Then we are circling a town with the most impressive acropolis on the hillside

'Oh my goodness. It's like Athens,' I say.

'It's The Temple of Athena Lindia. This is Lindos.'

'It's magnificent,' I shout back. 'What an amazing way to see the island.'

We fly over a large bay and a fishing village but I can't take my eyes from the temple. I marvel at the stone walls and the historical significance of the fortified citadel. And, as I look down at the hillside I wonder where Alexandros, Milos and Dorika live. They said they had views of olive trees from their home and I think of the children going to school and Alexandros' tourist shop and of Mariam.

What sort of person had she been?

I wish I had a photograph of her.

I'm distracted by Nikos calling out. 'That's Butterfly Valley but there are no butterflies until June. You'll have to stay here, Mikky. You'll have to stay on the island with me – forever.'

We both laugh.

I don't know how long we are airborne but the sun is higher in the sky. I giggle at the silly thought of me staying here so long. I laugh excitedly because I've also overcome my fear of flying. Adrenaline rushes though my body and I recognise its powerful influence from when I kite-surf on the ocean. I know what it's like to feel the rush of speed and my body appreciates the anxiety, skill and control as I skim waves and somersault with precision.

'How about some acrobatics?'

'No! Definitely not.' My happy mood evaporates.

'Hold on.'

Before I can hold on he lifts the nose of the gyrocopter high into the sky. We are climbing higher and I'm screaming. The engine is slowing and we are shuddering and shaking, losing speed and I grip the seat thinking we might fall backwards but suddenly the nose tilts forward and we are suddenly hurtling at great speed toward the ground.

My head is dizzy. I scream. I can't breathe and just when I think we will hit the field we lean to the left in a shallow ascent, flying sideways, rising gradually. My body slumps against the perspex door and I squeal as the grass seems to rush toward me and then it's blue sky. He changes course and suddenly

145

I'm leaning over his shoulder and I think I may fall. I shout.

'Stop! STOP!'

He brings the gyrocopter level and we head out to sea and I'm swallowing the bile in throat. My head is buzzing and my stomach is heaving.

'Once more?' he laughs. 'You must remember, Mikky. You're on my side. We're a team. We stick together. We want the same things in life. We'll do a deal together so don't mess up. Don't fuck with me or there'll be trouble-'

'I won't.'

'Let's just make sure.'

He sends the gyrocopter into a spiral wobble, rotating the joy stick and we spin. I close my eyes and grip my camera between my knees. My head somersaults. I'm disorientated and dizzy. My vision is blurred. The gyrocopter sways and lurches and my stomach slides to the floor. It rises again and fear hits me in my stomach. I think I might faint so I dig my nails into the palm of my hand. The next thing I know is we are bumping along the grass toward the open shed.

We slow down but my body is still somersaulting.

Anna's face appears to be rushing toward me. She flings open the door and I unhook the harness, fall out and retch on the grass. My knees are weak. Anna steadies me as I stumble.

'I need a bathroom,' I whisper.

She points to the old cottage and takes my arm. I'm grateful for her stability and when my knees buckle I hold her tighter.

The cottage is a dilapidated small, stone building. The main door leads into a large room with an old wooden table, two chairs and a small sink. Anna pulls me past a smaller room with a mattress on the floor into a shabby, small bathroom.

I throw up missing the broken toilet basin, heaving my

breakfast onto the filthy tiles. Then when there's nothing left I lean my arms on the cracked sink and sob. I cry with fear, pain, anger and frustration - all mixed in my gut from the times I've been bullied and beaten. Finally, I weep with self-pity at my humiliation in New York and my overwhelming despair of having such a formidable opponent as Nikos.

He wants the Torah as much as me.

Finding a clean tissue in my pocket I wipe my face and dry my eyes. There's a trickle of cold water and so I rinse out my mouth. My forehead is clammy and my T-shirt clings to my back. I'm fighting my sickness and I sit for a while resting my head on the cold tiles trying to ignore the stench of sewerage and urine seeping up from the floor.

Outside I lean against the wall, in the shade, at the back of the cottage. My head is gradually calming and my vision has stopped swaying.

Nikos was testing me, teasing me and he frightened me.

That's the second time. I might have thought the incident with the speargun was an accident but now, after today, I know he's trying to spook me.

He has to be in control.

In the fresh air I calm my shaking hands by taking out my camera and snapping a close-up shot of a wild, red poppy growing between the sandstone rocks. When I've finally stopped shaking and I'm back in control of my body and mind I step out of the shade and walk confidently back across the field with my jacket slung over my shoulder.

Nikos is kneeling, inspecting the front wheel of the gyro-copter. Behind him Anna leans over his shoulders and she's covering his neck and cheek with kisses.

My step falters but when Nikos sees me he stands up and

Anna is knocked off balance. She falls to the ground as he waves cheerfully.

'Hi princess, feel better?'

'Bastard,' I mutter but I wave back enthusiastically. I've made a promise to Mariam's children. He's not going to win.

Nikos drops me at the hotel saying he has work to do. Just before I open the car door I ask:

'So, did I pass your test?'

His brown eyes smile and he kisses me dismissively on the cheek. 'I'll let you know, princess.'

'When can I see the Torah?'

At first he doesn't reply but I wait out his silence until he speaks. 'Tomorrow.'

'You said today.'

'I have to do a few things.'

'You're stalling me.'

'I've got to get it.'

'Where is it?' It never crossed my mind he didn't have it nearby - unless he's lying.

He grins. 'Sorry princess, I'd have to kill you if I told you.'

'You're not the only one who has contacts, Nikos. I've been dealing with these types of guys for years.'

'What types?'

'Janus figures. The ones who buy looted artefacts illegally and sell them legitimately through art galleries and antique shops. How do you think I make money to live the way I do?'

He doesn't reply and just as I'm about to climb out of the car he grabs my wrist.

'You never told me how you knew about the Italian.'

'You never asked.'

'I'm asking now.'

'I'd have to kill you if I told you.'

He lets go of my hand and laughs. 'Let's hope it doesn't come to that.'

I go straight to the reception and spend half an hour organising a rented car to be delivered later this afternoon. I'll need wheels if I intend to follow Nikos.

I eat lunch alone in the hotel. A Greek salad and grilled tuna. My mind is whirling with the events of the morning and in particular I'm thinking about Nikos and his behaviour. He's reckless but charming. He's insulting yet funny. He's dangerous and also very intelligent.

I'm going over our conversations in my head, thinking of our flight in the gyrocopter, wondering if Nikos trusts me enough to get me involved in the deal he wants to make with the Italian. Short of sleeping with him, I'll do anything to see the Torah.

I've been asked to verify it and nothing else and then my job is done.

But what happens then?

I can't let him sell it.

If it's the same Torah that Mariam went to Turkey to collect then it belongs here. I will not let her efforts be in vain. It's the least I can do for Milos and Dorika, and I have a sudden urge to see them. I want to help them heal. I want to do something useful so that their mother didn't lose her life for no reason.

But Nikos wouldn't be easy.

What if he does want me to negotiate a deal with the Italian?

It will take time.

The Italian will have to trust him – us – and he will want to know he's buying the real thing. He says that the Italian has contacts in the Archaeology Museum in Athens and that if it's authenticated by Stelios then it will be enough for him.

But is that true?

Is that enough?

How much will the Italian pay for the Torah?

I order another glass of white wine and chat briefly with the waiter about how I might spend the afternoon. He's surprised when I tell him I haven't yet been to the old town and he shakes his head in admonishment and smiles cheekily revealing a gold tooth.

'I'll go after lunch,' I promise realising it's time for me to do some investigating of my own.

Sipping my wine I realise how Nikos is playing with me. He's like the Prince of Hearts. He's holding all the cards and I'm the joker – especially after this morning. He scared me in the gyrocopter and yesterday he almost harpooned my hand.

Is he nuts?

I look down at my bare fingers.

Why haven't I worn Eduardo's ring? Why am I not wearing it now?

What's wrong with me?

Eduardo is kind and loving. He's my type of guy – uncomplicated, intelligent and a thinker. He's adventurous and yet he's careful. The opposite to Nikos. So, why am I not excited at the prospect of spending the rest of my life with him?

I'm finishing a sweet filo pastry stuffed with dried fruit when Stelios strolls into the restaurant. He seems to be looking for me so I wave at him.

He's six foot, willowy and pale. He pulls out a chair and

slumps beside me with his legs akimbo. His hair is tied neatly back with a leather strap and he's trimmed his beard.

'Did you have a good morning with lover-boy?'

I ignore his grumpy tone and offer him my plate. 'Want some? It's delicious.'

'He's a notorious flirt...'

'And you're bothered - why?'

'Because you're better than that.'

'What if I said I'm only doing it because I want him to trust me. Because I want to see the Torah?'

'Then you're wasting your time. He's playing with you.'

'How are we going to see the Torah then? You're not having any more luck than me.'

'I spoke to Elias this morning. He's the one who contacted Simon. I told him I can't waste any more of my time here on the island and that I need to see it-'

'And?'

'He couldn't get hold of Nikos this morning but he's going to arrange for me to see it in the morning at his house.'

'Do you think Nikos will agree?'

Stelios stares at me. 'What are you playing at, Mikky?'

'Nothing.'

'Maybe you're not the person I thought you were.' He stands up. 'Maybe you're not the person Simon Fuller thought you were either. You've behaved appallingly. You've wasted your time since you've been here and-'

'Wasted?' I stand up and face him. 'Who are you to tell me I've wasted my time? You've done nothing, Stelios.'

'We need results, Mikky. I'm not on a holiday like you. I take my work seriously.'

He walks away but I grab his arm.

'There's more to all of this,' I whisper.

We stand glaring at each other and I'm conscious of the other diners watching us.

'What?' he asks.

'I don't know, but something isn't right – and I think I'm being followed.'

'By who?'

'That bald guy...' I stutter trying to formulate my thoughts. 'That foreign man from last night. He was outside the hotel again when I got back at lunchtime.'

'Mikky? You're impossible. You're completely crazy. Of course there're foreigners working here. It happens. They live here. I thought you would have known that–'

'But this guy is different–'

'You're making things up to justify your pathetic behaviour.' Stelios pulls his arm angrily away. 'If you want to see the Torah then meet me at midday in the reception. I'm not going to be put off any longer.'

'Wait, Stelios. Don't be so angry with me. Wait! What are you doing this afternoon?' I call to his retreating back.

He seems to hesitate and then he turns around. His eyes look tired and confused and he shrugs in weary resignation.

'Do you want to come to the Jewish Museum with me?' I ask.

There are eight gates leading into the Old City. Seven built since the medieval times and we enter through the eighth gate, the newest one, built by the Italians. We pass the dry moat and limestone walls and make our way through narrow passageways and small squares to the Jewish Quarter and the Kahal Shalom.

'It's the oldest Jewish synagogue in Greece, on Dossiadou and Simiou Streets. There are only about forty Jews that live in Rhodes now,' Stelios explains. 'But the synagogue is still used for prayer services on a Friday night and for High Holidays and special occasions by visiting Jews and their friends and family.'

Inside the building, the tevah – the prayer reading table – faces south east toward Jerusalem. The floor is decorated in black and white mosaic, a typical design throughout the old city.

'Only two Jews came back from the camps,' Stelios tells me and he nods at a plaque on the wall. 'That's a list of those who never came home. The Germans rounded up members of the Jewish community and they were deported to Auschwitz.'

I think of the story that Alexandros told me. How Jews were tricked into thinking there was work and I shake my head in despair thinking of the tragedy that befell so many families.

'Do you think the anonymous donor is Jewish?' I ask.

He shrugs. 'Maybe. It would make sense if they were.'

'Perhaps I should try and find the donor – if there are only forty Jews on the island it might be one of them?'

'Perhaps they're not from here, Mikky. The donor could be a Jew who once lived here and moved abroad to America or even to Africa. Greeks emigrated all over the world – the donor could be living anywhere. Trying to find him could take forever.'

Stelios takes a yarmulke from the reception table and places it on his head and points up to the balcony.

'They built the balcony in 1934 for the women. Until then they were only allowed to sit behind those screens in the adjacent rooms. Come and look at the museum.'

I follow him into a number of high-arched rooms where displays of clothing and artefacts once belonging to the Jews of the island are on show. The wall is lined with illustrative texts informing visitors of the history of the Sephardic Jews who came to Rhodes. Stelios explains their history.

'By 1492 many Jews had been thrown out of Spain and they found refuge in the Ottoman Empire. In 1522 Suleiman the Magnificent of the Ottomans, wanted to repopulate the island and he invited the Jews to start a new community here and they brought with them their customs, traditions and language; Espanyol also known as Ladino. The offspring of the Jewish people from Spain are known as Sephardic Jews after the Hebrew name for Spain,' he says.

'I'm familiar with the term Ladino,' I reply. 'It's almost an extinct Roman language and it descends from medieval Spanish spoken by Sephardic Jews. It's also called Judeo-Spanish.'

He smiles in appreciation. 'You know your history.'

'I know music. The Sephardic Jews were banished from Spain and they went to all parts of the Mediterranean. Ladino is an endangered language. There are probably only two hundred thousand people who speak Ladino now. One of the most well know Ladino singers is Yasmin Levy. When she sings it's like listening to ancient ballads and lullabies. She's often accompanied by guitar and sometimes there's a hint of flamenco in her music. She sings from the heart and it's very moving.'

'She's Spanish?'

'She's from Israel but she spent a lot of time in Andalusia. I went to her concert once,' I say. 'Her music is very special and the Ladino language is quite different to Castellon Spanish.

154

She appeared last year in the National Theatre in London, as the Woman of Song in Salomé.'

I don't tell him that I have Salomé's face painted on my breasts - along with the bloody head of John the Baptist and that wrapped around my waist are colourful veils from her tantalising dance for Herod. It's a haunting tattoo from my former life - when I was looking for reason, purpose, meaning and love. I explored all religions and music, and the Ladino music had been part of my past and still resonates with me now. Growing up in Spain I listened to its melancholic sound and its soulful tunes had lulled me to sleep on many occasions leaving me comforted and loved. Ladino music had filled my soul and allowed me to explore my emotions. It was only more recently that I embraced rock music. It blocked out the sound of my crying soul and my fearful insecurity.

My parents had no roots, no community and no religion. I searched for meaning in my life, a God or someone or something to believe in. I took refuge in churches around the country, the only places where I felt safe and where my parents usually couldn't find me. Many times I sheltered from their drunken arguments and my mother's cruel jealousy in the sanctity of the Catholic Church and the calmness of quiet chapels.

Stelios interrupts my thoughts. 'Many Rhodians, including Jews; left the island before the war. In the 1930s they took their families and emigrated. That's why the Greeks understand immigrants so well. They went to America or Africa searching for business opportunities and a better economic lifestyle.'

I walk alongside him looking at the photographs and memorabilia and as we move into another room where more posters are on display he continues his explanation bringing alive the history and people of the island.

'This was initially the women's prayer room. Some Rhodians returned in the fifties as tourism began to reach here. Tourists started arriving with their foreign money on private yachts or by boat and in the 70s the government decided to build an airport. Although the Dictators were in power from 1967 to 1974 many Rhodians came back to the island and started businesses.'

I pause to stand to look at a glass cabinet.

'It's a sixteenth century Sephardic Torah,' I say with surprise gazing at the beautiful script.

'Not as old as the one that should be here,' he replies.

'Where do you suppose Nikos is keeping the Torah?'

He shrugs. 'I have no idea. Perhaps Elias is looking after it for him.'

I gaze at the old scroll. 'This Torah is four-hundred-years-old and the one Nikos has is over nine-hundred-years-old. What would an Italian businessman pay for that, Stelios?'

Stelios shrugs. 'Hundreds of thousands.'

'Nikos spent two hundred thousand Euros on the building in the old city and he reckons he needs at least three hundred thousand to reform it into a boutique hotel...'

'He would certainly get that and far more if he sells the Sefer on the black market.'

'That's what I'm worried about.'

I walk around thinking and humming to Yasmin Levy's Una Noche Mas. I read the information on the posters and imagine the fear of the local people as the Germans arrived on the island. I can't imagine the terror of the sound of Nazi jackboots stomping along the cobbled streets or being forced to leave here and sent to a camp in Poland. It's a memory that nightmares are made of, and although it's warm in the museum, I shiver.

'What next?' Stelios asks minutes later when we are outside.

The street is peaceful and tranquil, a haven in the otherwise busy city. My mind is a mixture of the past and present but my heart is filled with sadness and melancholy.

'I need a drink,' I reply.

Chapter 9

'You don't develop courage by being happy in your relationships everyday. You develop it by surviving difficult times and challenging adversity.'- Epicurus, Philosopher of the 4th century BC.

We find a bar and order chilled beer. I tell Stelios about my gyrocopter flight this morning and how we flew over the city and down to Lindos.

'Nikos told me he trained to become a commercial pilot but it bored him,' Stelios says.

'At the end of the flight he tried to scare me. It was like he was doing loop-the-loop in an old war plane.'

Stelios laughs. 'I'm sure you're exaggerating again, Mikky. You're very funny.'

I give him a hard stare but that makes him laugh more so I ask. 'What else do you know about Nikos? What's his background?'

'Elias and his brother were bought up on the island. Elias stayed here and has done well but his brother, Nikos's father, went to Athens. He made a series of bad investments. He and Elias were never close but I believe Elias has bailed him out a few times.'

'What about Nicos' mother?'

'Another bad choice. His mother is a bit of a loose cannon at the golf club. She has a bit of a reputation with the men.'

'That might explain why he's a misogynist,' I mumble.

Again, Stelios laughs and says. 'Nikos put himself through pilot school. He flew with a commercial airline for three years but then he got bored, more recently he started working with his father helping refugees but it sounds like he's been looking after his own interests.'

'Could his father be involved in all this?'

'I don't know what to think. All I know is that it's my job to see if it's worth investing more time and money to have the Torah authenticated.'

'Don't you think it should be returned to the island?'

'It's not for me to get involved, Mikky. It has nothing to do with us. If it's stolen or forged or Nikos can't provide us with a legitimate provenance then it will be up to the Culture Crime squad - Interpol probably, to do something about it.'

'You'll report it all officially - to the Museum?'

'Of course. I'll do everything by the book. That's my job and that's why Simon Fuller asked me here.'

'Come on.' I stand up. 'Let's see the rest of the town.'

We walk companionably through the medieval town centre and Stelios points out the Memorial to the Jews in the Square of the Martyrs. We continue through the Burgo - the commercial centre, and to the Collacchio - the historical centre. We spend a few hours exploring the Archaeology Museum and the Palace of the Knights. I link my arm through his as he points out the Inns of each Nation that represented the Knights who belonged to the Order of St John.

There's something nagging at the back of my mind but I can't fathom what it can be. There's something I've missed. Something I've overlooked.

159

'Some old buildings have already been converted into small boutique hotels, look at this one Stelios.'

I stop to peer into a landscaped courtyard. It's a small restaurant with beautiful flowering bushes and dining tables laid with crisp linen cloths. It's an oasis of peace away from the busy streets and evening nightlife and I understand Nikos and his dream to build a luxury hotel in the heart of the city.

I am thoughtful, emotionally lost in a timeless sense of wonder and when I see the ruins of the Temple of Venus from the third century before Christ, I unhook my arm from Stelios and lose myself in photographing this wonder,

'It's unsurprising that the town is a UNESCO heritage site. I'd like to spend weeks here,' I say sighing dramatically.

'Wait until you see Simi Square and the Municipal Art Gallery let alone the Museum Reproduction Shop,' he says.

He doesn't have any idea that I am a master forger and I reproduced one of Vermeer's most famous pieces of art and I smile at the irony of his words.

As we wander through the streets I turn periodically wondering if the eyes of the bald man are watching me. I secretly scan the streets looking for the man who I fear and who walks in my shadow. I snap photographs thinking I might spot him amongst the crowds of tourists who babble around us; Polish, Italian, Spanish, Scandi and Dutch.

I isolate their sounds in my head identifying their origins and wonder why the world cannot always be this harmonious. When I voice my opinion, Stelios replies:

'It's power and greed, Mikky. They're two very dangerous components. All you have to do is look back through history. The Romans, Turks, Byzantines, Italians and Germans - they've all wanted a slice of this island and they've all left their mark on it.'

'An architectural legacy.'

'An archaeological one,' he smiles. 'When the Turks occupied the city they built minarets, hammams and domed mosques and the Greeks were forced to leave the Old City. Other villages on the island prospered like Lindos when the local people began bringing their foodstuffs into the city and clothing, silverware and perfumes,' Stelios explains. 'In the sixteenth century the Turks left gunpowder in the Palace of the Grand Masters and in 1856 there was a violent storm and lightening struck a tower and the gun powder exploded. It did more damage than any other invading force.' He points out where the damage was done.

'How long were the Turks here?'

'Until 1912. Then the Italians arrived and they began to rebuild everything. You can see the Italian architecture and influence on the island like in the hotel where we're staying.'

'But being here in the Old City it's like being transported back in time,' I marvel. 'So when did Rhodes finally belong to the Greek people?'

'It came under the control of the British until 1948 and then they gave Rhodes and the other Dodecanese Islands their independence. It was after the war.'

'That's some occupation. I'm surprised they're all so kind and friendly to strangers–'

Stelios laughs. 'The word stranger and guest is the same in Greek – Xenos. We like to share what we have and to make people feel comfortable with us.'

'I remember Athena telling me the same thing,' I smile wishing I could shake off the nagging voice in the back of my head.

It's getting dark when we find a restaurant tucked in a backstreet, away from the tourists, overshadowed by a ficus tree and where bird cages hang from low branches. Over dinner of fried squid, salad and white wine we talk with easy familiarity.

'I'm pleased we're going to finally see the Torah tomorrow,' Stelios says. 'I can go back to Athens after lunch. I'll take an afternoon flight.'

'Really, you're leaving?'

'There's nothing else here for me. What about you, Mikky? When will you go home? Where is home?'

I sit contemplating the question. I can't leave. I haven't resolved anything yet. I shrug and reply. 'I'm a little unsettled at the moment.'

'Unsettled? There's nothing to it. Once I see the Torah tomorrow, I'll know if we need to get it to Athens for further tests.'

'And what if it's the same one that Mariam had with her in Turkey?'

'Then I'll speak to Elias and it can be returned to Athens or the Jewish Museum here.'

'But if Elias paid for it - he won't want to hand it over so easily.'

'Of course he will, there will be some sort of deal made, he won't be out of pocket I'm sure.' Stelios munches on the soft squid.

'Who will reimburse him, or Nikos, if they did actually pay for it?'

'We don't know how much he paid.'

'Exactly.'

Stelios shrugs. 'It happens all the time. All around the world.

People pay for forged or stolen artefacts and they don't get reimbursed. Sometimes they get caught and get put in prison. There's that big case on at the moment in New York about the Han Ceramics, did you read about it?'

I nod vaguely. It had been in the papers the night of my art exhibition but I hadn't paid much attention to it. Instead I think of Dino and how he bought artefacts that he believed were originals and he tried to sell them. His lawyers would have to prove that Dino was innocent and that they were good imitations.

Had he realised they were fakes?

What if the Torah was a fake?

'Elias has done very well building three hotels. Could he absorb the cost of the Torah - and help Nikos financially with his boutique hotel?' I ask helping myself to more salad.

'There's no doubt he has the money but whether he'll want to do that is another matter. I suppose Athena will also have to agree.'

'Athena? Is she involved with the hotel business?'

'She's a lawyer.'

'Here, on the island?'

'I'm not sure, she goes to Athens a lot. She's done a lot of Human Rights litigation for the government.'

'Wasn't it her dowry that gave Elias the land to start with?'

'Probably.' He eats slowly and seems to consider my question.

Large twisted grape vines grow on the wooden beams over our heads and yellow lamps provide a softness to our surroundings, and occasionally a small colourful bird lets out a greeting from his cage. We eat in companionable silence and eventually I ask:

'Why didn't you go with Mariam to Izmir?'

'She didn't ask anyone to go with her.'

'But you knew about the Torah?'

'Yes. She - the Jewish Museum - made us aware of it. It's not often that someone makes such a generous donation. Not many people knew about it.'

'Who else could have known what she was doing?'

He shrugs. 'She went over on the ferry to Marmaris and they drove to the Izmir province.'

'They?'

'The Syrian lawyer provided her with a bodyguard.'

'What happened to him?'

'I think he died in the earthquake too.'

'Wasn't she frightened? Didn't she worry that someone might have thought it was valuable? How was she going to get it out of the country?'

'I don't know.'

'You haven't done your research very well, have you?' I snap.

It's a childish remark and he glares back at me, wipes his mouth with the napkin and tosses it into the middle of the table.

'The Syrian lawyer has gone missing.' I stab the table with my finger. 'So the mystery donor must be pissed off - they must wonder where the Torah is? They must want it back.'

'They probably assume that if Mariam died in the earthquake then the Torah was destroyed or lost too.'

'What would you do?'

'Me?'

'Yes, if you were the donor? Wouldn't you want to make sure the Torah was safe? Wouldn't you want to know what happened to it, Stelios?'

'I suppose so.'

'What if she was followed? What if someone knew she was going to get the Torah and followed her to Turkey and stole it.'

'It's possible but who?'

'Someone from the Museum in Athens might have told the wrong person.'

'No.'

'She sent photographs to Simon just before the earthquake. She had it with her. Who took it out of the rubble?' I ask. 'Was it a coincidence that someone found and sold it on the blackmarket or was she being followed and someone took it?'

Stelios doesn't reply but stares thoughtfully into his wine glass so I continue speaking.

'I've rented a car. I'm going to see Alexandros, Mariam's husband, first thing in the morning. I'll be back by midday to come with you to see the Torah. He might remember if there was anyone else she told about going to Turkey. Maybe there's some paperwork or an email or some information that's been overlooked. It's worth checking. She might have mentioned to someone that she was going over there.'

'Nikos hinted that he bought the Torah from a dealer in Turkey. Anyone could have picked it up after the earthquake.'

'What if it is the same Torah and Nikos won't hand it over to us?' I insist.

'Of course he will. Elias and Athena will be there.'

'I'm not sure he's that decent.'

Stelios laughs. 'He's not a bad person, Mikky. He likes to push the boundaries and he presses people's buttons to get a reaction but he's just a kid at heart.'

'He has a strange relationship with his sister.'

'Anna?'

165

'I met her on Sunday - and again this morning.' I lean across the table. 'I wandered onto the beach on Sunday evening and found this girl - the girlfriend that Nikos had been sitting with at the meal - she was unconscious. She'd been injecting herself....'

Stelios looks at me with disbelief.

'It's true. She was really ill-'

'Did you tell Nikos?'

'Well, this girl came along - who I realise now was Anna and she was furious with me for interfering. She dragged the girlfriend along the beach and Anna wouldn't let me help her. Then she accused me of being drunk.'

Stelios laughs. 'We did drink quite a lot.'

'It's not funny! What about those girls on the yacht yesterday? They're Romanian and when I tried to ask them about Cristina-'

'Cristina?'

'The girlfriend who was on the beach,' I explain. 'They appeared to know who I was talking about but then Nikos came down into the cabin and stopped us from talking.'

Stelios refills our wine glasses and I continue speaking.

'Don't you think it's odd that he has these girls with him. They're not models, Stelios, they're like...' I let the words hang in the air and I stare meaningfully at him. 'Did you pay them?'

'For what?'

'Come on, Stelios. I know what happened on the boat. Did you pay them? Is Nikos renting them out? He's treating them like prostitutes.'

Stelios leans across the table and glares into my eyes. His pale skin shines in the orange light and his voice is stern and serious.

166

'If you haven't noticed I have very white skin and lots of freckles. A fact that Nikos kept talking about on the yacht. I'm not a gung-ho, tough-guy, action man with an intellectual inferiority complex. But I did drink too much wine and the hash was strong. I didn't feel great so, as soon as you guys disappeared in the water I told Yannis. He's a good guy and he let me go downstairs and use his bunk - where I dozed off. I didn't have sex - or a threesome.' He speaks through his teeth as if controlling his temper.

'I'm sorry but Nikos led me to believe-'

'I don't care what Nikos said. I'm a married man and my wife has just had our first baby - only six months ago. I love them both and I would do nothing to jeopardise my marriage.'

I breathe a sigh of relief and smile. 'Congratulations.'

'Not all men are like Nikos, Mikky. There are kind, generous and loving men who mean what they say and have no ulterior motives. Believe it or not there are some guys who can genuinely have women as friends. They don't see them as sex symbols or as a replacement for their mother's - or sister's affection. We're not all suppressed, aggressive, testosterone filled teenagers with no conscious thought, training or sensitivity. Some men, like me, like Elias, like Alexandros just want to love one woman and have a happy family. Now, I'm going to the bathroom before I really get angry.'

As he walks away from the table I realise I've overstepped the mark. I had assumed - or rather Nikos had led me to believe the worst about Stelios and I was wrong. I sit smarting over his words and his rebuke and that's when I catch a glimpse of the bald man walking past the taverna. I want to leap out of my seat but I've been making too many assumptions and too many mistakes.

It's time I listened and learned.

I watch the man disappear into the crowd and I sigh. There is something strong in Stelios' manner, a quiet, principled dignity that reminds me of Eduardo and I think of him holding his baby; a tall gangly father, all arms and legs, cradling a delicate little girl and loving her so completely.

Eduardo would make a wonderful father.

Stelios returns to the table. 'I've paid the bill. Let's go.'

I thank him and on the walk back to the taxi rank I link my arm though his, determined to redeem myself in his eyes.

'I'm sorry Stelios. I'm not the awful person you think I am. I'm very professional and I would never let Simon Fuller, you or anyone else down,' I say.

'Let's see what happens tomorrow.' His response is gruff but I'm pleased that he doesn't pull his arm away from mine.

When we arrive back at the hotel the receptionist calls me over to say that my car has arrived. I say goodnight to Stelios and spend a few minutes signing the documents. I've decided to leave early to be back for midday. Afterwards, feeling restless and thoughtful, I wander outside to sit on the terrace. There's a couple in the far corner kissing so I deliberately sit where they can't see me. I order a brandy nightcap while I check my iPhone. The evening breeze cools my jumbled emotions and I take pleasure in the illuminated garden and quiet shadows. It's at times like this I wished I still smoked. Even a joint would be a welcome relief. It would relax the tension in my neck.

I text Eduardo and I'm pleased when he replies back straight away:

Me: Did you have a good day? How's work? XXX

E: Did you see the Torah?

Me: Not yet. XXX

E: So what did you do today?

Me: I went to the Jewish Museum. XXX

E: Who with?

Me: Stelios XXX

E: And dinner?

Me: I'm having an early night. I've been thinking of you. XXX

He doesn't reply, so I text again.

Me: Can I call you? XXX

E: My shift is just starting.

Me: I'm sorry. XXX

I wait ten minutes and when there's no answer I text Josephine.

Me: Hope all is well? Did you ever meet Elias and Athena Pavlides on a yacht in the Med?

I am about to text Simon when suddenly I'm cast in shadow. I sense a figure standing beside me and I turn. He covers my lips with his hand and grabs my wrist. His accent is foreign and his voice urgent.

'I want to talk with you. No harm will come to you here in the hotel. We have things to discuss. Okay?'

I nod.

He takes his hand from my mouth. It's the young bald man

who has been following me. I glance around to see if anyone has noticed but the few guests on the terrace are engrossed in conversation with their partners and they pay us no attention. He pulls out a seat and sits beside me.

'I could scream,' I say.

'Please don't. It's not necessary.' His accent is Eastern European. I have met people like him before. Russian Mafia – cold calculating – murderers. My wrist is sore and I'm sure he could have broken it with no effort.

'You've been following me. Who are you?'

'My name doesn't matter,' he says.

'Where are you from?'

He pauses. 'Albania.'

'What do you want?'

'You must verify the authenticity of the Torah as soon as possible. Nikos is looking for a buyer on the blackmarket.'

'What do you know about the Torah?'

'Trust me.'

'Why have you been following me?'

'To protect you.'

I laugh sarcastically. 'From whom?'

'All of them.'

'All of who?'

He says nothing but his piercing blue eyes and a raw, ragged scar on his forehead send a chill through my stomach.

'Why do you want to protect me?' I insist.

'Because they're ruthless and greedy.'

'And how do you know all this?'

'Trust me. Stelios has an appointment to see the Torah with Elias and Nikos. You must go with him and verify it in the morning.'

'Then what?'

'Then we can have it returned to the Jewish Museum.'

'Is that what you want?'

'It's what my client wants.'

'Who is your client?'

'It doesn't matter.'

'What happened to your head?'

He raises a hand and touches his skin. 'An accident.'

'You were with Mariam in Turkey, weren't you? You were her bodyguard.'

He stands up. 'I don't matter. This is about the Torah. Don't fuck up!'

The sun rises before five o'clock and the streets are empty. I jog quickly, pushing myself and panting hard, needing to exercise, clear my head and sort myself out. I run on unfinished pavements and in the street, imagining the view from the gyrocopter. I pass the closed tavernas and the bar where Stelios and I walked only the night before last. The bald Albanian had been standing outside the taverna. Waiting. He had been following me. If he was Mariam's bodyguard then he had been employed by the Syrian lawyer. The only person who knew the donor's identity.

I stop to lean against a street lamp for a few seconds gasping for breath but it smells of urine so I walk slowly up a dirt track past sleeping villas, small apartment blocks and fields of olive trees. I remember Nikos' story on the yacht about the old couple who wished to be buried together. I think of Mariam and Alexandros and then of Eduardo but I can't imagine a lifetime with someone I love. Was he right. Had I been more excited coming to Rhodes than a lifetime with him?

I loop my way around the track back to the hotel. I have no more answers only more questions jostling for position and priority in my head.

Back in the hotel I run a quick shower. Afterwards I pull a Foo Fighters T-shirt over my head and slip into dark jeans and boots.

I'm in a hurry.

I want to get to Lindos and back before I see the Torah at midday. I think Alexandros may shed some more light on the Torah and I have a photograph of the bald man that I took from the Yannis's yacht. Alexandros might know the Albanian who I hope will lead me to the mysterious donor.

I'm annoyed with myself for not asking Simon more details about the whole affair but on reflection, I suspect he told me nothing so I wouldn't get too involved. His instruction had been clear, view the Torah with Stelios and pass on his best wishes to Alexandros.

I pick up the car key and find the rented silver Skoda outside the hotel parked against the hedge. I gun the car into life revving the engine but in my haste I realise I forgot my camera. Cursing my forgetfulness, I turn off the engine, climb out and slam the car door. I'm ten metres away when the explosion rocks me off my feet and debris falls like a heavy meteoric shower.

'What the f-' I shout and instinctively crouch down covering my head protecting it from shards of flying glass. The damaged exhaust pipe lands inches from my face and my hired car is in flames, its engine smouldering and beside it the hedge is on fire.

A gardener quickly tackles the small blaze diverting the spray from the hosepipes watering the garden and I sit on the hotel step watching him. His colleague joins him circling the car with a fire cylinder to extinguish what's left of the flames, dousing the nearby trees and shrubs.

The receptionist appears behind me. She's a different girl to the one last night.

'Are you okay? Is that your car?'

'I'm fine. No,' I lie.

I wait until my knees are no longer shaking and as a small crowd gathers I slip away. I'm still shaking as I run up the two flights of stairs to my room. It takes me only a few minutes to grab my clothes and toiletries, stuffing them inside my holdall. I throw my camera, that saved my life, around my neck and empty the safe, slipping my passport in my back pocket and my engagement ring on my finger.

Downstairs in the reception the crowd has grown.

Staff are reassuring everyone that it's safe.

There is no crime in Rhodes.

In the street I mingle casually with the locals, guests and tourists as two uniformed police officers drive up in a marked car. I slip away from the Palacio Hotel, lucky to be alive. Once I'm on the main street I jump onto the first bus that comes along and swing my bag onto the seat beside me. Outside the window, just a few metres away, the bald man is scanning the streets. I duck down behind the seat as the bus gathers speed taking me in the direction of Rhodes old town.

Chapter 10

'One thing I know, that I know nothing. This is the source of my wisdom.' - Socrates, Philosopher of the 5th century BC.

I negotiate my way through the cobbled streets, getting lost in the maze of narrow alleyways before locating my destination: The Knight's Suites Hotel with the stunningly beautiful and enclosed courtyard I'd passed only yesterday afternoon with Stelios. Although it's early, I'm greeted by the receptionist with a warm smile who tells me I'm lucky and there's only the last suite available. I am still shaking as I walk up two flights of stairs. Although the room is luxurious with a king sized bed and stunning rooftop views across the town to the harbour, I have more important things on my mind.

I send a message to Simon Fuller.

Someone tried to kill me this morning! Supposed to finally see the Torah at midday. Will text you. MX

I phone the Palacio Hotel and ask to be put through to Stelios' room. It's almost eight o'clock and his voice sounds sleepy as if I've woken him.

'Someone just blew up my rented car,' I say.

'What?' I can imagine him swinging his legs out of bed and rubbing his tired face.

I tell him what happened this morning.

'Who would have done it.'

'Nikos?'

'Don't be crazy, Mikky.'

'I mean it, Stelios. He tried to shoot my hand with the speargun on Monday and then when we went in the gyrocopter he really freaked me out. I told you he was trying to scare me.'

'Why?'

'I don't know,' I lie.

I haven't told Stelios about my conversation with Nikos and how he wants me to help him do a deal with the Italian but it still doesn't make sense.

Why try to kill me?

'We've an appointment to see the Torah at midday. We'll find out then if Nikos is involved,' he says decisively.

'Where was he last night?' I ask.

'You're reading far too much into it all, Mikky. He wouldn't kill you over a Torah. You haven't even seen it yet. It's all a coincidence...'

'What if it's to do with those Romanian girls. The ones from the boat and Cristina the one who was ill at the party. Maybe he's using these girls as sex slaves. He's sex trafficking, Stelios.'

'Don't be crazy, Mikky.'

'I'm not - think about it. He was trying to set you up on the boat - wasn't he?'

The line goes quiet. 'I wasn't interested.'

'I know but he wanted you to be. He did his best, didn't he?'

'Let's not get everything out of proportion. We'll go and meet Elias and see how Nikos behaves. It's only a couple more hours. Give me half an hour to jump in the shower and I'll meet you downstairs for breakfast.'

'I've moved out of the hotel.'

'Where are you?'

'I'm not telling you - or anyone. Where are we meeting today?'

'Elias is sending a car for us. We are going to his home.'

'Then find out where he lives and I'll get a taxi. Text me his address.'

Having been awake early I'm now very hungry. I wander downstairs to the patio and order breakfast in the shady courtyard sitting with my back against the wall. The gated door allows me a view of the street and I watch the faces of the strangers that pass.

The rented car had been parked outside the hotel overnight so anyone could have attached a small device to it. There had been no sign of anyone near the car this morning when I went jogging but it doesn't mean to say it hadn't already been rigged last night.

Who would want to kill me?

Nikos?

Elias?

Stelios?

The bald man?

But why?

It's a shot in the dark but I am beginning to wonder if Elias isn't aiding Nikos. Perhaps they are working together. But on the other hand - why would Elias entangle himself in this mess - he has a successful business - why ruin it?

What would Elias say when one of his guests is almost killed outside his hotel?

I spend the next hour writing names of all the people I've met since I arrived on the island: the Pavlides family - four members, Nikos, Anna, Stelios, Cristina, Yannis and then finally I add Alexandros.

It's random but now I know I can't trust anyone.

I spend the next hour studying the images of the Torah that Mariam sent Simon Fuller last September before the earthquake in Turkey killed her. It is essential that I am definite about the identity of the Torah and I am suddenly filled with excitement, determination and purpose.

Today I will finally see the Torah.

Elias and Athena's home is within walking distance of the hotel, at the far end of the village, set back from the sea and surrounded by an unimposing garden. Like the Palacio Hotel, their Italian style villa is charming with understated elegance.

I pay the taxi driver and almost immediately Elias opens the front door. He kisses me on both cheeks.

'Come in, come in, Mikky. I heard about the incident this morning. The rented car...it was yours. It was lucky no one was injured.'

'Incident - you're joking?' I reply barely concealing the anger in my voice. 'It was deliberate.'

His smile fades.

We stand alone in the vast hallway beside the sweeping stair-case. The centre piece on a mahogany table is a magnificent sculpture of a racing horse. It's amazing and for a moment I pause, distracted by its beauty and the tightness of its black marble muscles.

'It was a petrol explosion, a fault in the car I believe. An unlucky accident. It was fortunate you weren't inside.'

'More like a bomb. Someone tried to kill me.'

'A bomb?'

'I started the engine but I forgot my camera and so I went back inside. It was timed to go off several minutes after I switched on the engine.'

'No, no, no. There must be some mistake.'

'I'm telling the truth Elias.'

'Don't worry I will speak to the local police. We take the safety of our hotel guests very seriously. No-one could be more angry than me. Come, Stelios has just arrived. Come into the dining room. It's better we go in here. The table is large and we'll be able to see the Torah at its best.'

When Elias opens the door Athena turns around to face me. She smiles and opens her arms, greeting me like an old friend.

'Elias has told me what happened this morning. Are you alright?'

'I'm shaken-'

'But not stirred?' adds Stelios standing beside me.

'That's not funny.'

'Who would have done this?' she asks, glancing at Elias.

'It's already sorted.' Elias waves his hand in dismissal. 'It's all been taken care of there's and no damage done - well no-one has been hurt. We'll have to sort out the hedge but the main thing is that Mikky is alright and so are all the other guests. No harm done.'

Nikos's brown eyes regard me carefully as he hugs me in

greeting. 'Are you alright?'

'It was deliberate,' I say stubbornly.

'Do you think so?' Athena looks closely at me.

'Why would anyone do that?' asks Nikos.

'It could have something to do with the Torah?' I suggest glaring at him but Elias puts his arm around my shoulder and guides me to the long dining table.

'Let's move on. There are more important things to discuss this morning.'

Stelios shakes his head. 'I don't think it's anything to do with the Torah or they would have targeted me but they haven't.'

'Who's they?' asks Athena.

Stelios shrugs.

'Is it some sort of conspiracy? Elias?' she asks.

'No, I don't think so. It's not good to dwell on these matters...'

'It's someone who doesn't want me on the island.' I sound petulant.

'Who wouldn't want you here, Mikky?' Nikos puts his arm around my shoulder and smiles. 'I'm pleased you're safe.'

I shrug him off and push him away. 'I thought perhaps you might know who did it, Nikos?'

'Me?' He looks aghast.

'Nikos, do you know anything about this?' growls Elias.

'Of course not, why would I?' He holds his palms upwards and shrugs in Greek fashion. 'We're friends, Mikky, aren't we?'

I turn away, my emotions are colliding but my anger is now subsiding. I have to control myself and not let accusations take over. I've been making too many assumptions and so I take a deep breath and step back from them all. To refocus, I take in the details of the large colonial room.

At the far end, rectangular windows overlook a tropical garden. Beside me on the long dresser are family photographs, pictures of Arianna and Michalis and several images of Elias and Athena showing expensive holidays abroad; skiing, yachting - there's even a photograph taken at Ground Zero and my heart lurches.

New York.

One photograph in particular interests me and I lean closer to inspect the faces. It shows four people, very beautiful women who have the same aquiline nose and high cheekbones. Athena is much younger in the picture. She's probably in her early twenties and standing in front of her is her daughter Arianna as an unsmiling teenager. Beside her is a middle-aged, attractive woman with a wide smile who I assume is her mother and the last lady, the eldest woman, has hunched shoulders and grey hair. The similarity between the women is unmistakable.

'That's my mother and grandmother.' Athena lifts the frame and hands it to me. 'It's one of my favourite photographs and it was taken shortly before my grandmother died almost fifteen years ago.'

'Four generations of women. It's beautiful,' I say truthfully, remembering her mother had died only last year. 'There's an amazing likeness in you all.'

'That's a compliment coming from a photographer,' she smiles and takes the frame from my hands and replaces it on the unit. 'It's lovely to see you, Mikky. I'm so sorry about what happened. Nikos was just telling us what a lovely day you all had sailing on Monday.'

'Yes, and he also took me on his gyrocopter yesterday,' I add without smiling.

If Athena notices the edge to my voice she ignores it and pours coffee for us into china cups.

'Didn't we have fun.' Nikos' eyes gleam and I am looking for a hint of malice but he's flushed and excited. He's restless and charged.

My mobile pings and I pull it from my pocket. The message is from Simon.

Urgent - Call the police. Italian now arriving tomorrow - THURSDAY. Tell Stelios everything. He will protect you. Look after yourself. SX

Nikos claps his hands together and directs our attention to a damaged cylinder placed upright on a dining chair in the corner of the room. 'This is it.'

I place my iPhone back in my pocket.

As a precaution Stelios pulls on a pair of latex gloves and hands a pair to me. He takes the lead picking up the cylinder and carrying it to the table where he studies the outer casing. I stand beside him, looking over his shoulder, noting how dried blood has seeped into the cardboard container.

I think of Mariam and I shudder, overcome with a sense of loss and despair. I remember the faces of her two children, their innocent eyes and sad demeanour and, I remember my promise to them last Sunday.

I will get this Torah to the Jewish Museum. I'm filled with an angry sense of duty. I know that nothing will stop me from taking it from Nikos. I will call the police. I'll call Interpol or whoever it takes.

I hold my breath as Stelios pulls the scroll reverently and very slowly from the tube. The cylinder is probably sixty

181

centimetres in length and the whole thing probably weighs about twelve kilos.

Elias and Athena are focused on his actions and it's only Nikos who looks at me and when he sees me glaring at him, he winks.

'Where did you get this?' I ask him.

'It doesn't matter,' he replies.

'Actually, it does.'

I look from him to Elias and then to Athena. I need them on our side. 'Morally, it matters very much, Nikos. You're going to have to provide us with the provenance. We need to know its origins and where it's been. So you'll have to tell us.'

'The casing is damaged.' Stelios ignores my outburst and turns the cylinder in his hands.

'From the earthquake?' I ask.

'Probably.'

'And the blood?' I ask softly.

Stelios ignores me.

'Mariam had just left Selçuk when the earthquake struck. She was in a car when the road split in two and they ended up in a ravine. There's blood on the cylinder.' I point to the marks on the thick cardboard.

'Don't prejudge,' Nikos says. 'It might not be the same one.'

'Do we know how it got here to Rhodes?' Stelios asks but doesn't look up.

'How did you get this here, Nikos?' I suddenly remember what Alexandros said to me in the hotel the day I arrived. A sudden feeling of dread comes over me. It might be harder than we think to return it to the museum. Perhaps Nikos and this family won't be prepared to release it to us.

No-one answers the question and silently we watch Stelios

lay the Torah on the long dining table. He indicates for me to stand the other side and nods at me to hold the top edge. Very carefully we lay it flat on the table and he unravels a few metres of the ancient parchment.

The room is silent but I hear Athena's breath catching in her throat as she plays with a golden charm hanging around her neck.

'It is beautiful, isn't it?' I say smiling, pleased she appreciates its beauty.

'Do you know where... it's from?' she asks.

'The specific origin would be hard to establish. The Sephardic Jews were exiles from the Iberian peninsular and they settled in many places across Europe and the Middle East as we know it today,' I reply.

'So it could be from anywhere?' she insists.

'The one that Mariam had gone to collect was from Syria. The war has led to many artefacts being looted and sold on the black market.'

'Aren't there specialist scribes who need to look at this?' she asks.

Stelios glances up. 'There are Sofers - Jewish scribes - who analyse the content of the parchment, the letters, the style and the way it's written. I'm not here to validate it. It's my job to ascertain if it warrants their time - and also the financial investment to investigate it further on behalf of the Archaeology Museum in Athens.'

Athena nods, bites the corner of her mouth and glances at Elias. We are all looking at the Torah but listening to Stelios.

'For the Jews there is no old and new testament. The bible that the Christians call the New Testament are not part of the Jewish scriptures. The Torah refers to the Five Books of Moses:

Bereisthith is the equivalent to Genesis - In the Beginning. Then there's Exodus - The Names, and Leviticus - And He Called. Finally there are Numbers - In the wilderness, and Devarim which is the equivalent of Deuteronomy - The Words.'

Stelios removes a magnifying glass from his pocket and leans over the scroll, analysing and peering intently at the markings. 'The scriptures are normally written on parchment, animal hide that's soft like a leather jacket. It's normally cow's hide slaughtered the Kosher way. The edges are harder in texture. No-one touches a Torah because of the sweat from our fingers. Normally, the Rabbi or those asked to read from it, follow the text with a Yad, that's a hand with a pointing index finger. They don't touch it with their skin. The scrolls are also normally kept in an ark - as in the Ark of the Covenant, also referred to as the Ark that Moses sailed - it's a special cabinet in the synagogue.'

Elias leans across the table. 'It looks very...intricate. Can you understand it?'

'I can understand the important things like for example there are some clues to the age of a Torah and also its Sephardic origin. Look at this, normally the Torahs have forty-two lines in each column. This is an older Torah and it has forty-five lines. Most of these letters are elongated which is also another sign of its age. In new Torahs these letters 'nun' and 'yud' are normally separated. However in this one they are joined.' Stelios stands back from the table and passes the magnifying glass to me. 'Take a look.'

He knows I have no experience in scripts, scrolls or Torahs but I know he's asking me to check the marks with the ones consistent to Mariam's photographs. I spend a few minutes studying the parchment then I move to the right corner and identify the inch tear and the water mark in the shape of a fat serpent, slightly bigger than a thumb print.

I return the magnifying glass to Stelios and remove my gloves. I take my iPhone from my pocket and flick quickly through the images for the photographs Mariam sent to Simon before she died.

'What's wrong?' asks Athena.

'What are you doing?' Elias leans to look over my shoulder.

'Mariam, the girl who was sent to recover the Torah from Turkey, was with the Syrian lawyer in the hotel in Turkey and she sent photographs of the Torah to Simon Fuller.'

Athena gasps.

Elias places his hand on my arm. 'Before the earthquake?'

'Yes.'

'Impossible,' says Nikos.

I continue speaking, 'As we all know Mariam died and the Torah was lost.'

'She sent the photographs before the earthquake happened?' Athena repeats. Her eyes wide and round in disbelief.

'Yes. She was in the hotel with the lawyer. It was the only place with an Internet connection. Simon Fuller asked Mariam to go to Turkey to collect it on behalf of the museum and so she contacted him and sent him the photographs straight away,' I confirm.

'Impossible,' Nikos argues. 'This isn't the same one. It's not possible. I don't believe you.' He looks at Elias and Athena as if pleading for their support.

'Where did you get it, Nikos?' I ask softly. 'You've successfully wriggled out of telling us anything significant since we've been here. You've fobbed us off. You've given us no information and you've made us wait three days. You certainly haven't been honest.'

'I have–'

'If you'd bought it legitimately then you would have nothing to hide,' I insist.

'You can't prove it's the same one,' he argues.

'Yes I can.' I stare defiantly at Nikos. 'Where did you get this?'

'I bought it from a reputable dealer in Turkey.'

'When?'

'It doesn't matter.'

'Who did you buy it from? Give me his details and I can check him out. It's too much of a coincidence that two Torahs have turned up at the same time in the same location. It could even be a forged copy.'

Elias looks at Stelios. 'Is it a fake?' he asks.

Stelios rubs his cheek. 'Mikky is right. We need to establish its authenticity. We need to run some carbon-dating tests to see if it is one of the oldest Torahs. It's hard to tell with the naked eye–'

'Then what's been the point of all this messing around if you can't tell us.' Nikos circles the table his hands in his pockets.

Stelios speaks calmly and directs his gaze at Elias. 'We need to verify that it is or isn't the same one that Mariam collected in Turkey and Mikky can definitely do that.'

I lift my iPhone. 'I have the photographs Mariam sent to Simon.'

'Impossible,' Nikos shouts.

Elias coughs, clears his throat and glances at Athena but it's Nikos who raises his voice.

'You haven't got a clue, have you? This has all been a performance. You can't prove it's the same one,' he shouts.

'You don't know anything about these things. How do we know your photographs aren't fake?'

Stelios peers inside the tube as if he's not listening to Nikos, and so I reply.

'Look at these photographs. It's impossible they could be fake photographs.' I hold out my iPhone and Elias stares at the images and I continue speaking. 'There are certain similarities that we can't ignore between the images that Mariam sent of the Torah and this one on the table. See the slight tear here, between these two words and also this water-mark in the shape of a fat snake? These are the same marks on the pictures Mariam sent to Simon Fuller.'

I place my iPhone beside the parchment for them to compare.

Elias and Athena lean forward but Nikos raises his voice.

'That doesn't prove a thing. You can't base all this on a few photographs.'

'We will be able to.' I'm thinking of the bald Albanian when I add, 'I believe I may be able to find the donor who will also verify and testify to it being the same one.'

'The donor?' says Elias. 'Who is it?'

Stelios looks at me in surprise.

'No one is going to pay a fortune to legitimately donate this to a museum and not follow it through. Would you spend thousands - only to let it be stolen? The donor wants it taken to the museum.'

'So, if it's the same Torah then it will be returned to the Jewish Museum?' Athena's question is crisp and dry and she sounds suddenly like a lawyer.

'Yes.' I square my shoulders defiantly.

'That's the plan,' Stelios adds. 'I'm here to tell you if it's worth the financial investment to research further. It's worth the time and money to find out more about this. We need to take it to the scribes, run tests and I think we should–'

'You don't know anything.' Nikos shouts. He turns away from the table and begins pacing the floor. 'You've wasted our time, you don't even know if it's the real thing.'

'It's real alright.' Stelios frowns bristling with indignation.

'Is it valuable? Is the museum going to pay me for it?' demands Nikos.

'How much did you pay for it?' I ask. 'Can you prove what you paid?'

But it's Athena who asks quietly. 'Can you say that it is definitely the Torah that Mariam had with her in the earthquake?'

I've spent days studying the photographs, memorising every detail and fortunately my photographer's sharp eye can see it's the same tear that this Torah has.

'I believe it is,' I reply quietly. 'These photographs show a tear and this watermark in the top right corner that are consistent with these marks here.' Again I point out the tear and the watermark.

Elias and Athena lean over the parchment, taking it in turns with the magnifying glass to check for themselves.

Nikos glares at me. 'This wouldn't stand up in a court of law. You don't know for sure. You can't possibly say it's the same one.' He grabs the cylinder and shoves it at Stelios's chest. 'Roll it up and put it back. I'm going to get some expert advice. I'm not messing around with amateurs.'

Stelios lays the cylinder back on the table and begins to roll up the parchment.

Athena glances at Elias but he seems to be lost in thought then he suddenly looks at me and then at Nikos.

'Go on, put it back in there, Stelios. I'll take it somewhere else.' Nikos orders. He paces nervously as Elias speaks to him in Greek. Nikos rattles something back at him and Elias seems to accept what Nikos says then he nods and steps away from the table.

'What?' I ask. 'What did you say?'

Stelios is rolling the Torah into the cylinder.

Elias walks over to the window and that's when it dawns on me. That's when I understand the game they're playing. They all know it's the same one but they want to keep it.

'We can take it back to Athens for verification or we can take it now to the Jewish museum where it belongs,' I say.

'No!' Nikos cries. 'I'll go somewhere else. There's a lot of people who would want this–'

'A woman died because of this,' I shout leaning across the table.

Nikos folds his arms across his chest and his eyes flash defiantly. Suddenly I remember how he almost speared my hand and how he scared me in the gyrocopter. He threatened me and this morning my rented car was blown up.

'You won't intimidate me. It doesn't belong to you, Nikos and you know it,' I say quietly.

His cold eyes glare at me. 'Prove it.'

'This is the same Torah that was in the earthquake. It was donated to the Jewish Museum on the island. A lady from here died in Turkey but I guess you know about all that, don't you? How did it come to be in your possession, Nikos? How did you know about it? Was it from one of your refugees - from Syria - did they tell you about the looting of artefacts? Was it stolen from her before the earthquake even happened? Did you kill her?'

Elias steps toward me. 'Nikos hasn't killed anyone.'

'Shut up!' Nikos shouts. 'I'm not wasting any more time.' He snatches the Torah from Stelio's hands and although it's heavy he holds it easily in his arms. 'It's mine, and that's that.'

'You can't take it.' I run to block his path, standing between him and the door. 'It doesn't belong to you.'

'She's right.' Stelios stands to my left blocking his exit.

I reach out to take it but Nikos shoves my hand from his chest. 'Get out of my way you stupid bitch before I slap you.'

Athena gasps.

Stelios takes a step forward but I place my hand on his arm. 'Touch me and you'll regret it,' I hiss.

'Nikos. Nikos. Stop!' Elias growls. 'There's no need to speak like that. We can come to some logical and financial agreement.'

Nikos leans into my face and I smell stale Ouzo on his breath. He waves the tube in my face.

'Don't think you can get your hands on this. If you come within spitting distance, I'll take you down. And you,' he glares at Stelios. 'If you think I'm angry now, you've seen nothing.' He storms out of the room and we listen to the sound of his quick footsteps clicking across the marble echoing in the hallway.

My body is shaking and I turn to Elias and Athena. 'That's stolen property. We'll have to inform the police - Interpol.'

'Nikos doesn't believe that the Torah is the same one,' Elias argues. 'He wouldn't steal it and he wouldn't get it illegally. Nikos isn't like that. I know that boy, he's a good lad-'

'It is the same Torah,' I argue.

'We can prove it, if we have to,' Stelios adds.

'Elias, I made a promise to Mariam's children. Nikos isn't keeping it. The International Art Squad and just about every other culture crime specialist unit in Europe will work to get it returned to the Jewish Museum. It will involve a lot of time, money, effort and energy but he won't win. I'll make sure of it.'

Athena looks at Elias but he continues to stare silently at me. Suddenly he blinks and walks toward the window where he stands thinking until I say.

'There's something else.'

Elias turns to look at me. 'Simon just emailed me to say there's an Italian businessman. He's arriving tomorrow on his private yacht and Nikos is going to sell it to him on the black-market.'

Elias continues to stare at me as if he's digesting this information very slowly.

'Can you help us stop him?' I ask.

'How can I do that?'

'Call the police, Elias. Speak to Nikos. If necessary I will go onto the Italian's yacht. A young woman from this island lost her life. She has two young children.'

'I'll notify the authorities in Athens.' Stelios stands tall beside me and I breathe more easily, reassured by his presence.

'What do you think, Elias?' Athena's calm legal voice cuts through our dialogue and she is staring inquiringly at her husband. 'Do you believe them or do you believe Nikos?'

Elias's voice is deep and confident. 'It can't be the same one. There must be a mistake.'

Athena nods her head in satisfaction and she sighs. 'That's what I thought you'd say.' Her knowing eyes stare defiantly at me.

'They're all in it together,' I say.

The taxi is taking us to the old city but Stelios is looking out of the window. I can feel his anger and confusion but he won't meet my gaze.

'How could I have been so naive to think Nikos would just give up the Torah?' I moan.

Stelios doesn't reply so I continue.

'I assumed that with Elias and Athena there – they would have wanted to do the right thing but they are all from the same mould. I thought she was a lawyer – is she crooked?'

'Not at all. She works for the government but she's always supported her husband and he's highly regarded in the tourism industry.'

'So, a scandal could hurt their reputation?'

'Of course, but they are not directly involved. It's Nikos who has taken it. And remember, he's not their son only their nephew.'

'It's hardly the point. Elias has made it perfectly clear whose side he's on and it's not ours. He's endorsing Nikos's bad behaviour.'

'That's hardly relevant now.'

'So how will we get it back? Do you have a plan?'

He looks at me. 'Our job is done here. We will track Nikos through the authorities. I'll pass on this information to my superiors and they will decide what's best.'

'You're not going to do anything else?'

'What else is there to do? I'll go to the Archaeology Museum here on the island and inform them and they can liaise with the police – Interpol or whoever. Nikos won't get away with it but it will take time.'

'But what about the Italian – he's arriving tomorrow. What

if Nikos sells the Torah to him? You know how these artefacts disappear. It could be gone forever.'

'The Italian could be a legitimate collector.'

'Asians are the big buyers right now. Once it gets sold to China, Japan or even to one of the Russian states we might never see it again.'

Stelios replies. 'You are assuming...'

'Let's find Nikos?'

He shakes his head. 'That will make no difference at all, Mikky. He'll laugh at us or flex his muscles. You already think he's tried to kill you. What more do you want? Do you want to die?'

'I'm not giving up. Are you?'

'I have a wife and daughter in Athens. I've done what I came here to do. Simon asked me to look at it to see if it needed further investigation. That's all. I'll fly home after I've spoken to the authorities at the Archaeology Museum here on the island. I'll tell them what's happened.'

'What about brokering a deal with the museum - what happened to that idea? Isn't that what Nikos wanted?'

'It was obviously a scam. All Nikos wanted us to do is to verify the Torah so that he can sell it. He needed to verify that it's not a forgery or they would come looking for him if he sold them a fake.'

I gaze out of the window and pieces of the picture fall into place.

'He never paid for it,' I say.

I feel the heat of Stelios's eyes.

'He never bought it from a dealer,' I repeat. 'If he did, he would have told us who it was or how he got it. He doesn't have the money and I really don't think Elias would invest in something like this. I'm beginning to think he stole it. I think he knew about the Torah from the beginning and he followed Mariam to Turkey. He stole it.'

'In the earthquake?'

'Maybe he was following Mariam when the earthquake happened...'

'But he wasn't hurt?'

'Maybe he was lucky. If he was in the car behind them he may have had time to swerve or stop before he followed them into the hole in the road.'

Stelios stares at me. 'It's nothing to do with us, Mikky. We've done our job. We've done what Simon asked us to do. It's time to go home.'

'So that's it then? It's all over?'

I gaze out at the busy streets where crowds of people are wandering around the city; tourists, Greeks, Rhodians and as I scan their faces my photographer'e eye picks out the bald Albanian.

He is waiting at the gate to the old city near the harbour. I don't have my camera but I twist in my seat and raise my iPhone. Using the zoom I take a quick photograph of him before he turns away. I have one good shot.

'It's him.' I show it to Stelios.

He squints in the sunlight. 'Who is he?'

'He's interested in the Torah,' I insist.

'I've never seen him before.' He picks up his phone and dials a number and although I can't understand what he is saying I realise he is speaking to his wife and making baby noises and chuckling happily.

I leave Stelios at the gate leading into the old town. He's going to the Archaeology Museum and I have no desire to go with him. I'm angry and despondent so I wander around the quay looking at the yachts wondering where the Italian will berth tomorrow. I need to find out his name and so I send a message to Simon.

It might all be over for Stelios but it certainly isn't over for me.

I sit on a bench in the shade of a ficus tree cursing my stupidity. I have been outmanoeuvred by Nikos.

Did he try and kill me?

If so why?

He asked me to be involved in his negotiations but then he tried to scare me.

Why?

It takes the Albanian only an hour to find me and he slides onto the wooden seat beside me. I continue to stare out at the sea and I ignore him.

'What happened?' he asks eventually.

'Did you blow up my car this morning?'

'No.'

I glance at the scar on his forehead. 'Nikos has the Torah that Mariam went to collect in Turkey.'

He nods in satisfaction blowing out his cheeks. 'Good.'

'But Nikos has taken it and he's disappeared.'

'Elias didn't stop him?'

'He won't believe it's the same one. Maybe Elias is in on it too?'

The Albanian shakes his head and clasps his hands between his knees. 'I'd be surprised. What about Stelios?'

'He's gone to the Archaeology Museum. He's going to report

it and hope the police will arrive in time.'

'Before the Italian arrives?' His cold blue eyes hold no emotion and I reply.

'That's his plan.'

'His plan?'

'Yes.'

'Not yours?'

'Nikos has to be stopped. He could be anywhere but I'm going to find him before he meets the Italian tomorrow.'

'Where is he?'

'I don't know. He's got a gyrocopter in a field somewhere at the back of the Palacio Hotel. There's a cottage but it's disgusting I can't imagine him being there. He's also bought a building in the old city that he's developing into a small hotel. I think it's where he keeps the girls.'

'Girls?' he repeats.

'I think he takes young girls - refugees. He promises he will help them, you know, find a job and earn money but he gets them hooked on drugs and they become indebted to him. He makes them pay him back the money they owe him by turning them into prostitutes.'

'That happens in Albania. The gangs control girls through drugs too.'

'I'm not going to let him get away with it. I'm going to get the Torah.'

The Albanian's lips turn up in a smile but his cold eyes don't change. 'The donor will be pleased.'

'You know who the donor is? Who is it?'

He shakes his head. 'I can't tell you.'

'Then why don't you go and get the Torah?'

'You're the experts. You were going to get it. You and Stelios were dealing with it.'

'Well, you tell the donor from me that if you want me to get the Torah and return it to the museum, you'll have to do something for me.'

'What do you want?'

'Your email?' I hand him my iPhone. 'Put it in there and I'll send you a photograph.'

'Of what?'

'A girl. Her name is Cristina – she's Romanian. I want to know how she arrived here and when.'

'Why do you think I'll be able to help?'

He adds his contact details and he hands me back my phone.

'You're Albanian, aren't you?'

'Is she from Albania?'

'Do you have children?'

'Nieces and nephews.'

'Then imagine this is your niece – the prettiest one – the most vulnerable.'

'Where is she?'

'That's what I want you to find out.'

He scratches his bald head. 'What has this to do with the Torah?'

'Don't you understand? Nikos is sex trafficking girls from Eastern Europe. He's been working with his father in Athens with the refugees from all over and probably from Syria too. Somehow he separated the daughters from their families. He seduces them and lures them into staying with him. Maybe he offers them excitement, a job or money and stability. He probably even promises that he will help reunite them with their families. But he gets them hooked on drugs. At first it's a bit of hash, then some ecstasy tablets and then cocaine. He knows men who have parties on boats with drugs and alcohol. At first the girls think they're on holiday but once they get hooked, they have a debt to settle with Nikos. They're too ashamed and embarrassed to return home or to tell anyone.'

'This has nothing to do with the Torah.'

'Maybe not but it's one way of finding Nikos. You have contacts. You must do - you found me. Are you Mafia? Who is the donor? A wealthy American Jew?'

'Why are the girls so important?'

'Because he's stealing their identity, their youth and optimism. He taking everything that is sacred to them. He's making them perform sex acts they don't want to do. But it's not only that, it's about trust. They're coming here because they're escaping the violence in their own country. They have nothing, no safety or security. And he is taking advantage of them. It's not right. He should be stopped.'

'Why should I get involved?'

'Because it's the only way I'll help you get the Torah. Email me when you know something.' I stand up.

'What guarantee do I have?' he calls.

'You don't.'

'Then why should I help you?'

'Because your only other hope is Stelios and he's going back to Athens.'

I walk through the Burgo where the Jewish Museum is located and past the Martyr's Square without stopping or slowing my pace, weaving in and out and dodging tourists from a cruise ship that has docked in the port. I follow in their wake along the busy streets into the Collacchio - the historical city centre – wondering how I will find the building that Nikos bought.

'Mikky.' Stelios hails me with a wave from across the street. 'Mikky? Where have you been? I've been phoning you.'

He guides me to a busy cafe terrace and we order strong coffee and chilled water.

'I don't know what plans you have but I'm going to try and get a flight home this evening,' he says.

'I'm staying. I'm going to see this through.'

He sighs. 'I've spoken to the Museum here on the island and I've called the Curator in Athens. I told them what's happened and how we believe that Nikos has the Torah. It will be dealt with via the lawyers, the International Crime Squad and Europol. I've an appointment to talk to someone later this afternoon. They will serve Nikos with the necessary papers and he will have to hand it in or return it–'

'That could take months. He'll have sold it by then, Stelios. The Italian businessman arrives tomorrow and if we don't find Nikos today, it will be too late.'

'Interpol will be involved and the lawyers will submit papers to him by the end of the week.'

'It's probably already too late. We have no idea where he is.'

I finish my water and place the empty glass on the table.

'Perhaps we should appeal to Elias,' Stelios suggests.

'You saw his face – and Athena's – they're all in it together.' I stand up. 'Have a good flight home, Stelios.'

'Wait! What are you going to do?'

'I've just had an idea.'

'It's dangerous, Mikky. You already think that someone tried to kill you. What if it was Nikos?'

'And what if it wasn't?'

'Who could it be?'

'What if it was someone that we haven't thought of?'

'But why target you and not me?'

I shake my head. 'I have no idea but I'm going to find out.'

'Where are you going?'

'I've got an idea. I think I know someone who might help,' I smile. 'I'll phone you.'

Chapter 11

'The real destroyer of the liberties of the people is he who spreads among them bounties, donations and benefits.' - Plutarch, Historian of the 1st century BC.

I spend the next few hours searching the commercial harbour then I make my way to Mandrake Harbour where pleasure boats and private yachts are lined up along the quay. I find the yacht moored, swaying gently on the water.

'Yannis?' I call. 'Yannis? Are you there?'

I pull the rope that tethers it to the quay and I climb on board. There's no reply so I sit for a while on the deck and wait, conscious of the local Greeks watching me and guessing they will call Yannis.

It isn't long until he appears sauntering along with his hands in his pockets. When he sees me he smiles and waves.

'Kalimera,' he calls.

'Welcome aboard,' I laugh.

He jumps effortlessly onto the deck beside me.

'I need to talk to you. How much for an hour's cruise?'

He starts the engine and replies. 'Make yourself useful. Untie the ropes.'

I release the buoys and toss the coiled rope on the deck just as I saw Nikos and Stelios do only a few days ago. Yannis calls out, waves and jokes with the other mariners and once we are out of the harbour we glide across the open sea where the breeze is fresher. He doesn't bother with the sails and it's the engine that drives us. I stand beside him and gaze behind us at the V-shaped wake in the water. We are not followed.

The hazy Turkish coastline looks equidistant to Rhodes. We sail between the two countries, two cultures and two lifestyles and I think of the treacherous sea and the fear that immigrants face after they've left the turmoil and uncertainty of their own country.

Suddenly Yannis kills the engine and the boat rocks gently caught on the swell of the sea. I'm conscious of the isolation and the gentle rocking of the yacht. Yannis leans against the wheel and stares at me.

'What's here?' I ask. 'Why have we stopped.'

We stand a few metres apart. My back is against the rail.

'This is what happens,' Yannis replies. His eyes are hard and his tone severe. 'Isn't this what you want to know?'

A ripple of fear shivers through me. If I want to get away from Yannis there is no escape. Nowhere to run and nowhere to hide. I'm a strong swimmer and I quickly calculate the distance to land but I know I wouldn't make it easily – if at all.

'The sea is a funny thing,' Yannis continues. 'If you're on a yacht watching the sunset with an icy cocktail in your hand and your lover beside you then it's romantic but if you're on a boat with strangers, men you don't know and there's nowhere to escape then the sea is your enemy. There's no-one to call, Mikky. There's no help. And all the shouting and screaming in the world won't save you.'

My heart is thumping erratically. I glance down into the galley. On the shelf is a diver's knife and it glistens in the sunlight. I look for the box where Yannis took out the speargun on Monday and I swallow, calculating my options.

'Both situations are equally as dangerous,' Yannis continues. 'Depending on the lover or the stranger.'

Glancing at me, he pulls a bag of white powder from his jacket pocket. I've seen stash like this before. I know how they inject girls first to get them hooked on drugs. My mouth is dry and I lick my lips. He raps a taut plastic wire around his knuckles and watches my reaction. His boyish charming smile is teasing and his voice coaxing.

'You want to try some, Mikky? Smoking hash is just the start. It's relaxing and it lowers your inhibitions. A few E's makes you feel cocky and confident then it's the hard stuff.' He waves the bag teasingly in the air. 'Snorting cocaine reaches the brain slower than smoking. It takes about fifteen to thirty minutes until you feel its peak effect. You know, increased confidence and energy, mental alertness, paranoia, indifference to pain and fatigue...'

I'm calculating the distance to the nearest shore. I'm fit and healthy but the blades of the boat could easily chop me in pieces. He could make it look like an accident.

Yannis continues speaking.

'Impure heroine can be injected, dissolved or diluted into veins. The rush is accompanied by a dry mouth and a heavy feeling and then nausea, vomiting or severe itching. It slows your breathing and it can lead to a coma and sometimes permanent brain damage.'

He stares at the bag. Holding it high in the air against the afternoon sunshine.

'Withdrawal symptoms normally occur anytime between twenty-four and forty-eight hours after the last intake. Withdrawals, do you know what that is like, Mikky? They call it cold turkey - and it includes muscle and bone pain, diarrhoea, vomiting and cold flashes - goose bumps and jerky leg movements. It's not very pleasant...'

'Why are you telling me this?'

'In case you want some, do you? It's good stuff. It's the best.' He steps forward but I hold up the palm of my hand.

'No!' I shout.

'Don't worry.' Yannis folds the bag and puts it back in his jeans pocket. He points to the horizon. 'I thought I could trust you, Mikky. You're not like the others.'

'Others?'

'The other girls.'

'Who?'

'Immigrants. They come from there.' He points to the Turkish coastline. 'Mostly they're refugees from Syria, sometimes Afghanistan or Somalia and they come via Turkey. Nikos has a network of contacts from Syria to Romania, bringing in stolen goods, looted artefacts and human trafficking. The merchants charge them one thousand dollars per person for a passage to Europe. They bring them over in a Zodiac that normally carries twenty people but they squeeze forty on board. They cram them in, families, children, old people and pregnant women. They're all escaping. They've spent everything they have and they think they will be looked after here. The traffickers tow a jet-ski behind the Zodiac and once they get near the Greek coast they sink the Zodiac. The merchants escape on the jet-ski but the immigrants flounder. Sometimes they drown or go missing.'

I remember televised reports of immigrants arriving in Italy, Croatia and Greece and I can barely imagine the fear they must face let alone the discomfort and worry.

'How often does this happen?'

Yannis stands beside me looking at the Turkish coastline.

'Normally every two or three months. They're mostly families that want to reach their Syrian relatives in Europe. They are given papers and they can then go to France, Germany or wherever.'

I study Yannis. He's good-looking and charming and although he had me worried I know I'm safe with him.

'Isn't that what you wanted to know?' he asks quietly.

'How long does it take them to get papers?'

'Depends – about a week.'

'Do you pick up the refugees?'

'Frontex do that.'

'Who's Frontex?'

'The European Border and Coast Guard Agency. The Eastern Mediterranean is patrolled by them. They help the refugees. The Greeks asked for help – they couldn't cope. In 2015 almost nine hundred thousand migrants arrived this way. We Greeks know about being immigrants. Many of our families left here in the 50s after the war. There was nothing to stay here for. Rhodes was destroyed and families, some of them pregnant women, lost their lives and their property. Some returned in the 70s but others did not. We understand migrants. But not the merchants, the traffickers are people smuggling – human trafficking. It's a very important and lucrative industry in Turkey.'

'And the smugglers are the Turks?'

'Not always – normally they're the nationality of the refugees who trust these people with their savings. They believe they will be looked after and that they're coming here legally or will find work.'

I study the coastline and imagine the fear of the sea, leaving your homeland and your country devastated by war.

'They have nothing,' I say.

My legs are weak and I sit down leaning back against the rail. Yannis sits beside me and we rock on the waves to the rhythm of the yacht.

'You don't have to be an accountant to work out the profit they make,' he adds.

'Tell me about Nikos. How do you know him?' My voice is almost a whisper.

'I've known him for a few years. He comes to visit family on the island but in the last year or so he's been here more frequently. He told me that in Athens, in the summer, it's easy to meet daughters or girls of wealthy or sometime not so wealthy families. The girls are genuinely looking for work and he seduces them. They think he's in love with them. He insists in trying the goods first – to see how willing they are – and to see how easily he can manipulate them but more recently he's been involved with other girls – foreigners – immigrants.'

'Like those two girls with us last Monday?'

'They're Romanian. I think there's three or four of them here at the moment.'

'And he's sex trafficking?'

'They stay at his house.'

'And he forces them into prostitution?'

He nods. 'I think so.'

'Does Elias know? How does he get away with it?'

'His sister Anna is supposed to look after them. He makes out they're friends of hers. They go to the parties together – you know the type of party where rich boys have private yachts.'

'Anna goes along with this?'

'She's a little strange – I haven't seen her for a few months.'

'I saw her yesterday. Nikos took me on his gyrocopter. They seem to be very close.' I remember how she was wrapped around Nikos's neck, kissing his cheek.

Yannis doesn't react so I ask.

'Is this how he pays for his lifestyle? The gyrocopter can't be cheap and Nikos seems to like the good life...'

'I think so.'

'And you?'

'I'm not like him,' he says angrily. 'Nikos has asked me to help but I refused.'

'To do what?'

'He planted cocaine on my yacht.' He nods at the bag inside his pocket. 'He's threatened me and now he's attempting to blackmail me. He uses coke to control the girls.'

'How many are there?'

'Possibly four.'

'I've only seen three. One was very ill on Sunday night at Arianna's engagement party – Cristina.'

He nods. 'I was there.'

'You saw her?'

'I didn't stay for long. The whole town – everyone was invited. My family know Elias and Athena but I am not comfortable with Nikos. He's changed. He's become very....unsafe.'

'So why did you bring me out here, Yannis? Are you frightened of him?'

'This is where they sometimes exchange. When the girls are separated from their immigrant families they are brought here. The girls are transported by schooner and they're taken around the island to a bay near Lindos.'

'They don't come into Rhodes town.'

'They avoid the coastguard. They use a gulet - you know the Turkish boats? They're traditionally a two or three-masted wooden sailing vessel built in Bodrum or Marmaris.'

'Is it large?'

'They vary in size between fourteen to thirty-five metres. They use them for tourist charters - some of them are not properly rigged for sailing and they use a diesel engine but this one has red sails.'

'It sounds like a pirate ship.'

'They flaunt it, so it's never suspicious. Occasionally the coastguard take a look - perhaps they even turn a blind eye - I don't know. Maybe Nikos pays someone. But I brought you out here Mikky so that you would understand and feel their fear. I thought you might be able to do something to help.'

I can't tell Yannis about my past life. I can't tell him how I understand fear and the effect drugs had on me. They were a part of my life; a part of my past. I know terror. I know rape. I know darkness and drugs.

'There was no need to frighten me, Yannis. I'm on your side... So, Nikos takes money after the girls have sex with men?'

'Sometimes; depending on the party; he negotiates a fee upfront. He leaves them and comes back for them.'

'And why don't you go to the authorities? Why don't you tell the coastguard or the police?'

'Because his uncle is one of the most successful men on the island. He won't believe Nikos is a bad boy. Neither for that matter would my family or any other local people.'

'What about the police?'

'I can't go to them.'

'But you have evidence - what about the cocaine he planted

on your yacht?'

'How can I prove it was him?'

'Well, I believe you - why wouldn't they?'

'Look, when I was a young boy I was caught stealing. It was nothing big or major but I have a criminal record. No-one would believe me over Nikos.'

'We need to convince Elias then?'

'I doubt that will be possible. He adores Nikos.'

'Tell me something,' I say changing the subject. 'Did Stelios have sex with the girls here on the yacht last Monday when Nikos and I went swimming?'

He shakes his head again. 'Stelios was wasted. He was drinking to keep up with you and Nikos. He's not that sort of guy and with his pale skin I felt sorry for him so I took him down to my cabin so he could sleep it off. It was cooler there.'

'And the girls?'

'They watched a DVD in the other cabin. They're only kids - they love animation films. You know, the musical with the two princesses in the ice. It's their favourite,' he smiles. 'They knew all of the songs.'

'So, why are you telling me all this?'

'Because I only found out how dangerous Nikos is last night. He forced me to go out and help him and I'm ashamed.' Yannis' eyes darken. 'The crew on the gulet were rough. Three Turks. I didn't like them and Nikos swapped the girl - Cristina - I think she's the one from the party last Sunday night.'

'What?' I reach for my iPhone and flick through my pictures and show him the photograph of Nikos and Cristina laughing at the party. 'Is this her?'

'She looks worse now. She looks very bad. Not smiling and not happy.'

'Swapped? What did you swap her for?'

'A package.'

'Package? How big?'

'I couldn't see clearly but it was long and cylindrical.' He uses his hands to indicate the size of the Torah.

I think quickly. The Torah came over from Turkey last night.

'Do you know that he wants to sell a valuable scroll – a Torah – to an Italian tomorrow?'

'No. Are you alright, Mikky? You look terrible.' He places an arm awkwardly around my shaking shoulder.

'A woman died trying to bring a Torah here to the Jewish museum last September. She has two very small children and they are growing up without a mother. They'll never know what it felt like to have that security and love. I know what it was like, Yannis. I was adopted and my parents were very cruel to me. I know what it's like to grow up without a loving mother.'

'Come on.' He stands up and starts the engine. 'I'll help you.'

'We must go to the police, Yannis. Tell them the truth and I will back you up. I will stand by you. Don't be afraid of your police record. I'll speak to Elias if I have to. I must get the Torah back before tomorrow.'

The yacht glides into the harbour and after we haul the buoys over the side and secure the ropes I turn to Yannis.

'You said you thought there were four girls – so can you tell me where the other three are?'

The instructions Yannis gives me are comprehensive even with my limited knowledge of the old city. I walk purposefully contemplating our conversation and his silly schoolboy prank stealing from tourists that had given him a criminal record and his insecurity with the police.

His was no crime.

Now he said organised gangs appear in the summer and steal bags, wallets and bracelets which ruins the utopia of Rhodes where all religions and people normally mix harmoniously.

'We are Rhodians first and foremost,' he explained. 'There is no snobbery, no jealousy at others' success. Menial jobs aren't just done by immigrants. We work alongside foreign workers, sometimes second and third generation Albanians but they too are Rhodians.'

Josephine calls me just as I am passing Martyrs Square and I pause to sit near the monument under the shade.

'Dino has been arrested,' she says.

'When?'

'This morning.'

'But he's innocent.'

'That's why I haven't answered your texts, my darling. I've been so busy. Trying to rally some support and get his friends involved. But they're like rats scurrying from a sinking ship.'

'I'm sorry Josephine. I wish I could help.'

'Are you alright, Mikky? How's it going? Have you seen the Torah?'

'Didn't Dino used to come to Greece?' I ignore her question. 'Didn't you sing and meet his friends?'

'Sometimes. I used to be invited to parties and we sailed around the Med,' she replies.

'Do you know who his friends were?'

'Not really.'

'Did you know the name of the couple I texted you, Elias and Athena Pavlides?'

'There were so many people, Mikky. It was so long ago.'

'Was there a wealthy Italian businessman with his own private yacht who collected artefacts?'

'There probably was but it's over ten years ago, Mikky. Why?'

'Can you find out?'

'There are lots of Italians with their own yachts but I'll try. What's happening?'

'Nikos is going to sell the Torah to an Italian tomorrow and I have to stop him.'

'Are you in trouble?'

'Me? No. Not at all.'

I hang up my call with Josephine and walk across the square to the Albanian. He waits until I pocket my phone.

'Everything okay?'

'Have you found out anything?' I reply.

'Not yet.'

'Nikos brought the Torah over to Rhodes by boat last night. Some pirates were looking after it for him somewhere in Turkey. Their boat is a brown gulet with red sails and it's crewed by three Turkish men. He swapped a refugee called Cristina for the safe passage of the parchment. You must find that boat. You must find her.'

'I'll check it out.'

'God knows what they're doing to her – or what they've done. I also think they're bringing drugs into the island.'

'Who, Nikos?'

'I think he's involved with the people on the gulet. They run the illegal stuff under the pretence of it being a tourist boat.'

'You know the police are looking for you, Mikky? You hired the car that got blown up. They want to talk to you. Don't you think your life is in enough danger?'

'Nikos has bought an old property to do up as a boutique hotel. It has grey shutters. The girls are living there. They mostly work at night, private parties that sort of thing, sometimes on the big yachts with visiting foreigners. Maybe Nikos is also setting these girls up with the Italian tomorrow?' I sit with my elbows on my knees and my hands clasped. 'Did you find Nikos?' I ask,

'Nikos is not in hiding.'

'What's your relationship with the Jewish museum?' I ask.

'I'm employed to find the Torah.'

'So why aren't you getting it? Why don't you do something or are you happy to watch me do it all for you?'

His face darkens and when he says nothing I continue to bait him.

'You were with Mariam in Turkey. You were in the earthquake, weren't you? Tell me. You went with Mariam and you were supposed to escort her back here to the island?' I grab his arm but his muscles are made of steel. He pulls my fingers gently away.

'Tell me the truth,' I hiss.

'I was paid to protect her.'

'By whom? The Syrian lawyer or the anonymous donor?'

'Both.'

The Albanian sighs and looks around suddenly conscious of the tourists walking past us.

'I was employed by the Syrian on behalf of the donor as Mariam's bodyguard. It was supposed to be simple and straightforward. I met Mariam off the ship in Marmaris and I

213

drove her to a hotel in Seljuk, near Izmir, Ephesus. But as we were driving away from the hotel there was an earthquake and it was like a war zone. Buildings were collapsing around us. Debris was falling on the car and I thought we'd got through it but then the road opened up. A crack widened in the street and the car dropped into the void...' He uses his hands to signify how the car dropped. 'I couldn't do anything. I was trapped for ten hours. Hundreds died and thousands were injured. When I got out of hospital I found out Mariam had died. I contacted the lawyer and told him the Torah was gone.'

I watch the troubled emotions as they cross his scarred forehead wishing I could snap photographs of the horrific images trapped in his eyes.

'You never saw it again?'

'It was stolen.'

'How do you know?'

'We were being followed. A man in a white car – and as I was laying there, after the quake – I thought someone was coming to rescue us. He began digging and shoving the debris out of the way to get to us.'

'Who was it?'

He shrugs.

'You see didn't him?'

'He was like a giant shadow and I kept losing consciousness.'

'If someone was following you, then why wasn't he injured in the earthquake?'

'He must have been lucky. He was in the car behind us – so he probably braked in time.'

'Do you remember anything?'

'Just a shadow.'

'Was it Nikos?'

'I can't be sure.'

'Could Nikos have known that the Torah was being donated to the Jewish Museum before Mariam went to Turkey?'

'Maybe.'

'How could he know?'

'People talk.'

'Mariam would never have imagined it would cost her her life,' I say.

On the branch of the ficus tree over our heads a bird chirps and I glance up.

The Albanian's voice is almost a whisper when he replies. 'I failed her and I failed my employee.'

'Who is the donor?'

'I don't know.'

'Have you spoken with them?'

'I have been in contact but I don't know their identity. They want you to get the Torah. Do whatever it takes and I will help you.'

I smile and sigh heavily. 'Thank goodness. At last there's someone on my side.'

'But,' he says. 'I'm under instruction not to help you with the illegal trafficking. That's another business and one that doesn't involve us.'

I stare at him in disbelief, my impatience and my anger rising. 'Right, well good luck. Stuff you and stuff the donor. You'll have to find the Torah on your own.'

I begin to walk away.

'Where are you going?' he calls.

I turn around and continue walking backwards. 'Can't you see? They're linked - the girls and the parchment and the common denominator is Nikos. I will find the girls. They will lead me to Nikos and I'm going to get the Torah.'

I leave the Albanian behind knowing he's staring at me and I follow Yannis's directions. The Albanian has told me nothing – except that someone was following Mariam. Someone knew about the Torah. Could it have been Nikos?

Did he follow her or did he employ someone to follow them?

My instinct, hunch or whatever you like to call it tells me Nikos knew all along. It wouldn't have been difficult for him to go over there or to organise someone to follow Mariam. Maybe it was one of the Turkish pirates? They kept the Torah somewhere safe in Turkey and smuggled it into Greece last night. That's why he stalled us. He left it until the last moment to bring it here. It was probably a relatively easy task – stealing a Torah compared to human trafficking.

And the fact that Yannis believed he swapped the Torah for Cristina, as if her life is worthless, makes me very angry.

How dare he?

Where was she now?

I walk quickly down the narrow Medieval streets ducking under limestone buttresses built to protect the buildings in an earthquake and cross a small square where a scrawny cat slinks stealthily into a deserted alleyway.

The Albanian is of no use. I had hoped that he might use his contacts to find the gulet. Stelios has gone to the authorities but it will take too long for anyone to fly over here.

I follow the cat's skinny body and ragged limp and at the far end of the alleyway, as I come out into the sunlight, two mangy dogs are humping so I clap my hands and shoo them away.

Across the square and down another narrow alley I pause at a solid brown door and look up at the façade. There are several narrow windows and an archway on the second floor which leads across the street. Fleetingly I imagine this as a boutique hotel rather like the one where I am staying and I imagine it painted and refurbished and guests stepping into the shade of a luxurious reception.

I take a deep breath and bang the door hard with my fist.

There's no answer so I thump harder.

A neighbour opens her window and looks down at me. She rattles off a string of Greek words and when I don't reply, her head disappears inside and she slams the shutter closed.

Suddenly the door creaks open and a face with big glasses and large nose appears through the gap.

'Anna?' I say. 'It's me, Mikky.'

She opens the door a little wider.

'Where is he? Where's Nikos?' I ask.

'He's not here.' She tries to close the door but I wedge my boot against the frame and shove my shoulder against the door. She squeals and as I push past her into the cool, dark interior my senses summersault with the awful stench of damp and mildew.

It takes a while for my eyes to adjust to the dusty darkness. The small room is cramped with heavy furniture and there's an overwhelming dank, mouldy, fetid smell that seems to have penetrated every pore of the place. I sneeze then spy a crack of daylight between black drapes at the end of the room. In a few strides I tug the curtains aside. The patio door is already broken so I kick it open and venture outside to an interior courtyard where there's a warm scent of sewerage.

'Nikos?' I call into the empty courtyard. 'Nikos.'

I look up at the balcony above that runs around the gallery.

'He's not here,' Anna says behind me.

'Where is he?'

'What do you want?'

'What happened to Cristina?'

'I don't know anyone called–'

'The girl from the party last Sunday. Nikos's girlfriend. The one that was injecting herself on the beach.'

'Get OUT!'

She pushes my shoulder but I step back and she loses her balance and so I say quickly.

'He swapped her last night – out at sea – for the Torah. Didn't he? Where's she gone? What have they done with her?'

Anna covers her ears with her hands and closes her eyes, so I grab her arm. 'Nikos is human trafficking. He's using these girls as sex workers and you're helping him. You're turning them into prostitutes. You're forcing them to take drugs.'

She moves with speed. She twists, turns and lunges at my throat, taking me by surprise, punching me with her fists. Her blows are heavy and misdirected but one lands on my cheek bone and my head ricochets against the patio wall. She punches me again. This time I block her fist then I land a heavy punch on her temple. Undeterred she grabs my hair and we're grappling with each other. I hold her waist but she shoves me against the wall, lifting her knee sharply into my stomach and I fall backwards losing my grip on her jacket and I slip to the floor. My head smacks against the concrete and she's kicking me, panting like a wild cat, shouting.

'Stay away from Nikos. Get out of our life. Get out!' she

hisses. 'Go!'

I roll away and leap up. My anger propelling me as my fist slams into the side of her head. Her glasses fly from her face and she knocks her head against door frame and the glass splinters. She tries to balance herself but I punch her again putting all my weight behind the blow and she falls to the ground. Her hair has escaped from its clip and it's strewn across her face. She lifts her top lip and snarls but I leap onto her, push her backwards and sit astride her chest, pinning her arms to the ground.

'I am so fucking angry, Anna. Tell me where he is – NOW!'

I lean my elbow across her throat and begin squeezing, using the weight of my body to cut off her air supply but I'm not prepared for her sudden tears nor for the sobbing. Heavy bursts. She cries out like a sad, lonely, hunted animal.

Feeling sick and dizzy I slide to one side and lean against the wall panting hard amazed at my violent instinct.

Anna's primeval wail fill the patio echoing off the cracking walls. It seems to come from somewhere deep inside and so I wait and watch, listening to her racking sobs until she sits up and wipes her face with her arm.

I fumble in my pocket for a tissue, wipe my bleeding nose and pass a clean one to her.

'Take it,' I order.

I wait until she's in control again.

'I want the truth,' I say quietly, dabbing blood from my sore and bruised cheek. 'Cristina was drugged. There was a syringe on the beach and you picked it up. You put it in your pocket. Then on Monday there were two other girls when Nikos took us on Yannis' yacht. Does Nikos pimp them out to private yacht owners?'

She doesn't answer so I pick up her glasses from the floor, wipe them on my T-shirt and pass them to her.

'How many girls are there?' I ask gently.

'Three.'

'He swapped Cristina last night for the Torah - so where are the others?'

She doesn't answer.

'You let him abuse these girls. You let him take advantage of them. Why?'

'I don't...I don't want him to...'

'You don't help them. Why do you let him do it?'

'He loves me.'

I think of her leaning over his shoulder yesterday, as I came out of the cottage after I had been sick from the gyrocopter but I remember being shocked that she was kissing his face.

'What sort of love?'

'You wouldn't understand.' Her breathing comes in ragged breaths. 'You'll never understand.'

'Believe me, I do. You must hate these young, attractive, girls around him. He sleeps with them, doesn't he?' I dab the swelling on my cheek.

'Only because they want him. It's them. It's their fault.'

'He grooms them. You must hate him making love to them-'

'It's not the same.' When she looks at me, her eyes are unblinking. 'It's awful,' she whispers. 'They tempt him. They tease him.'

'He promises them a new life. He promises he'll find them work as models-'

'He's kind-'

'He's manipulative and controlling. He makes money from them. He has no intention of helping them. He uses them to sweeten his business deals-'

'They like it.'

'What do they like? Having sex with strangers? Would you?'

'He says they like it. They were doing it in Romania before they came here.'

'And you believe him?'

'They need his help.They're young.'

'Exactly. How old are they? Sixteen?' She doesn't reply so I kick her leg. 'Anna, how old are they? Younger than sixteen?'

'He likes them young.'

'How old?'

'Thirteen.'

'It's illegal, repulsive and it's morally wrong - especially with you.'

'He's my life.'

'He's your brother.'

'He's more than that.'

In the dim light her nose and strong jaw line are similar to Nikos and as she struggles to sit up and lean against the wall beside me, I know I would like to snap her image. There's fire in her eyes. She's subdued but she's not beaten. There's righteous indignation growing in her belly and I don't trust her.

'You sleep with him.'

'Is that what you think?' she replies.

'I know you do.' The words seem to reverberate inside the room and echo off the walls. 'Did he rape you when you were young?'

She remains silent so I continue quietly.

'Did he groom you too? I imagine he bullied you, saying you were fat and ugly and no-one would want you and that you'd never find a husband...'

'He loves me.'

She crosses her legs and holds a tissue to the side of her mouth where I cut her lip.

'He's treated you badly, Anna. He uses you. He's your brother. He should respect and care for you. You should be able to trust him.'

'I do,' she cries. 'He's my life.'

I stand up and brush the dust off my jeans, my body aching, sick to my stomach. 'You deserve better, Anna. You deserve a proper life with a man who loves you. A decent man you can call a husband. You deserve a family of your own.'

'He is my family. We look after each other.'

She stands up and although she's smaller and broader then me our faces are close together and I can smell her dank breath. Her eyes glisten behind her spectacles.

'How old were you the first time?' I whisper.

She shakes her head and stares at the floor taking refuge in its darkness not meeting my eyes.

'He had no right. You weren't his to take. I'll find him, Anna. I promise you - I'm going to get the Torah. It no more belongs to him than those innocent girls do.'

I turn away and pick up my bag. I dust it down and sling it over my shoulder and just as I open the door and step into the street a small childlike voice echoes behind me.

'I was eight,' she whispers.

I need a drink. My cheekbone is aching and my face is tender and swollen. Anna had a good punch and even my ribs are sore. But worse than that I'm angry. I can't believe the mess I've made of the whole situation. It was supposed to be simple, verify the Torah and give it back to the Jewish Museum. I'd thought Elias and Athena would have been more supportive. After all it was Elias who phoned Simon and asked for his help. Had he been put up to it by Nikos or was he more involved in all of this?

Does he genuinely believe Nikos is a good person?

My hotel is only a five minute walk and I slip through the door from a side street and sit in the shade with my back to the wall. A full grown ficus trees provides a shelter from the evening sun and I wonder what to do next.

How will I find Nikos before tomorrow?

Do I wait at the harbour and wait for the Italian yacht to arrive?

I order white wine and although I'm not hungry I ask for a plate of shrimps. I eat slowly and it grows dark around me. The street and patio are illuminated in a dusky yellow lamplight that's both tranquil and reassuring.

I check my iPhone and there's no message from Stelios. He's probably taken the plane back to Athens. He's reported it to the authorities. There is nothing left for him to do here. He was right.

What am I thinking?

Why do I think I can take the Torah away from Nikos?

It's impossible. And as for the girls and sex trafficking, how could I single-handedly stop him?

Would Elias listen to me?

Above me in the night sky stars begin to twinkle, mapping out a destiny unknown to me and I imagine joining the dots of The Big Bear or one of the other great constellations with a giant pen.

I wonder what Eduardo is doing and if he thinks of me.

Mallorca is one hour behind Greece. I check my watch. His shift is finished but he hasn't texted me.

Does he care?

I reach from my phone and text Simon.

The Torah is definitely the same one. Nikos has taken it and disappeared. Stelios has alerted the authorities. Mx

I yawn and stretch. I order another glass of wine from the bored waitress hovering in the doorway.

Then I text Eduardo:

Me: Hi, I saw the Torah today XXX

He replies straight away:

E: Great! Are you coming home? Xxxx

Me: Nikos is sex trafficking young girls from Romania XXX

E: Tell the police and come home Xx

Me: I will XXX

E: When? X

Me: I'll look at flights. XX

E: When? X

Me: Now XXX

E: Txt me your arrival? XXX

Me: Nikos has taken the Torah. He's going to sell it to an Italian businessman arriving tomorrow on his private yacht. The Italian will provide false provenance and sell it on the black market XXX

E: Don't get involved. SF said to verify it and nothing more. Tell the police. COME HOME! X

Me: Ok xxx

E: X
Me: XXX

I'm filled with warmth and a tinge of happiness. Eduardo wants me to go home to Mallorca. I think of Stelios with his baby and how, in the past few days, Nikos has tried to kill me. If only Eduardo knew.

I finish my wine, draining the glass when a shadow appears over me and a voice says.

'I've been looking for you.'

The Albanian places two glasses of wine on the table and he sits beside me. 'I thought you'd need another glass. You're a hard woman to find.'

'Thanks.' I take the wine gratefully.

'What happened to your face?'

'I walked into a door.'

'It looks more serious than that.'

'She's worse off than me.'

'She?' He raises his eyebrows.

'Nikos' sister, Anna. She's a tiger.'

He shakes his head and sips his wine and then says.

'I have a message for you.'

His deep-set piercing blue eyes look tired.

'If you get the Torah back then I can give you information about your friend Dino Scrugli.'

I sit up straighter and lean across the table clutching my glass. 'Dino? What do you know about him?'

'He's in prison.'

'Do you know him?'

'The donor knows who sold Dino the illegal paintings and is prepared to come forward and testify on his behalf.'

'The donor? Is it someone in the art world?'

He stares at me and refuses to answer. I stare back at this stranger wondering how my worlds have collided. My past and my present.

'Dino's bought artwork and now he's been framed. Who is the donor?'

'First, get the Torah.'

'How does the donor know about Dino?'

My mind is clicking and whirling. The donor must know all about me. The donor must know that Dino is my friend - or rather Josephine's friend - and how much this will mean to her. I wonder if the donor also knows Josephine is my birth mother. Had the donor also been a guest on Dino's yacht?

I think of us all in New York together only five days ago. Josephine had been making enquiries to help Dino and now this.

'Is the donor an American? Why has the donor offered me this information? How do I even know it's the truth?' But even as the words spring from my lips I know the answer.

It's the donor's way of getting me to trust them. But why?

I think of Miles Davenport and all the other gallery figures, dealers and black-marketeers like my friend Theo Brinkmann in Bruges and his daughter Marina Thoss who helped me frame Steven Drummond. All of them deal in millions of euros, pounds and dollars. Anyone one of them would have the finances or would know of someone who could afford to buy the stolen Scroll. They deal with philanthropists who buy and sell, and donate to museums and charities anonymously, but no-one can help me find the donor of the Torah.

'I want the donor's name. I'll pay you.'

'I am already paid - more than enough.'

I sigh and rub my thumping head. 'Okay. So how does the donor suggest I get the Torah without any help?'

But the Albanian doesn't answer so I say.

'In case you haven't realised I'm a foreigner on this island with no-one to help me...'

My phone bleeps in the darkness and vibrates on the table. When I pick it up Stelios speaks quickly and urgently.

'Mikky are you alright?'

'Why? Of course.'

'It's Yannis. They've burnt his yacht. He's on his way to hospital.'

'What?'

'I'm in the harbour. I wasn't sure if you were on the boat with him.'

'I'll meet you there.' I'm already standing up.

'He's very bad, Mikky. He might not make it. They're flying him to Athens.'

Chapter 12

'All men's souls are immortal, but the souls of the righteous are immortal and divine.' - Socrates, Philosopher of the 5th century BC.

I push my way through the tourists and local Greeks who have left their shops and businesses to stand looking into the harbour, and find Stelios standing amongst the crowd, gazing at the burnt out yacht bobbing lifelessly on the sea. The police have cordoned off the area but they can do nothing about the rancid smell of burning wood and canvas that fills the air. The cabin interior is still smouldering and the mast lays on the oil-slicked water. On the quay several ambulances with flashing lights are parked and a wave of sickness washes over me.

'What happened?' I ask.

'They pulled him out of the cabin.'

I lean against Stelios' shoulder and let him put his arm around me but my vision is blurred with my tears.

'They'll take him in the ambulance to the airfield.'

'It wasn't an accident,' I reply. 'It has to be Nikos. He must have done it. Yannis didn't deserves this.'

I push away from him, waving my arms in frustration, conscious that people are staring at me. Stelios follows and puts his arm around my shoulder again pulling me into the shadow of the old wall where we stand silently and watch the ambulance pull away. The siren startles me and I think of Yannis inside, fighting for his life.

'Did you see him?' I ask.

He shakes his head. 'No, but I need to speak to the police - to the Inspector in charge. Why do you say Nikos did it?'

'Because I went out with Yannis on the yacht this afternoon.'

'After you left me?'

I nod in assent and tell him what happened. 'He told me how Nikos brings in immigrants and how he takes the prettiest girls and separates them from their families. He promises them work and gets them hooked on drugs. He buys them clothes and lends them money then he tells them that they have to repay him. He farms them out as prostitutes. He tried to get you interested in them - remember last Monday? He was filling them up with drinks, hash and Es...'

Stelios guides me to a taverna. 'Come on, let's have a drink in here.'

We order brandy and I cup the bulbous glass in my hands trying not to shake.

'Your face is a mess, what happened?'

'Yannis told me where Nikos's property is in the old town, so I went to find him but Anna was there.'

'Anna did that?'

'She's tougher than she looks.'

I tell him about my conversation with Anna and he listens without interrupting and when I've finished he says, 'Elias called me earlier. The police want to talk to us.'

'I thought you were going back to Athens this afternoon.'

'I was but now-'

He sighs and raises the glass to his lips wincing at the sharpness of the alcohol as it touches the back of his throat.

'What did you do this afternoon, Stelios?'

'I spent my time at the Archaeology Museum filing my report. It took longer than I thought. Why? Don't you believe me? Do you think I'm involved? Do you think I would have done that to Yannis and his yacht?'

'No, I'm sorry.'

'Mikky, this is dangerous. It's getting out of hand.'

'I have to find Nikos. But how can I find him? Even Yannis didn't know where he lived.'

'He rents a small house near the hotel.'

'Really? How do you know?'

'I asked Elias.'

'Can you get me his address?'

'Elias wouldn't give it to me.'

'The Italian arrives tomorrow. We have to stop him from doing a deal, Stelios. Did you tell Elias?'

'Let Interpol handle it. I told him I've informed the authorities.'

'It will be too late by the morning.'

We order more brandy and watch a group of tourists stagger into the street laughing and singing out of tune. They head away from us toward the harbour.

'Anna told me that Nikos has been abusing her for years,' I say quietly.

Stelios lets out a lungful of air and slams his glass on the table.

'There was always something - dangerous about him. It's best that you stay away, Mikky. I'll go and speak to the police again down in the harbour. I promised Simon I'd look after you so go home. Go back to Eduardo and have a happy life. I see you're wearing his ring now.'

I look down at my hand. I'd forgotten I was wearing it. It seems so natural to have it on that I've hardly given it a second glance.

'Leave here, Mikky. Let the police do their job. After this fire they will be determined to catch whoever did it. Nikos can't hide from anyone now.'

'I can't believe he's done that to Yannis,' I say.

But at the back of my mind there's another question that's not making sense. If the Albanian is working for the donor and he knows Nikos has the Torah, then why can't he just go and get it?

Why is the donor determined to get me involved?

Why me?

I'm very drunk. The wine at dinner time followed by four brandies with Stelios has sent me into a drunken rage. It's anger rather than common sense that propels me into a taxi and to Elias's palatial house near the hotel. The Italian villa stands illuminated but the windows are in darkness. It's past two o'clock in the morning when I ring the bell and lights come on in the upstairs window.

'Elias? Get out here now – where's that fucking nephew of yours? Where's Nikos?' I shout out.

Dogs bark in the distance but I stand my ground, swaying and shouting up at the window until the front door opens and Elias appears in his pyjamas looking sleepy and dishevelled.

'What's the noise? Mikky, what's wrong?'

'I'll tell you what's wrong. Your nephew has set fire to

Yannis's boat. Where is he? Where's Nikos? How do you let him get away with everything?'

'What are you saying?'

'Haven't the police been here yet? You can't shield him forever.'

'Nikos?'

'He set fire to Yannis' boat in the harbour. They've taken him to Athens. He might even die.'

'Who?'

'Yannis might DIE!'

'Nikos wouldn't do–'

'Well he HAS! He's also trafficking prostitutes but I suppose you know nothing about that either?'

Athena appears behind Elias. She pulls a long gown over her shoulder and folds it at the waist. She looks tired and her face is creased in a worried frown. She stares at me like I'm a distraught witch sent to ruin their lives. They both look as if I've woken them and I feel a surge of pleasure at creating a disturbance in their idyllic lives and I shout even louder.

'Nikos seduces young girls and forces them into prostitution. He's got four Romanian girls hooked on drugs and–'

'Stop shouting,' Athena's urges. 'Please! Mikky, come inside.'

'I don't want anything from you. You both condone his behaviour but someone has to stop him. You're disgusting – you're as bad as he is. Just tell me where he is. Where does he live?'

'What do you plan to do?' asks Athena.

She's remarkably calm and she makes me appear even more hysterical and slightly deranged. She makes me think about her question and my actions but I can't remember all the good ideas I had earlier and so I shout.

'I'll get the police. I'll go to his house and...and...and-'

'Mikky,' Elias says soothingly. 'You're drunk. None of this is true. I'm sorry about Yannis but this has nothing to do with Nikos - or with us. We'll do everything we can. His parents are friends of ours-'

'You should be ashamed,' I shout. 'That poor man may not survive. How many other lives has Nikos ruined? The night of your daughter's engagement party there was a young girl - I found her on the beach. She was drugged and I thought Anna was going to look after her but she DISAPPEARED. Nikos swapped her at sea for the Torah...'

My breathing is ragged and my chest is heaving with emotion. I want to cry. Suddenly a powerful mass of brandy and shrimps erupts from my throat and I throw up over their lawn.

They stare at me and in their silence I feel suddenly powerless. I spit and wipe my mouth on the back of my arm.

Athena doesn't move and it's Elias who walks toward me.

'I think you should go home to bed, Mikky. You've been drinking. We can sort this out in the morning.'

'Get away from me. Get off.' I push his arms away. 'The police won't believe me. They don't want to know. That's what Yannis said. He said they'd never believe him over you. He had a criminal record and he hardly did anything...'

My tears begin to fall and I stagger away wiping them with the back of my hand and I shout over my shoulder.

'It's my fault Yannis is on his way to hospital. He was trying to help me and now he's paid the price for telling me about Nikos.'

I stagger away into the darkness of the shadows but I turn around to spit on their lawn one final time. When I turn back to look at them, Athena has already disappeared. Only Elias is still standing in the doorway. Watching me, making sure I leave their land.

They are still in control.

I'm lying in bed but I can't sleep. My head is thumping, my heart racing and my stomach is churning. My mouth is dry like the inside of a caged lion's compound and I'm restlessly alert. Blood seems to be chasing at a great speed through my veins and I'm charged with adrenalin. I mull over the past few days, going through conversations, thinking about the yacht trip, the speargun incident and my blown up rented car.

I'm convinced that Nikos is responsible. I knew about the Italian and he wanted to keep me close to him and then scare me off. He had no intention of involving me in the deal and I've been duped. The Torah wasn't even on the island. He delayed us - playing for time - until the Italian arrived.

Tomorrow.

I glance at my watch. Today.

I can't sleep so I reach for my camera and flick through the images looking for clues or hints - something I may have missed. I see the pictures of the engagement party the day I arrived. The picture of the Albanian holding binoculars watching us leave the harbour and pictures of us on the yacht. The girls are posing, Yannis smiling from behind the wheel. Nikos tanned, flexing his muscles lifting his T-shirt. Stelios revealing his ginger chest hair and the girls laughing - so innocent - so young.

It looks like a fun and happy day but I remember the fish that Nikos speared, narrowly missing my hand. I had been incensed and he had laughed.

He loved danger - just like in the gyrocopter. He was a good pilot but I couldn't trust him. He knew I was frightened and it excited him. I think of the old cottage and the land where he housed the gyrocopter. He definitely didn't live there. There was no sign of anyone staying there. He must live somewhere else, somewhere nearby to the hotel.

I examine the random images that I snapped as we took off from the field. There are a couple of shots of Anna looking wistfully up at the sky, tracking us, then I'm taking a video. Beside me, Nikos waves and says something I can't decipher. The background noise is loud but he points at the ground.

I climb out of bed and transfer the video to my MacBook Air.

I take a glass of water and swallow two paracetamols and check my bruised eye in the mirror before sitting at the table.

The video is jerky as we fly over the Palacio Hotel. I recognise the unfinished roads where I jogged in the mornings and the unpainted, cement building next door. I follow the pock-marked road and a cluster of small houses, mentally mapping them in my head to behind the hill where there's a big field and beyond that a small villa.

What's Nikos pointing at?

On my computer, I play around with the video, dimming the sound of the whistling wind and I hear Nikos muffled voice. 'That's where I live.'

I rewind it and watch it over and over, memorising the area and remembering the route of my early morning run. I google a local map and narrow down the search and it's almost four o'clock in the morning by the time I've finished.

'Found you, you bastard.'

I text Stelios:

235

Found him! Nikos is three streets up from the hotel on the left, in a villa in a large field behind the hill. Let's surprise him. I'll meet you at six-thirty outside the hotel? MX

Then I set my alarm and collapse on the bed falling into a deep, dreamless, contented sleep.

After two hours sleep, I'm pacing outside the hotel waiting for Stelios, constantly checking my watch surprised there's no sign of him. The rented car has been taken away and there's a small crater in the asphalt where the car once stood. The burnt hedge has been trimmed. I had been lucky.

Yannis hadn't been so fortunate.

I imagine an intensive care nurse like Eduardo looking after him, gently and calmly. Eduardo my angel who had cared so tenderly for me. I twist my engagement ring around my finger. I walk into the reception and tell them Stelios isn't answering his phone.

'He checked out,' the receptionist tells me looking at the computer. 'He settled his bill last night.'

'It must have been late?'

'I don't know what time it was,' she shrugs. 'My shift has only just started.'

I turn away. He must have caught the last flight to Athens, after we'd been drinking and he left without saying goodbye.

He's gone.

Outside, I stand on the steps of the hotel listening to the early morning birdsong and watch two tortoiseshell butterflies playfully dancing.

I don't blame him.

Why would you stay here another night when you could get home to your wife and baby?

He's sensible, I say to myself. I should be doing the same thing. Leave Nikos alone. Tell the police everything and book a seat back to Palma.

Get out now. Go back to Eduardo.

I look down at my engagement ring and turn resolutely back and walk inside the hotel.

'I need to book a flight to Palma. It will probably be via Madrid,' I say.

'You can book online or I've a number of a travel agent here who can help. They won't be open yet but I'll get you the phone number.'

She turns away and begins to rummage through a contact sheet on the desk behind her. That's when I walk away from the desk and stand outside in the early morning air and take a deep breath.

'I've never run away. I don't need Stelios,' I say aloud. 'I can do this on my own. I made a promise to return the Torah to the museum. Nikos isn't going to get away with this.'

I find my bearings with maps on my iPhone, wishing I had my Phantom 4 drone so I could send it up in the sky to look for Nikos' house. I glance up at the sky imagining the gyrocopter flying overhead and I make a mental note to buy a nano drone - one that I can pack and bring everywhere with me in future. It would save me a lot of hassle.

I pass the empty concrete building that has nettles and weeds growing around its base that will one day be an apartment block and perhaps it may even be a dowry for a blushing bride.

I pass the waste ground and the three houses then I turn left into the unsurfaced road, walk over the hill and there before me is a villa.

It's a twenty minute walk and already the sun is rising and I am perspiring. My head is thumping from lack of sleep and too much alcohol so I pause and wait for the rush of nausea to pass. I sip water from a bottle, rouse myself and still feeling dizzy I move cautiously forward.

A black Mercedes is parked in the driveway. It's the car Nikos collected me in from the hotel and I feel a surge of elation.

Found you!

Parked beside it, is the old blue Fiat I saw parked in the field on Tuesday morning. It must be Anna's car.

There's no gate and so I walk into the overgrown garden where there's been a futile attempt to put up a wire fence. It's seen better days and half of it has collapsed. A few stone steps lead to a wooden door and I pause. There's no bell so I walk around the verandah, tip-toeing on the wooden decking, past shuttered windows.

In the back garden, under the shade of an umbrella, Nikos is eating toast and scanning his mobile. He hears my footstep, glances up and smiles.

'Mikky? How lovely. You're just in time for breakfast. Sit here.'

He pulls out a seat and I sit down. The table is adorned with toasted rolls, marmalade and fresh fruit.

'This is a lovely surprise,' he says. 'That's a nasty bruise on your face. How careless. Coffee?'

I shake my head as he tops up his own cup with the thick, dark liquid. His phone, laying on the table, shows pictures of last night's devastation in the harbour and a picture of Yannis' smouldering yacht.

My head is thumping and my throat dry.

'Did you do that to Yannis?' I croak.

He laughs. 'Me? What little faith you have, princess. I thought we were friends. I thought you liked me.'

His hand rests on my wrist and I move it away.

'You like a lot of girls.'

'Jealous?' He places a slice of peeled orange in his mouth.

'Where's the Torah?'

'Is that what you've come for?'

'Yes.'

He nods and wipes his lips free of juice. 'Why should I give it to you?'

'Because then I'll let you keep your other dirty secret.'

'Blackmail?'

'Call it what you like.'

He laughs and chews the orange. 'Don't you realise I can keep both.'

I lean back and fold my arms. 'Is this where you bring the girls? After you've separated them from their families. Do you bring them here from Athens? Do you have to rape them first or get them hooked on drugs?'

His eyes narrow in the sunlight and I continue talking.

'You promise to help them. I guess you take away their passports or any identity they have and you feed them and buy them clothes. They think you care because you can be quite charming. But then they're in your debt. You tell them there's a way to repay you and you make them sleep with foreigners who arrive on their yachts, don't you? Do you just work in Athens and Rhodes or on other islands too?'

I lay my hands on the table and lean closer to him. A tic

twitches in his left eye. 'Where do you keep them? Where are they now? Are they here - upstairs?'

'You're a curious one. I thought you'd be trouble, Mikky.'

'I'm more than trouble Nikos. I'm your worst nightmare. I'm not going to let you get away with this.'

He strokes his cheek and I continue.

'You tested me on the yacht, didn't you?'

'I know you like me.'

He strokes my hand and pats my wrist and when I feel the strength of his fingers I pull away.

'You almost speared me in the hand...'

He laughs. 'A genuine accident.'

'Like my rented car? How did you know it was mine? Of course, silly me, you know everyone. It wouldn't have taken you long to find out from the reception that I'd rented a car.'

He chuckles. 'You have a very low opinion of me.'

'I should call the police.'

'I'm above the law, Mikky. There's so little crime on the island. It's only brought here by foreigners - people like you - who cause trouble. Besides, Elias is my uncle. In his eyes I can do nothing wrong. He'll never believe you - he won't trust what you say. I'm the son he never had-'

'You tried to scare me in the gyrocopter. You pretended you wanted me to help you broker a deal with the Italian. But you don't need me. You actually wanted me to leave Rhodes. You thought you could scare me away - especially once you had the Torah authenticated. You thought your vicious temper and your empty threats would frighten me, make me run...'

He continues smiling and lifting his coffee cup he sips slowly. His chestnut eyes never leave my face. The tic twitches.

'But why hurt Yannis? Why did you do that?' I ask.

He replaces his coffee cup in the saucer. 'It wasn't me. I'm the make love not war type of guy. Haven't you realised that yet?'

'You tried to lure Stelios into your game. You even pretended that he had slept with the girls while we went swimming and I believed you...'

'He wanted to fuck them.'

'Yannis took him into his cabin after the hash you gave us made him ill and he slept.'

He shakes his head. 'Yannis talks too much. He deserves what he got....'

'I thought he was your friend?'

'First you, then Stelios, you're really pushing my patience today.' He stands up and brushes crumbs from his jeans.

'Stelios?'

'He thinks he's some sort of action hero, just like you, coming to my home and threatening me. He turned up two hours ago thinking he'd surprise me. He thought I'd hand him the Torah,' Nikos laughs. 'The guy is nuts. You're both stupid.'

'Stelios is here?'

'Didn't you know? He began blackmailing me-'

'Blackmail?'

'Like you, he thought he'd mention these girls and then I'd just hand over the Torah - you're both so predictable but, I hate to tell you princess, that's not the plan,' he hisses. 'I'm respected here. Elias loves me. I'm his son. He's encouraging me to build my hotel - he believes in me.' He stabs his chest with his finger. 'And I'm not about to let two idiots take it all away from me. I don't want the bloody Torah. I don't want anything to do with it but it will pay for the restoration and refurbishment of the building and nothing you do or say - is going to stop me.'

'Where's Stelios?' I glare at him.

'You're very demanding...first you want the Torah then Stelios. Maybe what you really need is a decent man. A man to give you a good time. Is that what you've come here for? Is that what you want? You're lucky, Mikky. I'm always ready for sex after breakfast. You want to give me a blow-job?'

He reaches for his buckle and unhooks his belt.

'You're a tease. But not any more, princess. Today is your lucky day.'

'Fuck off, Nikos.'

I stand up but he lunges forward and grabs my wrist. I twist from his grasp and when he snatches my hair I pull away and kick him in the groin with my boot. He groans and doubles over clutching his balls.

'I'll find Stelios myself,' I hiss.

I leave Nikos gripping the table and swearing at me. I run inside the villa calling for Stelios but in the hallway Anna blocks my path.

'Where's Stelios?' I bunch my hands into fists. 'Tell me where he is. NOW!'

She points upstairs and I run pushing the doors open randomly. The first room is empty with a double mattress on the floor. In the second room a girl is curled up on a single bed. Beside her, on small unit, small packets are laid out, neat bundles of coke, hash and other drugs I don't recognise, and syringes and a box of latex gloves.

Anna follows me and stands in the doorway.

'It's not Cristina, Lily or Lisa. Who is she?' I demand. 'Where's Stelios?'

Nikos's footsteps echo on the marble tiles downstairs and

he's shouting angrily in Greek.

I push past Anna and find Stelios in the last room. He's lying drugged on his back in the middle of a king sized bed. I lean over, slap his cheeks and he groans but doesn't stir.

I pull on his wrist to heave him onto my shoulder but he's tall, gangly and surprisingly heavy. That's when my skull splits open and I sink to my knees and the lights go out.

Chapter 13

'Let no man be called happy before his death. Till then, he is not happy, only lucky.' - Solon, Lawmaker of the 6th century BC.

I wake with a thumping head beating in unison with my heart and hazy vision. My head feels as if my skull is cracked wide open. My throat is dry but I retch onto the floor where I lie.

Anna's face is grotesque as she bends over me and I push her away. Behind her Nikos paces quickly, shouting and gesticulating furiously.

They are arguing in Greek.

When I groan Nikos stops pacing. His eyes are cold and angry and I think he might kick me but Anna pushes his foot away and speaks urgently. I can't understand what she says but her tone seems placating and cajoling.

I lean on my elbow until Anna pulls my arm and lifts me to a sitting position so I'm leaning against the bed holding my head.

'What have you done?' I raise my bloodied hand to my head.

'Head wounds bleed more but you'll be fine.' She pushes a towel into my hands and whispers. 'Don't annoy him. He has a terrible temper and he can be unkind.'

Nikos goes to the window and stares outside, remaining dangerously silent and still.

'What now, Nikos? What are you going to do? Kill me? Or sedate me like you've done to that girl in the other room and to Stelios? You can't continue. Too many people know. They know about Cristina and you swapping her, and the other girls-'

His head jerks around and he stares at me as if seeing me for the first time.

'What?' he says, moving quickly. He leans over me and instinctively I shrink away from him. 'What do you know?'

'You swapped her for the Torah on Tuesday night. You swapped her with those men on the ulet with the red sails. You sold her-'

'I didn't sell her. It's mine.'

'You followed Mariam, didn't you?'

'You have no proof.'

'The bodyguard remembers you,' I lie. 'He saw you. He knew you were following them as they left the town. You left him trapped in the rubble and you stole the Torah while Mariam lay dying. You could have saved her.'

'I couldn't,' he shouts.

'She was ALIVE.' I shout back.

'She was dead-' he stops suddenly.

'But her bodyguard was alive. You could have saved him, Nikos.'

He waves his arm and turns away and he has his back to me when I say.

'You won't get away with it. Stelios reported you to Interpol. There will be no deal today with the Italian. Even Elias knows what you're like. I spoke to him last night.'

When Nikos turns around his eyes are blazing. He spits at me. 'You've ruined everything. You were supposed to leave after you saw the Torah. You were both supposed to go-'

'Give me the Torah and I'll say nothing.'

'You have no bargaining power. You can't tell me what to do, Mikky. I have it, remember?'

'You can't sell it to the Italian. Stelios has already informed the authorities. They'll find it. The International Art Crime Squad are already onto you. They'll get you in the end,' I threaten.

'You're lucky to be alive - both of you.' He lunges at me and when I recoil he laughs manically.

'Frightened? Oh Good. Anger, fear they're both the same to me. I like it when you're frightened. I saw it in your mask under the water that day. You were terrified. You swam away from me and God I was so hard. I wanted you then and it hurt.'

He begins unbuttoning the belt on his bulging trousers.

'You were better after the gyrocopter trip. That really scared you. You were begging to get out. I wanted you then and I would have done...Get out of the way, Anna.'

He shoves his sister to one side and pulls on my legs, dragging me by the ankles. My head bangs on the floor and Nikos throws himself on me, collapsing with his full weight on my chest and I'm pressed against the hard, cold tiles.

I scream and struggle.

'You've been teasing me all week you bitch. Think of it as a farewell present. Think of me as your last fuck.'

My head is split in two and he leans his arm across my throat choking my air supply. My shoulders are weighed down. I wriggle, trying to use my fists but he holds my wrists and laughs. He presses his hardness into my crotch and I've no strength left to push him away.

'Come on, princess. I will enjoy it more if you try and fight me off. You'll enjoy this...' He pushes my thighs further apart. 'You're a feisty one, Mikky. I like it when you're frightened and angry. Go on struggle bitch! Scream if you like.' He smacks my face hard. Then his hand pulls at my jeans. He rips the zip and the button flies off. I scream and thrust myself forward trying to bite his shoulder. His hand is rubbing against me and he wedges himself between my legs, his eyes gleam excitedly and his teeth are clenched together.

'No! Not her,' Anna screams.

Nikos's face registers surprise then he collapses. His head falls on my heaving chest and his inert body is heavy.

'What the f-' I push Nikos's leaden body away and wriggle out from under him. I kick off his heavy legs and he groans but it's Anna who scares me more. Her eyes are wide in disbelief. She mumbles something in Greek, and dragging him by the shoulders, she rolls him so that he lays with his bleeding head in her lap. His eyes flick open, then they close again and she wipes his hair lovingly from his face.

When I stand my knees are shaking. I'm breathless and my head spins. I hold onto the edge of the bed.

'Nikos, Nikos, I love you...' she whispers, caressing his cheek. 'More than you'll ever know. Why do you need them, Nikos? All those tarts, those cheap girls and now HER. Why am I never enough?' Tears slide down her cheeks.

I sit on the bed and pick up the bloodied towel from the floor and hold it to the back of my skull. Laying on the floor is a heavy onyx statue and I guess she hit him with the same one she used on me.

'Nikos, Nikos,' she murmurs over and over again, stroking

his head. She kisses his face and his lips.

'Stop!' I say.

'He needs me.'

I shake my head. 'You don't have to-'

'And what would you know? It's my duty. He said that's what sisters do who love their brothers. He told me I was special and that no-one else understood him, only me. Only I know him.'

'But he raped you when you were a child?'

'How would you understand a love like ours?'

'Try me?'

I sit on the edge of the bed waiting for my dizziness and nausea to pass while at my feet Anna holds her brother's head. His blood trickles onto her blouse but she doesn't notice.

'We were always left alone. He was my big brother. Our father worked hard. He always came home late - he was always at some meeting or working and our mother, well she never came home for another reason...'

'She had lovers?'

'I was eight and Nikos was fourteen. He looked after me but sometimes I was frightened. He used to come into my room and ask me if I was alright. He cared about me. He would climb into my bed so I wasn't alone any more. He used to stroke me and make me feel safe.'

'And he touched you?'

'I remember his shadow on the wall, illuminated by the cars in the street and he'd whisper to me-'

'It was wrong, Anna.'

'He said he was looking after me and I had to look after him. If it felt so good, then how could it be wrong?'

'But you were eight. You were only a child.'

'I was mature for my age.'

'It doesn't matter - it was still wrong.'

'He made me feel special but then I got fat and ugly with teenage spots. He said no-one else would want me and that I should be grateful to him for still touching me. He said that no-one else would make love to me or know how to touch me like he did.'

'But for all these years, Anna.' I sigh and rub my hand over my sore head, pulling the towel away to check the bleeding. 'Why didn't you tell anyone? Ask for help?'

'He said he'd call me a liar. He said no-one would believe me. He said he would kill me if our parents found out. One night he tried to strangle me and...and, I was so frightened. I used to wait for his shadow on the wall. At first I wanted him to come and look after me but then he made me do other things...'

'You should have told your mother.'

'She thought we were friends. He'd smile at her and say how he looked after me but she didn't care. I did try and tell her one day - but she told me to stop making things up and that I was a liar. You see, Nikos had told her that my imagination was wild and that I made things up. He made out I was unstable but because he promised to look after me - she was happy. She didn't have to bother...'

'No-one held him to account for what he did?'

'They thought he was kind. He would pretend to be loving when others were around but in secret he terrorised me. Sometimes he locked me up in the dark or tied me to the bed-'

She looks away then adds in a small voice. 'He got excited and afterwards he was kind to me.'

'You never tried to fight him off?'

She wipes her eyes. 'He found other girls. I thought he would leave me. He told me that he never wanted me again – but he did – he always came back. Just like last night. He wanted me again. He realised what I meant to him. He knew I was loyal. It had been so long...'

I think I might be sick.

'He didn't set fire to Yannis's yacht or to my rented car, did he? It was you, wasn't it Anna?'

'My poor boy had been worrying so much. You've driven him crazy. Since this business with the Torah and then Cristina. It's all been too much for him. I wanted to help. We're family, we look after each other. It's what we do but you wouldn't understand.'

I can't keep the distaste from my voice. 'It's so wrong. It's also illegal and just for the record so is setting fire to Yannis' yacht and blowing up my car. We could both have died. Yannis still might not survive.' My voice is rising and I stand up from the bed and even though I wobble on my feet I am determined to call for help. I hold onto the bed and straighten my T-shirt and check my jeans.

Her eyes flare in anger. 'What do you know about love?'

'I know Nikos. He's a pathological liar and a psychopath. He's a bully, Anna. He's manipulated you. For god's sake, you were a child. He raped you and now you're doing bad things for him. Did he ask you to do it?'

'He loves me.'

'He should have been more responsible but he bullied and manipulated you. He lied to you as a child. Even when you were a teenager – of course other boys would have found you attractive but he damaged your self confidence. He wanted you for himself.'

'But he didn't want me. Don't you understand? He's told

me I'm ugly and fat and no-one would want me. He even told our father I would never marry. He told him to spend money for my marriage on a boat to help the immigrants. You see, he likes foreign girls. He finds their pale skin and translucent eyes attractive but worse than that, they're scared of him and sometimes he makes me watch.'

She pulls away, sliding her legs out from supporting his shoulders and when his head lolls onto the floor he groans.

'He even married my best friend. He told me he married her because she was ugly and that she would never leave him but she's not ugly-'

'He's married?'

'She's in Athens with his two children. He left her. He said she never understood him. She didn't understand his needs. She wouldn't do things... I was frightened he'd do the same with me. I don't want him to leave me. To cut me out of his life, so I...'

'So you what?'

'I was there for him. Whenever the girls didn't... he came to me.'

'I think we should call a doctor?' I nod at the pool of blood by her feet.

'I'll look after him.' She continues to gaze down at him. 'He's so handsome, isn't he? But he'll never stop, will he?'

'Stop what?'

'Wanting women. He likes to take them against their will. It's a game. At first he seduces them so they feel loved and safe. He tormented Cristina and he couldn't get enough of her. Day and night, he wanted her. She was terrified of him-'

I remember the pretty girl wrapped around him at Arianna's engagement party and the photographs I have of them on my iPhone.

'And you watched all this?'

'I gave her heroin to help her forget, so that he wouldn't hurt her.'

'You gave her drugs that night?'

'She didn't want to go with any more strangers but he'd arranged to take her to a private party after the engagement party. She was frightened. A man hurt her the last time so I helped her. She needed something to help her forget...'

'You're taking drugs to numb the pain too, aren't you? I saw them when I was looking for Stelios. They're in one of the rooms here and you also planted cocaine on Yannis's boat.'

'Nikos wanted him to stay silent.'

'Because of the swap? You know he swapped Cristina for a safe passage for the Torah. He traded her like a piece of cargo, as if she had no feelings or emotions. Where is she now? Who did he trade her with?'

Anna won't answer me, so I raise my voice.

'How dare you! She's a human being. No-one deserves to be treated like that. Irrespective of culture, race or religion. First and foremost we are human beings that's what separates us from animals. We have a brain. We have a conscience. We have morals-'

'You'd better go,' she says quietly. That's when she moves over to the cupboard and she pulls a gun. It looks like a revolver and her hand is shaking. 'I've never used one before but I will now. Get OUT!'

She waves it toward the door. It's the fear in her eyes that scares me but I say, 'I'm taking him with me.' I lean over the bed and slap Stelios' face and call his name but he won't open his eyes so I pull his arm over my shoulder and half lift him and half drag him to the door. I stand in the doorway with Stelios hanging over my shoulder.

Anna stands gazing adoringly at her brother still lying motionlessly at her feet. 'Just go. I just need more time. I need to be alone with him.'

'I need the Torah, Anna. It's only brought Nikos bad luck and it belongs to the Jewish Museum. Do you know where it is? Do you know where he put it?'

'It's not here.'

'Where is it?'

She shrugs.

I take Stelios's weight on my back and shoulders and bump him downstairs. He mumbles and opens his eyes for a few seconds and tries to put one foot in front of the other but he slips and we stagger on the bottom step.

Anna follows us. 'He'll be alright. It'll wear off. It's what Nikos gives the girls after their first night with strangers–'

'Are you joking?' I ask angrily.

'He'll need sleep and coffee.' Anna pockets the gun and she takes Stelios' arm and hoists him onto her shoulder and between us we carry him as if he's had too much to drink.

'Take the Merc, Nikos won't need it. The keys are inside.'

We place Stelios in the front seat and his head lolls forward as I click him into the seatbelt. When I walk to the driver's side of the car she has the pistol in her hand.

'What will you do with Nikos?' I ask.

'Just go. Get out of here.'

'He's abused you for years. He's never loved you.'

'Get OUT!'

We don't say goodbye. I slam the car door and drive down the rickety, pot-holed road feeling exhausted and when I look in the rear view mirror Anna has already disappeared.

I park the Merc as close to the boutique hotel as possible, hiding it in the backstreet, right up against a wall. I don't care if it's towed away.

I half carry and half drag Stelios to my room and he collapses on the bed. Even against the crisp white linen his face is pale saved only by his ginger beard and chest hair sticking out from his shirt. When I force water past his lips, he's groggy and he blinks open his eyes. He pushes the glass away so I leave him to sleep a little longer.

It's barely eight o'clock.

I've hardly slept and the aggression and violence of the past few hours have left me pumped up with adrenalin. The sickness that overwhelmed me earlier has receded.

I order room service; vast amounts of eggs, toast, buns and coffee. I am on my second cup and sitting in the small armchair staring out at the pretty courtyard below when Stelios stirs and rubs his head.

'Mikky? What time is it? Where am I?'

'It's just gone nine o'clock,' I reply. 'Coffee?'

He swings his legs over the edge of the bed. 'Are you alright? What happened?'

I spend the next few minutes telling him the events of the morning and how Nikos groomed Anna but that she still loves him.

'He tried to rape me but Anna rescued me,' I finish.

'I'm sorry Mikky. I had no idea. When you texted me I was awake. I had decided to catch the first flight to Athens but then I thought I'd do a quick detour to his villa, so I went up there-'

'You'd checked out of the hotel?'

'I checked out after we got back from the taverna last night. The brandy kept me awake. I couldn't sleep and it made sense just to leave first thing.' He smiles ruefully and rubs his hair.

'Without saying goodbye to me?'

He looks sheepish and he blushes. 'We'd said goodbye over all those brandies, don't you remember?'

This time it's me who turns away. 'I barely have any recollection of going to Elias and Athena's house. I was shouting at them. I woke them up-'

'You went to their house?' His voice is filled with disbelief. 'You could hardly stand, Mikky.'

'I was sick in their garden but I told Elias that Nikos was using girls as prostitutes.'

'And did he believe you?'

'The opposite. He thought I was a drunk and it just reaffirmed Nikos as a saint in his eyes.'

'What did he say about Yannis?'

'I don't know. I was ranting on at him but he did say he would check it all out.'

'Let's give him a chance to do that but first we must go to the police and tell them what happened.'

'Nikos is evil,' I say standing up. 'I can't believe how he's getting away with it.'

'And I can't believe he tried to rape you.' Stelios shakes his head in disbelief. 'I still find it hard to think he's controlling Anna like that. It's emotional-'

'It's psychological,' I reply. 'It was Anna who set fire to Yannis's yacht and I think she also blew up my rented car. She wanted to frighten me off and protect Nikos.'

'Do you think Nikos put her up to it?'

I shrug. 'We'll never prove it.'

We finish breakfast and go over the details and then Stelios says.

'You look terrible, Mikky. You haven't slept, have you? You must be exhausted.'

'I'll take a shower,' I reply.

'Okay, in that case I'll phone the hospital and see how Yannis is doing.'

I run the hot water over my head and remove the matted blood from the tender sore on my crown. I towel myself dry and choose clean black jeans and a Queens of the Stone Age T-shirt. I cover my bruises with make-up and add purple lipstick and black eyeliner. Then I wait on the balcony overlooking the small patio below while Stelios finishes his call to the hospital in Athens.

'Yannis has forty percent burns on his chest and neck. He's in intensive care. The doctor has spoken to a Police Inspector who is going to speak to Nikos. They're going to his villa.' He places his arm around my shoulder. 'I'm sorry Mikky, I should have been more help to you but he used chloroform to knock me out and then Anna must have injected me with some sort of drug. I really do apologise.'

'Why did you go to the villa without me?' I ask.

'I thought I could talk to him, you know, man to man.'

'Did you know Nikos is married?'

'I'm not surprised but no I didn't.'

'He's from Athens. Are you friends?'

'No.'

'Did you go to the villa to speak to Nikos about brokering a deal with the Italian? Did you want to do it behind my back?'

'No, of course not...'

'Or do a deal with the Archaeological Museum? It's not unheard of for Museums to behave that way.'

'No, Mikky. That wasn't my intention.'

'Then why did he drug you? Why not just send you away and laugh at you like he did before?'

Stelios pulls away from me. 'Probably for the same reason he wanted to have sex with you,' he replies angrily. 'He probably felt cornered – threatened – by both of us. The net is tightening. You pushed him too hard about sex trafficking and he was frightened of being found out.'

I stare at him and Stelios doesn't blink but he says softly.

'You can trust me, Mikky. I'm on your side. I did a very stupid thing going there this morning but I suppose he pushed my buttons last Monday on the yacht. He made me feel inadequate and I wanted to prove that I could do something worthwhile apart from getting drunk and falling asleep.' He turns away. 'I also feel very guilty about Yannis. He was a good guy. I wanted to do something for him.'

His mobile rings and when he answers it, he turns pale and his eyes lock on mine. When he hangs up he says, 'The Inspector says there's been a fire at Nikos's villa. It was started over an hour ago. They've managed to put it out but they've found a body...'

I lean back against the rail of the balcony and hold my thumping head.

'There were three people there, Nikos and Anna and another girl in one of the other rooms. Was it a male or female?'

'They don't know yet – the body is unrecognisable. The inspector wants to meet us. It's over, Mikky. It's finally over.'

'He'll get away with it Stelios. You know that as well as I do. Nikos has never been held to account for any of his actions.

His parents never reprimanded him and look what he's got away with - for years. Elias won't believe he's evil. He will protect him. I know he will.'

I pick up my iPhone and send a message to the Albanian.

'You can rest here if you like. Get your strength back, Stelios.'

'Where are you going?'

'I must get there before him.'

'Where?'

I gather my bag and I am at the door with my fingers on the handle when Stelios asks.

'Mikky, what about the Torah? Do you know where it is?'

I shake my head.

'Do you think it's gone up in flames?'

I shrug. 'Perhaps.'

'It can't have done... Nikos still has it, doesn't he? That's where you're going, isn't it? I'll come with you. Wait for me.'

He slips on his shoes and I am happy to have some protection but then his legs give way and he sits suddenly on the bed looking pale, sick and apologetic.

'Don't worry, stay here and get some rest.'

As I leave the hotel I am disappointed not to have someone with me who is on my side but my oath to Mariam's children is stronger than the nagging feeling of fear creeping around inside my soul.

I walk at a brisk pace between the tourists strolling in the mid-day sun, down old alleyways, past hidden squares, small tavernas, cafes and past shops to the street I recognise. The old house looks as unassuming, dilapidated and closed up as it did when I came here yesterday. The shutters are drawn and the door is locked.

I ring the bell and wait.

There's a scuffling sound from the inside and when the door opens a girl with a haunting gaze stares vacantly at me. Her eyes are rimmed with dark-circles and she wears a short purple kimono.

'Lisa? Nikos sent me. Can I come in?'

I slide past her and familiarise myself with the room and where Anna and I fought in the courtyard. There is a dim light from the inside patio and in a few steps I'm in the courtyard where the stink assails my nostrils.

'Is Lily here?' I look up at the interior balcony. It smells of cats, damp and sewerage and far stronger than I remember. Upstairs a door creaks open and a pale face appears over the balcony and looks down at us.

I can't tell the difference between them but the girls who looked young and happy are now soiled, dirty and tired.

'Hi,' I raise my hand and wave. 'Lisa, Lily? How many of you are here? Does Nikos have a special room here that he uses as an office?'

I find the staircase in the corner of the patio and climb them two at a time. My boots are stomping on the stairs and the girls back away obviously frightened.

'Do you recognise me?' I ask quietly. 'Lisa, Lily? Let's go. We're getting out of here. Get dressed...'

Anna's voice rings out across the courtyard. 'What do you want?'

She is on the far side of the quadrangle. Her hair is dishevelled and her eyes are wild and I think of the fire she caused on Yannis' yacht, my rented car and now Nikos's villa.

'I want the Torah.'

'You don't give up, do you? Leave. Go NOW!'

'You're working these girls as prostitutes. Look at them. You're the one who is hooking them on drugs - not Nikos!'

The two girls have moved backwards and are now cowering against the wall. They are shadows of the girls from a few days ago. Their pupils are dilated and one has bruises on the inside of her arm punctured by needles, the other has a cut on her left cheek.

'You should be ashamed, Anna. You pretend it's Nikos, yet you're turning these girls into drug addicts. Look at them!' I shout. 'You're a woman. You should protect them.'

'What do you think I do?' she replies angrily. 'Of course I look after them. You think I want this?'

'They're children.'

Anna shouts at them in Greek and they huddle together, holding each other awkwardly like small children.

I walk slowly toward Anna. 'Where's the Torah?'

'Stay away.'

I continue moving forward around the quadrangle toward her.

'So, this is Nikos's idea of a Boutique Hotel? He seduces girls and they start smoking that hash, then it's a few pills, then cocaine and then heroin? Is that how you work? I'm taking them with me. Come on, girls.' I signal to the girls to come with me but they cower away. 'Come ON!' I shout at them.

The girls don't move so I reach for the nearest girl but Anna's blow knocks me on the side of my head. Instinctively I block her next punch and shove her back against the wall but she thumps my arms and my face.

'You stupid fu-'

I twist her arm behind her back and throw her into a body

lock, slamming her cheek against the wall. Her glasses fall on the floor. Anna's face is bruised and there is a cut under her throat with enough blood seeping into her shirt to make me realise she is injured.

I hold her wrists but she is breathing heavily and panting like a wild tigress. I hold her until I feel the resistance drain from her body. The fight in her has gone. I lift the sleeve of her cotton shirt and her forearm is purple and yellow and marked by needles.

'Is Nikos dead?' I whisper and when I release my grip on her, she rubs her hand through her dishevelled hair. Her eyes are glazed.

'I was beautiful once. He wanted me....' She leans against the wall and sinks to her knees sobbing. 'I was young and beautiful...' she continues speaking in Greek so I step over her legs and follow Lisa and Lily into a large room. A king-sized bed and opaque mirrors are on the ceiling. Cameras have been set up in each corner and it tells me all I need to know.

That's when I feel the tip of icy cold metal pressed hard against the warm skin on my neck.

'Move and I'll kill you.'

Chapter 14

'It is frequently a misfortune to have very brilliant men in charge of affairs. They expect too much of ordinary men.'
- Thucydides, Historian of the 4th century BC.

'**M**ove!' Nikos jabs the gun hard into my cheek and grabs my collar propelling me onto the bed where the girls sit with dead, robotic smiles, barely moving like rigid statues on either side of me. His eyes are filled with fury and a makeshift bandage is wrapped around his head like an Indian turban. He's breathing heavily and is agitated.

'Where's the Torah?' I ask.

He ignores me and shouts something in Greek into the corridor and Anna appears in the doorway. He pushes her into the room and a small wail escapes her lips as she sinks to the floor at our feet.

'I promise you, Nikos, I'm going to return that Torah to the museum.'

'And princess, I promise you, I'm going to have you and if it's against your will then so much the better.'

'Was it Cristina's body in the fire?' I ask.

The girl in the kimono gasps and pulls her knees up to her chin. She says something in her own language but Nikos fires the gun. It's a muffled sound with a silencer and a puff of plaster falls from the wall above our heads and she screams.

'The police are on their way,' I shout.

He laughs. 'Nice try but there are not enough police on the island, princess. They are all at the villa. Sorry, no-one is going to rescue you.'

He calls to the girl in the kimono and barks instructions. The girl ties my wrists together behind my back and pushes me face down onto the bed so I'm lying on my stomach. She leads Anna meekly to the iron headboard and clicks handcuffs to her hands. Then following Nikos instructions she does the same with the other girl. Then she ties her own feet with rope. After she's finished Nikos ties knots around her wrists and even though her kimono falls apart he doesn't take his eyes from me or the gun from my face.

The girls barely look thirteen and they try and cover their semi-naked bodies hunching their knees against their chest.

I lift my head and twist around. 'The Torah, Nikos. Where is it?'

He rips the silk purple kimono from Lisa, revealing a patterned bra and black lacy pants. He laughs when she squeals.

'The Italian arrives in a few hours, you don't have to play these games,' I shout.

'Games?' he smiles.

He stands behind me and I feel his legs straddling mine. He places the gun under my chin. 'Princess, this isn't a game. This is your...due.'

'I'm not scared of you.' I reply. 'They know I'm here.'

'It's your turn, princess,' he says ignoring me. 'I love an audience, don't you Mikky? I'm going to fuck you so hard, you'll be gagging to tell me how you know all about the Italian.'

He reaches for his fly.

'No chance.' I say through my gritted teeth. My cheek is pressed against the mattress but I twist my neck to watch.

A flicker of annoyance crosses his face. 'Come on, princess. You've ruined everything. Now this is my moment. It belongs to me – it's payback time.'

He tugs the waistband of my jeans and I roll to one side kicking out but the knots tighten and I curse aloud as his laughter echos around the room.

The girls look at me with a mixture of fear, pity and curiosity as Nikos places the gun on the floor and pulls a knife from his waistband.

'I'll cut you, princess.'

His blade cuts my arm, slicing through the tattooed canvas of the screaming face in Scream. Blood pours down my hand between my fingers and when he thrusts again I duck and roll but he grabs my hair and twists my head, holding the pointed blade under my chin. He drags me onto my knees then, with his right hand holding the knife, he uses his left hand to unzip his trousers.

'I've got something for you.'

He tugs back my head and I scream.

His crotch is in my face and his iron grip is like cement. I cannot move. He unzips his jeans and takes out his swollen penis.

There's a sound behind him. His arm goes slack and he releases his grip. I fall to one side and roll away jerking my head around to see the Albanian has slipped a wire noose around Nikos' neck. He leads him to the bed and pushes him face down, expertly tying his hands. When Nikos struggles the wire rips into his skin and he curses. His jeans are still hanging around his knees and his erection has disappeared.

In one deft movement the Albanian slices the rope tying my hands and feet.

'I got your message,' he says.

'I didn't know you would come.'

'You've got the Torah?'

'Not yet.'

I struggle to my feet and grab the knife from the Albanian's hand and press the blade against Nikos's flaccid dick.

'Last chance,' I hiss. 'Where's the Torah?'

I find a small room with only a desk and chair, and a blue folder stuffed with Greek documents and a cylindrical tube. While I'm out of the room the Albanian works quickly and by the time I have returned Nikos is laying on his back on the bed. His feet and hands are tied reminding me of a star fish.

'What are you going to do?' Nikos lifts his head from the bed and continues to laugh, taunting me, making empty threats. 'I'll have you one day princess, I promise you. You won't kill me – you won't get away with it.'

I lean over him and whisper:

'Killing you would be so easy but there is something much more effective for men like you.' I pat his cheek and he wriggles uncomfortably. 'There's a cure to take the wind out of your sails and the passion from your loins. It's handy that my friend here knows all about surgery – well, I hope he does. I'm trusting him to do a very delicate operation on you, but hey ho, if he botches it up then it won't be so bad. Of course, you might bleed to death but you don't deserve any sympathy. A man like you is beyond redemption. Hopefully castration will cure your passion.'

'You can't – Elias will–'

'It will be too late by the time Elias finds out.'

The Albanian stuffs Nikos' left sock in his mouth and tapes it closed.

Nikos's eyes open wide in horror and although he looks a pathetic figure with a bloody bandage around his head and only one sock on his foot I have no pity for him.

'It's what you deserve, Nikos. You've always said you're above the law and that Elias would never believe me. So, think of this as divine retribution. Think of me as the devil.'

I turn to the Albanian.

'You'll clean the room and leave no trace?'

'It's what I do.'

I leave the room with my shoulders straight and my head held high knowing Nikos is watching my back. With me are Lisa, Lily and Anna but more importantly I hold the Torah in my arms.

Nikos's Mercedes is still where I left it, parked up against the wall so I usher the two girls and Anna inside the car. I negotiate my way through the narrow streets with the window down. Warm air circulates around us and a cool sea breeze blows on my face as we take the coast road south. The girls are silent and when I glance at Anna sitting beside me, her eyes are closed. She appears asleep or exhausted, as if she's given up.

Elias and Athena's villa is covered with pretty bougainvillea, yellow roses and early white jasmine. The sweet scents relax my shoulders and the tension eases in my neck. I'm exhausted but wired. Instead of shouting up at the windows like I did last night, I stand on the step and politely ring the bell.

Elias answers the door. He's dressed in a grey suit and his mouth opens in surprise.

'Come on.' I usher the two girls and Anna in front of me, guiding them toward the dining room - the room where we first saw the Torah.

'What are you doing?' Elias protests. 'Anna? Are you alright? What's happened? Where's Nikos?'

I ignore him and focus on Athena who is walking down the corridor toward us. She wears a beige skirt and jacket, and a curious look on her face.

'We heard about the fire, Mikky. Elias has been trying to find you. Anna? What's happened? Where's Nikos?'

I push open the dining room door and guide the girls in ahead of me.

'Sit here,' I say softly and the girls obey. They look young, frightened and insecure amidst the heavy furniture, beautiful paintings and tasteful artefacts. The framed picture of the four generations of women momentarily takes my attention.

'Anna?' Athena cries, 'What happened to you?'

I ignore her and say. 'These girls were brought over here a few months ago. They're Romanian.' I pull up their sleeves one by one. 'Nikos has them hooked on drugs but it's not too late to sort them out. They'll need help - and they'll also need a job or repatriation to their own country. They need to go back to their families.' I look at Athena. 'You're a lawyer. You will know the right people. I'm sure you'll make your husband do the right thing. Anna also needs help. She needs someone to look after her properly.'

I turn to leave but Elias steps in my way.

'What is all this, Mikky? What's happened? You can't just leave these girls here, without any explanation. Where's Nikos?'

I face him squarely then I hear Anna's heavy sobs behind me.

'What happened, Anna?'

Athena pulls Anna to her breast in a warm embrace. She speaks to her softy in Greek, soothing her hair and trying to look into her eyes but Anna doesn't reply. She leans against her aunt, closes her eyes and cries with silent tears.

'What happened to her?' Athena asks again looking at me.

'Nikos set fire to Yannis' yacht. He also set fire to my rented car. Anna wanted to take the blame for him. She thinks that's what families do when they love each other – amongst other things.'

Elias looks at Anna and then at me.

'Where's Nikos?' he growls. 'What happened at the villa?'

'The body in the fire belongs to another poor girl – not Cristina the girl Nikos brought to Arianna's engagement party – she was swapped to get the Torah to Rhodes. But I think it might be the body of another young Romanian girl. Nikos will have to speak to the police. He has a lot to answer for.'

'It's you they want to speak to. You've created mayhem in the past few days. I can't believe you are blaming–'

'You can't! How do you think I feel?' I shout angrily. 'Nikos tried to shoot my hand with a speargun, then he set fire to my rented car and he almost scared me to death doing somersaults in his gyrocopter. He's tried to kill Yannis and at least one girl is dead – so, ask yourself why?' I bang the table with my fist.

'It wasn't in my interest to do any of those things, Elias. I had nothing to gain. And why are you so blinkered about him anyway?'

My question hangs in the air.

'Where did you find these girls?' Athena's voice is low and measured.

'At the house Nikos bought in the old town - the one he wants to turn into a boutique hotel. He's been using it as a brothel. If you bothered to go there you'll see he has one of the bedrooms tarted up with cameras and mirrors-'

'I don't believe you.' Elias protests but Athena holds up her hand and replies.

'They can stay here and we will sort this out. Elias, let's call the police and tell them what we know.'

She hugs Anna and kisses her forehead, glareing at Elias she adds sternly: 'WE will sort this out. It's our duty.'

Anna snuggles up to her aunt. Her sobbing has subsided but she still doesn't open her eyes.

'Is there anything else?' Athena asks.

'Nikos will come back soon but he may be very sore. It might be best not to ask him too much.'

I find the Albanian sitting in the car, stony-faced and staring at the three restored medieval windmills overlooking the entrance to Mandrake harbour. It's late afternoon, still warm and I hang my arm out of the car window relishing the warm breeze on my skin.

The Italian businessman's twin masted yacht sets sail. The professional, uniformed crew busy themselves untying the ropes and tossing the buoys onto the deck. It's an expensive yacht, one of the biggest in the marina and I can't help but admire its sleekness as it glides between the smaller berthed boats toward the open sea.

'No sign of Nikos?' I ask.

He shakes his head. 'None at all.'

I am reminded of Yannis lying in intensive care and I know that when I leave Rhodes I will fly to Athens to see him.

'The Italian is sailing to Lindos to meet with friends for a late dinner,' the Albanian says. 'He didn't get what he came for.'

'Not this time but men like him never stop looking for these opportunities.' I don't add that I've come across a lot of millionaires like this Italian businessman and nothing fazes them. They are soon looking for the next stolen artefact, bribing corrupt officials and taking advantage of an illicit black market.

I turn in my seat to look at the Albanian. The scar on his forehead is healing but it will be a constant reminder of Mariam and the Torah. Unlike the scar I once had on my head, he probably won't have cosmetic surgery to remove it or cover it up.

'What did you do to Nikos?'

'I scared him.'

'What do you think he will do?'

'Who knows but it will take an unusual man to come back from the fear I put into him. Albanian Mafia is famous the world over and he knows it. I saw the fear in his eyes.'

'I wish you'd castrated him.'

He smiles. 'That would make you as bad as him. Is that what you really wanted?'

'I have a feeling that he'll wriggle out of everything. He'll blame Anna – or he'll lie so convincingly that the police and Elias will believe him.'

'You have little faith in justice.' His lips twitch into a hint of a smile.

'I have no faith at all.'

He seems happy to digest what I've said and we watch the tip of the Italian's mast as it finally disappears completely from view and I take a deep breath.

'We averted a cultural heist,' I smile, reminding myself to text Simon.

'It's over,' he replies.

'Not yet, you said the donor would tell me who framed Dino Scrugli?'

'He's a Chinese man, Wy Humung. He's based in Singapore but flies around Europe buying and selling. He's often been a guest on Dino's yacht. He was one of his guests last summer.'

'How do you know it's definitely him?'

'He's supplied the Archaeological Museums in Rome, Krakow and Poznan with fake artefacts. He forged a bronze bust and the Krakow Archaeological Museum paid a fortune for it. He also sold fake Han Dynasty Ceramics to the American Museum of Natural History in New York.'

I stare at a smaller excursion yacht leaving the harbour. I'd heard of the collection and now it triggers a memory of my visit to the Museum in the Big Apple, only last week with Eduardo, when I was excited at the prospect of my own art exhibition and filled with my own eager and expectant dreams. That was before I knew about Mariam, or met Alexandros, Milos and Dorika. I hadn't known Stelios or Elias and Nikos and I had no idea about the strange Albanian sitting beside me either.

He speaks slowly and softly. 'I got to know Mariam quite

well on the journey through Turkey. She was funny, attractive and intelligent. I'm just sorry I couldn't do more to save her-'

I reach over and grip his fingers and I'm surprised by the strength of his hand as he squeezes me in return.

'Let it go. Think of everything you've done since then to help.'

'What's your name?'

'Ioannis,' he smiles.

'Come with us tomorrow morning, Ioannis. Meet me at my hotel at nine o'clock. Alexandros is coming over with Milos and Dorika. I'm sure you understand why it's important that they take the Torah back to the museum with me.'

He shakes his head. 'I can't, Mikky. I'm sorry. I couldn't face them.'

He seems resolute and there isn't anything else for me to say so with reluctance I open the car door.

'I thought you were going to ask me who the anonymous donor is,' he whispers.

'There's no need. I've already worked it out.'

Saying goodbye to Stelios isn't so easy. For some reason my words can't come out. I'm tongue-tied and choked with emotion. How could I have doubted his intentions? He had been recommended by Simon and I should have trusted him. He's a gentle giant and I feel that I should apologise. I have to stand on tiptoe to kiss his bearded cheek and we both laugh.

'I hope your wife is tall?'

'The opposite. She's very small but we muddle along quite well.'

He pulls out his phone and shows me her photograph. 'She

took it, this morning. They were waiting for me at the airport.'

She is petite and smiling, and he flicks the screen to another image of her holding a tiny baby.

'She looks adorable,' I say.

'I wish you'd let me take one last look at the Torah,' he says, pocketing his phone and hitching his rucksack over one shoulder.

I shake my head. 'I can't. It's in a safe place. Let's leave it well alone.'

'I thought you would have taken it straight to the museum.'

'I made a promise to Dorika and Milos and I've phoned Alexandros. They're meeting me first thing in the morning. We shall take it to the museum together.'

'That's a lovely thing to do.'

'I think Mariam would approve and I feel that her death will not have been in vain. I am hoping it might even be closure, if not for the children at least then for Alexandros.'

'That file you found will be invaluable to the police. It showed all the financial records he kept. He recorded the girls and other illegal workers. You were right Mikky, he was human trafficking.'

'I'm pleased it's of some value and it will provide evidence against him. I saw it when I took the Torah. I guessed it was important but it was all Greek to me,' I grin.

'You did the right thing giving it to the police.'

I sigh and suppress a yawn. 'Well, I hope they will charge him. He deserves to be in prison.'

'I called Elias while you were making your police statement. He told me that Nikos hasn't shown up yet but he has spoken to him. He said Nikos is on his way to the police station and he's handing himself in.'

273

'What about Yannis and the girl who died in the villa?'

'He told Elias that it had nothing to do with him – he said that Anna did it. She set the villa and the yacht on fire.'

I shake my head. 'Will we ever find out the truth?'

'Does it matter? I think something good came of it all in the end. You saved the girls and Anna – and you got the Torah. You're quite a torrent of energy, Mikky. You're a female James Bond. I'm sorry I couldn't keep up with you.'

'Stelios,' I squeeze his arm. 'You've been a good friend. You called the police, you've liaised with the archaeological museum and Interpol and besides, first and foremost, you're a husband and a father. That's the main thing in life – all of this, all these other things – everything else is just stuff – possessions...'

'And what about you, Mikky? Are you any clearer on your future? Are you going back to Eduardo?'

The ring twinkles on my finger and I smile. 'Maybe.'

'Invite me to the wedding,' he laughs and kisses me goodbye. He looks more like a hippy than an archaeologist. He throws his rucksack into the taxi and climbs in beside it.

I wave at the car until he disappears and I'm left alone outside the walled city staring at the harbour. It seems much longer than four days ago since we sailed out from here on Yannis' yacht.

It's all over.

I won.

I punch the air with my fist and laugh.

I got the Torah and Anna and the girls are safe. With a spring in my step I know there is one last task for me to do.

I stroll through the busy streets alone. I'm exhausted but happy. I will phone Eduardo. I need to hear his voice. The events of the past few days have left me knowing what I want and knowing how vital Eduardo is in my life.

I'm ashamed of my outburst last Friday when Eduardo proposed to me in New York. How could I be so unfeeling and insensitive? It is the city where dreams are made - he made my dream come true by proposing to me and I must apologise and tell him. I can only attribute my bad behaviour to stress. After losing Carmen last year and coming to terms with the events that happened in Malaga - I shut myself away and painted my nightmares on canvas. But they are gone now.

That was my past life. Now it's time to move on into the future.

Eduardo is my life.

There's a lightness in my heart that I haven't felt before and inside my head I'm singing. I pass under the buttresses and remember how Stelios explained that they hold up the buildings in case of earthquakes and I think of Mariam and Ioannis and how they suffered in Turkey.

I dodge a black cat and smile at a waiter tending to his cage bird on the taverna wall and for the first time my stomach isn't knotted with fear and conflicting emotions brought on by Nikos. The nausea that has invaded me for the past few days has disappeared and I'm happy and light-hearted. I'm excited about tomorrow, and meeting Alexandros and Milos and Dorika. I imagine her green eyes and dark hair - an older version of Mariam - a woman I have thought about constantly all week.

I remember watching the children on the beach as they stared out across the sea to Turkey. Their expressions filled with confusion, bewilderment and sadness. Their loss can never be replaced. Like a ripened fruit it will change colour and Mariam's memory will fade. Her voice will become a distant sound, her touch a fleeting whisper and her laughter a happy thought.

They will grow up and have their own lives, each dealing with their loss, supported by Alexandros but if they know that her death was not in vain, and that the task their mother set out to achieve has been completed then her legacy will live on. None of this will have been for nothing.

I made my vow to them and I haven't let them down.

I start singing, I Can't Get No Satisfaction, and I play air guitar across the shady square and duck down the side-street, skipping and twanging my invisible strings.

I'll take a shower, have a nap and dine in the hidden court-yard of my hotel. I'm suddenly hungry and I'm thinking of succulent slow-roasted lamb when I see Anna's old blue Fiat parked up against the stone wall. I slow my step and glance inside.

A hand covers my nose and mouth. I struggle and kick but the body behind me is muscular and hard. A cloth covers my face and a strong sweet smell of pungent ether fills my senses.

Then there's nothing.

Chapter 15

'At his best, man is the noblest of all animals; separated from law and justice he is the worst.' - Aristotle, Philosopher of the 5th century BC.

I'm barely conscious when I'm dragged out of the car. Nikos is not gentle or kind when he lifts me like rag-doll and throws me into a bucket-seat. My stomach tightens with fear. I don't know how much time has passed but in my hazy subconsciousness I'm aware of an engine shuddering to life. My chest contracts. We're moving, propelled forward, and my insides go into convulsions. I'm shaking. I open a bleary eye to see the ground below me disappear, falling away and my gut lurches and that's when a dribble of sick falls from my mouth and into my lap.

The whine of the engine reaches a frightening pitch. The gyrocopter is blown and buffeted against the wind and I rock and sway banging my head against the perspex window. My neck hurts from hanging loose on my chest and I'm groggy and nauseous. I'm uncomfortable but I cannot move. My hands are tied and my legs are weak. I try to focus. My forehead is pressed against the cold window and all I see below me are blurred fields, small houses and thousands of olive trees.

It's the detail in the cockpit I notice. Stupid things. The way

Nikos's thick fingers grip the joystick and the way his nose tilts in my direction as he shouts.

Without headphones I don't hear him. My ears hurt and my head thumps. I can't focus or concentrate. I can only swallow the sickness erupting in my throat and choke and cough.

We land heavily and the gyrocopter bumps along the ground. My head and stomach are colliding worlds and when Nikos opens the door and drags me out by my leather jacket I'm violently sick on the ground, kneeling in soft sand, retching and spitting. The sea is only a few metres away and the cold breeze, although reviving, makes me shiver.

Nikos curses and handles me roughly, pulling me into the sea. I stumble with him but he kicks me and I yelp like a beaten dog. He wades knee high into the water, dragging me behind him and when the sea splashes my jeans, I scream with the cold. I think he might drown me but he puts his hand between my legs and heaves me up onto a floating craft. My face smacks against wooden planks and I struggle to sit upright but I have no strength.

He pulls the chord, the motor roars and suddenly we are out at sea. I am too weak to move. I struggle to see where we are going. The salty sea spray flies into my eyes so I close them and feel myself drifting off to sleep. I can't stay awake.

Strong hands are under my arms. I'm dizzy and my head is thumping and I'm pulled, hauled and dragged roughly up the side of a boat. I hear men's voices but I can't understand them - they're not Greek - they're speaking another language - Turkish?

I'm dragged across a wooden deck, pushed down a few steps and thrown into a tiny cabin. When I bang my head on the doorframe I cry out but the hard mattress is welcoming. It embraces me with the promise of gentleness but it stinks of cat wee and I gag. Behind me the door bangs closed. I am alone with only the soft lulling motion of the yacht rocking me to sleep.

When I open my eyes it's dark but there's a strip of light coming from under the door. I stretch and move slowly, my body weak and unstable. My binds have been cut. My hands and legs are free and I hold onto the frame walking unsteadily but the door is locked.

I rattle it, banging the wood with my fist but no-one comes near me. I feel my way around but there's nothing. Even the light bulb is missing from the socket and it appears there's only a mattress in the small space.

I sit huddled up with my knees at my chin, conscious of the swell of the sea beneath the hull of the boat. There's a scratching sound and it's very near me, then something touches my leg. 'Shit!' I stand up banging my head on the low ceiling.

Miaow.

There's a soft purr. I reach down in the darkness, hold out my fingers and a cat rubs itself against my hand.

'They've locked you in too, have they?' I whisper and sit back on the bed. The cat jumps onto my lap and kneads my jeans with its claws. It feels malnourished and skinny. I stroke the cat conscious of the heat, the overpowering stench and the rocking boat. It snuggles against my leg and my nausea gradually subsides. I concentrate on the events and try to remember what happened.

Anna's car was outside my hotel but I left her with Athena. Nikos must have used chloroform to get me here. Nikos must have driven me to the hangar where the gyrocopter was stored and we flew to a beach then onto this boat.

But where?

Who did the foreign voices belong to?

Who owns this boat?

There's a thud outside like a smaller craft has banged against the hull and then footsteps overhead. Someone has boarded the yacht. The steps echo and I'm suddenly alert. The cat straightens up and leaps off my lap and lands on the floor with a soft thud.

My body tenses and when the door opens I'm blinded by sunlight. I squint and rub my eyes. All I see is the vague burred outline of a man.

'Water,' I say. 'Can I have some water?'

He grabs my upper arm and pulls me up the steps. I trip and fall onto the deck banging my knees and elbows.

Nikos stands in front of me. His wild eyes are dark-rimmed. He's taken off his turban bandage and his hair is matted with blood but he's changed into a clean denim shirt.

'Where are we?' I look around.

I'm on a wooden two-masted gulet, probably thirty metres in length. Red sails are furled up against the two masts and the wooden decking is no longer laminated but scratched, uncared for and cracked. What would once be a luxury yacht is now my prison.

We are anchored in a secluded bay but there are no lights on the land. The sun is setting leaving a multicoloured sky on the horizon and the breeze is turning cooler. I inhale lungfuls of air as if I've been starved of oxygen.

'Sit there.'

He points to a rickety wooden director's chair and I obey him, leaning forward with my head between my knees cursing my own weakness, willing my body to be strong but it won't obey me. The boat rocks gently and I think I may faint. I pull in the muscles of my stomach and dig my nails into the palm of my hand.

Pain would be better than losing consciousness.

'I'm going to speak and you are going to listen.'

Nikos pulls my hair and lifts my face up to his.

'This is your only chance, Mikky, so listen very carefully. I want the Torah and you are going to give it to me. Where is it?'

I stare blankly at him wondering if he looks as bad as me.

He slaps me in the face. The pain is excruciating and I fall off the chair wondering if he's broken my nose. I lie on the deck with my face throbbing. I want to cry.

Nikos leans over me.

'There is no-one to help you this time. No foreigner – no knife wielding maniac is going to suddenly appear and rescue you, princess. No-one knows where you are but me. You're not going to be rescued. So, unless you tell me what you have done with the Torah this will get very unpleasant. You will tell me – sooner rather than later, princess. I promise you and I always keep my promises. I've got a lovely assortment of drugs that will make you tell me everything. You'll be screaming so hard – you'll think you've got spiders crawling all over you – you'll not know who you are by the time I've finished. So, get up.'

He pulls me by the arm and shoves me back into the chair.

'I'm waiting,' he says.

I gaze at him and when I speak my voice is raspy and it hurts my throat. 'I need water.'

'You're not getting anything until you tell me.'

'Is it for the money – or is there another reason?'

He slaps me hard on the side of the head and my neck recoils.

'I don't have to explain anything to you, bitch.'

'Is it because your father never gave you the attention as a child – or is it because he lost all the family money on failed business deals?'

He leans over me. 'You're not even worth fucking any more.'

'Does the money make up for the fact that your mother was a whore at the golf club?' I spit.

His hands bunch into fists and I wait for the blow but instead of hitting me he kneels beside me. His face is level with mine and he spits when he says, 'I've the perfect cocktail for you, princess. It won't take me long to prepare.'

He grabs my wrists and ties me around the waist with thick rope then drags me to the main mast. His smile is crooked and his eyes hard.

'You'd better finish me off Nikos, because if I get off here – everyone will know what you are really like. And they'll believe me.'

He leans into my face and his breath is rank. 'No, they actually won't. They don't believe Anna or those Romanian sluts. I told Elias I was helping them find a job and he believes me. I told him I rescued them. He knows I'm a good person. A kind person. There's nothing you can do, Mikky. You're a liar.'

'What about the villa? What about Yannis? I gave them the folder,' I shout.

'I told them it was Anna's. The folder isn't incriminating.'

'What about the dead girl in the villa?'

'She was a friend of Anna's.'

'The other Romanian girls knew her – they knew Cristina too.'

He laughs. 'The police won't find anything out. Besides the

girls won't be talking to anyone for a while. They're too scared. They know I'll find them.'

'They're safe now.'

'I know people, Mikky. I know people who will make sure they don't speak - ever.'

'Athena promised-'

'Athena? What does she know? She'll do what Elias tells her to do. Before you know it the girls will be shipped off to Athens - puff - gone - just like that.'

'Just like Cristina? What have you done with her?'

'Not me, she was on here with the boys. I don't know where she is.'

'You're a bastard, Nikos. You're a nutcase. A psychopath.'

He smiles, 'Call me what you like princess. You're a liar. You're powerless, helpless and quite frankly useless. Why you came to Rhodes is beyond me, or wait, maybe it's because you're the screwed up one. The girl who can't commit to a relationship. The girl who's fucked everyone and taken drugs but had a scary, scary upbringing. The girl who has to tattoo her body...'

He pulls my T-shirt at the neck and rips it open.

'Well, look at this. What a colourful portrait.... St John the Baptist no less and all that blood over your tits - how perfectly awful. How revolting. What do you do? Choose all the bad boys who treat you badly or are you a frustrated lesbian, Mikky? No, don't answer me. It'll take all the fun out of my little cocktail party. I'll be able to ask you lots of things in a minute. I might even video you. It's quite funny to see someone losing their inhibitions. The Turkish boys will be back after a night out. They are drinking in the harbour and they'll come back very drunk and argumentative and very, very horny. Perhaps you

283

like sucking cock? With your pretty mouth and those lips you'll be very good at it.'

He pats my cheek and walks away then as an afterthought, he suddenly comes back to me.

'Sorry princess, I forgot my manners. I will get you a drink but there's no hurry. Are you quite sure you don't want to tell me what you've done with the Torah? I've checked everywhere, you haven't taken it to the Jewish museum. Where is it?'

I shake my head.

'No worries, princess. I can wait.'

He disappears and leaves me tied up to the mast. My legs are aching and my back is arched against the solid mast. If I relax my body the rope cuts into my skin.

Crouched in the corner of the deck the black skinny cat watches me. It leans forward on its haunches, not moving, not blinking and eventually I close my eyes.

It gets dark and cold. I wait and wait. The pains in my legs and my body cause me to drift in and out of consciousness and I try and concentrate, studying the stars in the night sky. My body feels numb and I sag against the rope but it burns my skin. The purring cat rubs against my ankles, waking me, and then very slowly the sky begins to lighten and dawn breaks in a beautiful soft hue of colour. The sun rises slowly but I have no idea of the time.

It could be four, five, six?

My mind is foggy. I know Alexandros, Milos and Dorika are coming to the hotel to meet me at nine o'clock.

How long will they wait?

Perhaps they'll ask the receptionist and call my room. I try and focus. I concentrate on Dorika's disappointed green-eyes when I don't appear. It will be like waiting for her mother and

I imagine Milos's grin fading under his mop of curly hair.

Will they think I've gone without saying goodbye?

Will they think I've stolen the Torah?

There's a noise below and Nikos appears from the cabin. His face looks creased as if he fell asleep and his voice is gruff. He carries a mug of coffee that smells delicious and he places a bottle on the deck. He cuts me loose but my knees give way and I sink to the floor. I have no strength left.

'You made a big mistake, princess. You left me with that knife-wielding maniac. I thought he was going to cut my balls off - but he didn't have the balls himself.' He laughs at his joke. 'So, let's have some fun before the boys come back.'

He waves the bottle in my face.

'Vodka. Thirsty? I bet you're dying for a drink now. This is good stuff Mikky, and guess what? I've got some goodies to go with it. Want some?'

I shake my head.

'Come on, princess. You didn't say no the last time we were on a yacht. I know how much you like a drink. The boys will be back soon. We're sailing at seven. Come on, drink up. I want you in the party mood, my princess.'

He grabs my neck and forces the bottle to my cracked lips.

Seven.

That's all I can think about. Even if there had been any chance of anyone missing me - it would not be until after nine when Alexandros and his children are meeting me at the hotel.

We are sailing at seven o'clock.

The sun is already hot on my skin. The bottle bangs against my lips. I keep them pressed firmly together and the Vodka spills down my torn T-shirt as I wriggle from his grasp.

He laughs.

'This is a good game, princess. There are lots more bottles and we have plenty of time besides, look what I have here. See this – do you know what it is?'

He waves a tiny vial under my nose?

'This is my friend. It originates in Colombia and the best thing about it is that it's tasteless, odourless and colourless – so you can slip it into any drink or put it on any food. It's amazing how they find out these things, don't you think? The other good thing is that it blocks any memory of what happened – so if you're gang-banged – or gang-raped – you won't remember a thing? Now that has to be positive, don't you think?'

I crawl away from him, pushing my knees up against my chest. He sighs then smiles and pats my thigh.

'Unlike a lot of date-rape drugs, it will be impossible for you to identify anyone afterwards. It comes from the borrachero tree, now you know what that means. The get-you-drunk tree – even the pollen sends you a bit crazy with weird dreams.' He makes circles with his index finger at his temple. 'And you won't even know you've taken it. Perhaps a little scopolamine hangover – but only a little one.' He holds the vial theatrically up to the sun and shakes it before pouring half of it into the vodka bottle.

'But it's not as bad as you think, princess. Would you believe, in Ecuador they use the alkaloid legally? You know, in medicines it's used to treat Parkinson's disease and even motion sickness. So, you won't feel sea sick on this yacht.'

He swills the liquid in the bottle mixing it with the clear vodka.

'Would you believe that this has been around for so long that Joseph Mengele - the angel of death - used it to interrogate people in the Nazi camps? I love knowing all these little facts, don't you?'

'You're nuts.'

'You won't be saying that in a little while, princess. Now, come on, time for you to have a drink. Let's celebrate.'

'Celebrate what?'

'What do you think, the Torah of course. You can give it to me and I will let you go. How about that for a deal?'

I shake my head. 'I don't have the Torah.'

'Now that is a lie.'

'It's true.'

'Where is it?'

'I gave it to Elias.'

He laughs. 'No, princess. Nice try. He would have told me.'

'I'm not drinking that, you'll have to kill me first.'

'Now, that IS a possibility and then all I have to do is throw you overboard, weigh down your body and no-one will find you. The fishes will eat you... yum, yum...'

He places his hand on my knee and I shudder.

'You know it could all have been so wonderful between us. I really did think that you were my perfect woman but then you had to ruin it. You mentioned the Italian and you wouldn't tell me, how did you know about him?'

'It was no secret. Simon Fuller emailed me.'

'How did Simon know?'

'He works closely with the FBI, Interpol, Europol and the International Culture Crime Police from around the world.' I'm trying to impress him.

He holds his arms out.

'So where are they all now? Where are all these imaginary policemen?'

'They'll find you. No matter what happens.'

He yawns. 'I'm getting tired now princess and the fun is going out of this game. All you have to do is tell me where you've put the Torah. You're a naughty girl. You haven't taken it to the Museum. Do you intend keeping it for yourself because you're prone to a bit of thieving aren't you?'

'No.'

'No? Well, never mind. Just tell me where the Torah is, then we can forget everything. I can take you back to your hotel and you can get on a flight and go back to Spain, to London or wherever it is that you want to go. Deal?'

'I don't have it.'

As quick as a lizard's tongue he grabs my throat. His fist clutches my neck and he rolls me over so I am lying flat on my back, staring up at the sky. His hand tightens and I'm choking. He pushed the bottle against my teeth forcing them apart and I feel the liquid dribbling down my throat.

There's a sudden thud against the yacht, we are jostled enough for the bottle to fall away from my mouth. He's distracted and I use that split second to pull from his grip and I roll sideways, gasping and, with my shoulder, I wipe my lips, spitting, coughing and retching to make myself sick.

The black cat hiding behind the mast eyes me warily.

Nikos leans over the side of the yacht and calls to me.

'Oh, princess. Good news! The boys are back.'

There's another thud against the hull as their dingy hits against the gulet. Men's voices and clunking footsteps up the steel ladder break the stillness and the gentle rocking of the yacht. The first man reminds me of a weathered fisherman. He has grey hair and hard lined skin. The second is ugly and missing his front teeth but the third one is younger and more frightening. He's stocky and very drunk.

They are play fighting and when they see me they move closer as if I'm a specimen worth looking at. The youngest one squints and tries hard to focus.

'They like you, princess,' Nikos smiles and pulls me into a sitting position.

The youngest one unbuckles his trousers and drops to his knees, kneeling he inches toward me but he's drunk and when he tumbles over the other men laugh.

'Grrrr - tiger,' he whispers and grabs my ankle.

He smells of body odour and alcohol.

'Get off.' I kick out.

He pulls a knife from his belt and waves it drunkenly in front of my eyes. He moves quickly and I'm no match for his strength. I'm weakened from lack of sleep, food and water. I cannot fight him but I try to scratch his face as he loops his belt around my throat. It's a tight collar and I cough and choke. He pulls me onto my knees so that I'm on all fours, like an animal, and I scream.

'Nikos, I'll tell you,' I shout. 'I'll tell you where the Torah is. Get him off me.'

'Tell me now princess, and then he'll let you go.'

'Let me go first. I'll take you to it. We can go together.'

Nikos laughs and folds his arms.

'You've no bargaining power, princess. Besides this is far too much fun. I think he wants to take you from behind. He's pretty determined. I won't be able to stop him-'

'Please Nikos, please–'

'Don't worry, princess. I've got my bottle of tricks for you. You'll be thirsty afterward. Would you like a slug now? It will be less painful for you.'

He leans over me and pulls my head back and holds the bottle over my lips.

The young one is behind me, pushing my thighs apart. He tugs on the belt and yanks me by my neck.

'Woof,' he growls laughing. 'Woof. Woof. GRRRRR...'

'Nikos. Please, I beg you...'

Chapter 16

'I know that each one of us travels to love alone, alone to faith and to death. I know it. I've tried it. It doesn't help. Let me come with you.' - Giannis Ritsos, Poet of the 20th century.

'Begging are we, princess? That's good. I thought I wouldn't get this opportunity. You're beginning to turn me on again. Maybe I'll go first.'

He kneels by my face and squeezes my cheeks forcing my lips to pucker and the leather belt cuts into my neck.

'I'll do you a favour - the more you drink the less you'll remember. You'll thank me afterwards.'

Memories explode in my head. My past comes flooding into my present. There's roaring, shouting and suddenly I'm screaming, flailing my arms like I'm demented, fighting for my life. I'm fighting for my dignity. For Mariam. For her children. For the Romanian girls. I'm thrashing and kicking and the young boy lets the belt go and falls drunkenly to to the deck giggling. His friends stand behind him laughing. The one with no teeth is so drunk he sinks to his knees, wiping his rheumy eyes. I struggle to my feet, lunging toward the railing and I'm about to throw myself into the sea but the older fisherman realises and he reaches out and grabs the swinging belt from my neck.

I kick out. I punch and push but the young boy pulls a knife and slashes my face. The blade sinks into my chin. I lash out knocking him off balance but he recovers quickly and with murderous intent he pulls the belt from the drunken man's hand.

An explosion rocks the yacht: fierce lights and an almighty bang.

I cover my head. 'Shit!'

In the sea there's the small whine of an engine and then a gun-shot. Ioannis is astride a jet-ski circling in the water. I pull myself onto the railing and prepare to hurl myself into the water but Nikos lunges and knocks me off balance and presses his full weight on my body.

'Going somewhere, princess?' His dark eyes gleam and I know I'll never get away from him alive. My strength is sapping. I'm exhausted and blood trickles from my face. His stale breath is in my face and I know he will kill me. I reach out, one last attempt and my fingers feel the glass vodka bottle. In the melee it's been kicked and it's now within my grasp. My fingers tighten around its thin neck and I lift it up and smash it into the side of his face. He screams, holding his hand to his bleeding face. I wriggle away from his body and kick him in the chest. He falls backwards and in one quick movement, using the last of my energy, I leap off the side of the yacht and into the sea.

The water is icy. My head is submerged. The salt water on my sores is unbearable and open my mouth in pain sucking in lungfuls of water. My legs can't kick. They have no strength. I'm paddling with my flaying arms but they don't seem to move. I'm under water holding my breath but my lungs are tight and they are about to burst when I finally rise to the surface. I'm choking, spluttering, breathing in lungfuls of air. It's torture and I want to cry.

Ioannis turns the jet-ski in my direction then his strong fingers grip my wrist and I'm surprised by his strength as he hauls me out of the water. I swing my right leg up and over the seat, falling against his back, grateful for his strength.

He turns the jet ski around as a gun shot rings out. He cries out and slumps forward. Blood is seeping from his shoulder. I reach around him and grab the handle but I miss and I slide off into the water again. I'm ducking my head against gunshots as I regain my footing and scramble back on. With one last burts of energy I grip the jet-ski handlebars and twist us away from the yacht accelerating so fast that I think my arms might be pulled off.

'Ioannis?' I shout loudly but he doesn't reply. 'Ioannis?'

His body is limp but then he stirs and groans.

'Ioannis, where are we?'

'Over there - head for that white building,' he mutters.

'Are you okay?'

'Just keep going and hope they don't follow us.'

I look over my shoulder but the yacht is already gaining ground.

I rest my chin on Ioannis's shoulder. I'm leaning forward as if I'm racing a motorbike, jumping and banging over the sea. The jet-ski hits the waves crashing against the water and my head thumps and bangs. My throat is parched but I'm concentrating, trying to keep Ioannis upright so he doesn't slide off.

'I'm not going there, it's too far,' I shout. 'We'll never make it.'

The gulet is gaining on us so I turn the jet-ski to the nearest point of land. There's a shingle beach and as we get closer I spot a small taverna and a rustic car park.

The yacht is coming faster. It is closing in on us. A gunshot whistles over my head. I send the jet-ski into a crazy zigzag path which I know will take longer but at least we won't be sitting targets.

Suddenly, a car appears over the hill and cruises slowly toward the beach and stops. A young couple climb out just as I ram the jet-ski onto the beach. I call and wave to them.

'You have to run, Ioannis. Come on. Help me. It's not far - maybe ten metres.'

I pull him into my arms but he slides to the ground. I'm shouting in English to the young couple. 'Please, we need your car. It's an emergency. He must go to hospital. It's urgent.'

The boy runs down and between us we half drag and half carry Ioannis toward the car. We bundle him onto the backseat and I jump in beside him, letting his head rest on my shoulder.

The couple climb into the front.

'Go!' I shout. 'Take us to the hospital. How fast can you drive?'

'I've always wanted to do this,' he replies with a hint of an American accent. 'This is much better than watching a romantic sunrise. Are those men chasing you?'

He guns the engine and sends a stream of pebbles flying in the air. The car skids off the beach and onto the tarmac.

The girl turns in her seat. She sees my ripped T-shirt and St. John the Baptist's severed head across my naked breasts and Salomé's colourful veils, my bleeding chin and bruised face and neck. My left eye is so swollen it's almost closed. She throws a few towels at me and I wrap one around Ioannis's shoulder and with the other I cover my nakedness.

Behind us the gulet has come to a standstill in the sea. Two of the men are standing on the deck of the schooner staring at us. There's no sign of the third man and as the car rises up the hill I have a better view. Nikos is on deck, holding a dressing to his bleeding face.

'We need to get him to the hospital,' I murmur under my breath and although Ioannis doesn't reply and his eyes are closed there's the hint of a smile on his face.

'What time is it?' I add.

'Eight fifty-five,' the girl replies.

'I need to be in the Old Town by nine.'

She laughs. 'You'll be lucky. We're on the other side of the island.'

.

In the Euromedica Hospital outside the Old Town a nurse has cleaned up my face and a doctor puts three stitches in my chin. The wounds on my face are stinging, one eye is swollen and almost closed, my neck is bruised and raw from the belt.

Ioannis' shoulder wound is cleaned and strapped. The bullet nicked the top of his arm but he will make a full recovery and when he appears in my cubicle his eyes are twinkling and I attempt a smile.

'I borrowed your phone,' I say. 'I called my hotel to give a message to Alexandros but I've a couple more calls to make.'

'That's fine.'

He sits beside me.

'The police are on their way,' he says.

'I'm not hanging around. You want to come with me?' I ask.

'I'm not letting you out of my sight until the Torah is in the museum,' he smiles.

'Come on then. Let's find a taxi.'

In the car, as we drive toward the old city, I call Josephine.

'Any news on Dino?' I ask.

'That Chinese name you gave me last night is checking out - they think you might be right, especially after that exhibition last week the ceramics being declared fakes. I remember reading about it. It was in the newspaper the night of your exhibition - in the Review. Do you remember?'

I vaguely recall the headlines: Han Dynasty Ceramics - Fakes.

'It's a scandal and I never imagined it could have anything to do with Dino,' she continues.

'Do you think his lawyers in Italy will get him out?'

'I hope so. I've passed on that information. So we can only hope. But what about you? What happened last night?'

'I'll let you know later.' I don't have the time nor the inclination to go into details of the events of last night on the gulet with Nikos. 'I've got to see someone now,' I add.

'I meant about Eduardo. Have you thought about him at all? You've treated him very badly, Mikky.'

'I know.'

'Don't think all men and marriages are bad. I loved your father more than any man I ever met and I regret nothing about our relationship, only that it didn't last longer, and he was thirty years older than me. We couldn't have had a life together. He was the father of the man I married. It wasn't anyone's fault that we fell in love. The scandal at the time in Ireland would have killed him as well as any hope of restoring my husband's business. But my biggest regret is not being there for you, Mikky.'

'I know.'

'Your father was a kind man and so is Simon Fuller. I'm lucky you introduced us. And Eduardo is also one of life's decent men. He has principles and morals and he's kind and loving.'

'It's not that.'

'Then what is it?'

'What if we separate one day? What if it doesn't work out?'

The taxi stops outside the gates and the driver waits expectantly. I gaze out of the window at the old palatial villa and beautiful gardens as Josephine's voice whispers in my ear.

'There are no guarantees in life. You can only work at your relationship. It's taken me years to figure that out. There's no sense in running, Mikky. You'll wake up one day and realise there's nowhere else to go and no-one is waiting for you. It happened to me.'

'But he wants a family,' I moan.

'And I would love to be a grandmother - but not at your expense. You must do what is right for you. I just hope you come to your senses and that you haven't lost Eduardo forever.'

'Wait here,' I say to Ioannis.

The sun is beautifully warm on my face and I spend a few minutes enjoying the peaceful solitude of the private garden realising it is already the first week of May. My face is beaten and bruised and my body hurts but I don't remember when I last felt so at ease and contented. It's pleasant and cool under the shade of the palm trees as I walk to the front door.

Athena answers on the first ring. Her lilac dress shows off

297

dark skin and long arms.

'My goodness, Mikky. What happened?' She opens the door and stands aside to invite me inside. 'Would you like something to drink?'

'Thank you, water.'

After being awake most of the night I am exhausted. My stomach is still queasy and it begins churning, turning mini somersaults.

She guides me to the back of the villa and I wait until she returns and places a glass of water on an olive carved, glass-topped table. We sit opposite each other on the matching white sofas. Her eyes travel over my biker's boots, torn T-shirt, leather jacket and blood-stained jeans.

'Did Nikos do that?'

'Him and a few others.'

She doesn't look away and continues to look at my bruises and swollen face. 'The police have Nikos in custody. They phoned just now. He was on the yacht with three other men of Turkish origin.'

I recline further into the comfortable sofa. I could sleep for days but I force myself to focus on her soft voice.

'Elias is still determined to do what he can for him. He is after all our nephew. He hasn't had the best upbringing. I'm not making excuses for him but his parents weren't great role models. That was one of the reasons why we were so keen to have him come here and work with Elias. We wanted to keep him out of trouble. Elias always wanted a son. Nikos often stayed with us in the holidays and they got on very well. We thought he was settled. You know, after he took his pilot's licence. He seemed happy working with the commercial airlines but he was always restless. He also liked the good things in life; expensive toys, cars and then the gyrocopter...'

She sips her water and seems to consider what to say next before she continues.

'I had no idea that he was... he was always charming and funny. I know he's young and he makes mistakes but he's also very clever and he works hard. He's innovative and inventive. Elias paid for his pilot's training and when he said he didn't want to do that any more and he wanted to go into the hotel business Elias was delighted. They found the old building together last year and Elias was helping Nikos with plans and designs and they were very excited.'

'Did you ever wonder where Nikos got his money?'

'He was paid well as a pilot.'

'Didn't you guess he was living beyond his means?'

'Elias gave him money. Elias spoils him. He feels as though he has to make up for his brother's failings...'

'How's Anna?' I ask.

'Damaged – emotionally – and also the drugs haven't helped. Our doctor has recommended treatment for her recovery....she will also need counselling.'

'Did she tell you what happened?'

'Yes. It was as if she couldn't stop.'

'Everything?'

'Yes, and I'm ashamed.'

Athena looks away, across the garden, but she's not seeing it. She's caught up in a conversation in her mind and I'd like to photograph the puzzled and sad expression on her face.

She slides a golden charm hanging from a thick chain around her neck nervously up and down then glances back at me.

'It's not the sort of thing you expect. Not in your own family. I'm sorry we didn't know sooner. I wish we could have done something.'

'Did Elias believe her?' I hold my breath and wait.

'Of course, he had no choice.'

'Where is she now?'

'She wanted to go home to her mother. Elias took her on the plane with him to Athens this morning.'

'Was your daughter friendly with Nikos?'

She barely pauses. 'I know what you're asking but no. He didn't touch her. He's eight years older than her and she's never really liked him. She avoided him whenever possible.'

'And the Romanian girls - where are they now?'

'In Athens. They are cousins. They will be joining their families next week.'

'Will they testify against Nikos? Or is repatriation part of the deal to keep them quiet?'

She looks away and I take her silence for consent and my anger rises.

'And what about Cristina - the girl he brought to your daughter's engagement party? Yannis told me Nikos swapped her for the Torah.'

'Elias will visit Yannis in the hospital this afternoon.'

She plays with the golden charm at her neck and rolls it across her lips. It caresses the skin on her chin then she tucks it into her blouse and turns to me when I speak.

'You know that Nikos followed Mariam, don't you. He found out about the Torah from a Syrian refugee who travelled out of Syria with the Torah. He was in Turkey...'

She stares at me and I return her gaze and the silence between us is palpable and I think she might speak but instead she turns away as I speak.

'He was lucky not to be killed in the earthquake. Ioannis,

Mariam's bodyguard, remembers someone in the wreckage. He thought he was going to help them but instead he took the Torah. Nikos stole it out of the car while Mariam lay dying.'

Athena covers her mouth with her hand and her eyes fill with tears.

'Don't you want to know where the Torah is?' I ask.

'You have it, don't you?'

'I'm taking it to the Jewish museum with Alexandros and his two children this afternoon.'

'Good. That's as it should be,' she smiles then checks her watch, stands up and holds out her hand.

'Thank you, Mikky. I'm sorry but I have another appointment.'

I don't move. Then I lean back and look up at her and say.

'I think you met Josephine Lavelle on a cruise around the Mediterranean.'

Athena tilts her head to one side and I continue speaking.

'She's my birth mother. She gave me up for adoption when I was a few days old thinking I would have a better life without her but my adopted parents drank heavily and bullied me.' I hold up my damaged and scarred hand. 'My mother tried to cut my face in one of her jealous rages but I've got over it. She's dead now and there's nothing that will shock me. So Athena, there isn't much that I can't understand in this life. Do you want to sit down again and tell me everything?'

'Everything?'

'You're the anonymous donor, Athena. So, tell me, why can't you tell Elias?'

She sinks back onto the chair clutching the gold chain at the base of her throat then she leans her elbows on her knees and cups her face in her hands. She speaks quietly and I have to lean forward to hear her.

'I suppose it's shame. My grandmother was born in 1917. Just before the war in 1936 she fell in love with a Jewish boy visiting his family on the island. She was Greek Orthodox so it would have been a difficult situation anyway but with all the rumours of the war and the Nazis gaining power in Europe, he left Greece and went to America. He changed his name to Jacob and he never returned. He never knew she was pregnant. So, my grandfather married my grandmother on one condition. He made her promise she would never tell a living soul. He promised to raise my mother as his own child just so long as she never contacted or met Jacob again.'

'Your grandmother married your grandfather but she loved Jacob?'

'They were at school together. He loved her and he had always wanted to marry her.'

'No-one on the island guessed?'

'That my mother was half Jewish? No.'

I remember the photograph in the dining room of the four generations of women. 'You have your mother's dark hair and almond eyes.'

'Many people don't have your photographer's eye. Fortunately, my grandfather only saw in my mother a daughter he loved. They were happy together. But when Mama was dying last year, in the last days of her life, she told me this story. She said it was her secret and one that, like her mother, she carried with her all her life. She even gave me a letter she received from Jacob after she tracked him down in America, after both my grandparents had died. Jacob said he was pleased to know he had a daughter. And just as my grandmother had kept the secret, Mama made me promise not to tell a soul.'

'So you found out last August that your mother was part Jewish – when Arianna wanted to have an engagement party.'

She stands up and walks to the edge of the terrace. 'I'm so angry with them all. I want to acknowledge Jacob – to claim the Jewish part of me. I know the history of the island and I know some of the Ladino Jews who settled here. Our family were friends with many of those who were deported and sent to Auschwitz. My grandmother could so easily have been one of those sent to the camps. Imagine – a pregnant woman with a Jewish man's baby. Had anyone known about my mother, I may not have been born at all, or she would have died in the camps with my grandmother...'

She pulls her charm from her throat and swings it on the chain.

'My grandfather had unselfishly and unknowingly saved us all – or in my mother's case – given her life. He also gave me life. After Mama died last year I realised there was nothing to recognise the fact that I am or could be a part of the Jewish community.'

'Did you ever feel a connection to the Jewish community?'

She blinks. 'Not really, I was born in 1967 and now there are very few Jews left on the island. On Rhodes we have learned to live with each other in harmony; Muslims, Christians and Jews. First and foremost we are Rhodians.'

'So, how did you know Mariam?'

'Shortly after my mother died I went to Athens. My mother had several properties that I was selling and I met Mariam on the flight. We were sitting beside each other and we started talking. We got on immediately. It was as if we had met before and we had known each other for years, only we hadn't. She told me she was a trained archaeologist but couldn't find work

303

on the island. She was going to the Archaeology Museum and she mentioned her friend, Simon Fuller, who lived in England. He was an eminent professor of transcripts and scrolls and she was going to ask him if he had any work for her. At the same time, through a colleague at work in Athens I had found out about a Torah in Syria. Like many other artefacts it had been looted by the IS to fund their terrorist campaign so I contacted a Syrian lawyer and he began negotiating a deal for me. It all had to be done rather quickly. Naturally I thought of Mariam. I thought she would be the ideal person to collect the Torah but I couldn't approach her directly. So, I asked the Syrian lawyer to contact Simon Fuller. I suggested it would be easy for someone from Rhodes to collect it in Turkey. So many looted artefacts are turning up in Greece from the Middle East and a colleague of mine deals with these things. It didn't take long for me to find it.'

'It's amazing what you can do when you have money,' I say. 'So you became the anonymous donor.'

'I couldn't shame Elias with my family secret. The sale of Mama's property was far more lucrative than I had anticipated so I decided to invest it in my heritage – in our heritage.' She pulls the charm from her blouse and begins to twist it, letting it uncurl quickly. 'But after the earthquake I knew Mariam had died in vain. The Torah disappeared and worst of all, I could never tell anyone. I didn't know what to do. It had been my secret.'

'And Elias thought you were grieving for your mother and cancelled Arianna's engagement party last year?'

'Yes.'

'So how did you feel when Nikos turned up with the scroll?'

'I was shocked. I couldn't believe it. Of course, it came out in the newspapers that Mariam had been killed in the earthquake and that she had been going to collect the Torah on behalf of the Jewish Museum but then when Nikos said he'd bought one from a Turkish antiques trader, I said immediately that it must be the same one. But he wouldn't have any of it and he got angry-'

'He saw a way to finance his boutique hotel.'

'At first I thought it was a coincidence. I assumed that once you and Stelios assured us that it was the same one that Mariam had gone to collect, he would hand it over. Unfortunately, like Elias, I believed Nikos was a good boy who, underneath it all, would do the right thing-'

'But he wasn't.'

She shakes her head. 'I hoped Elias would see through Nikos but he didn't. Even after he took the Torah on Wednesday. He wouldn't believe Nikos was bad.'

I remember the morning we verified the Torah. I had assumed they were all in agreement to keep the Torah for themselves.

'How did you know that I am the donor?' she asks.

'Because you told Ioannis about Wy Humung. You'd said he's based in Singapore but comes to Europe. He's often been a guest on Dino's yacht and when I spoke to Josephine, she told me he was one of his guests last summer - and so were you. That's when he purchased the Statue of Stalin. You've been asked to testify at his trial.'

She nods. 'Yes, that's true.'

'Only you knew that information.'

'I gave myself away.'

'Not really, Athena. I had guessed before that. I could never work out why Ioannis wouldn't just go and take the Torah from

Nikos. Someone was protecting him – and it wasn't Elias.'

'I didn't want Nikos to get hurt. I know that the Albanian is tough but I didn't want him to get rough with Nikos.'

'That's why you said you'd help with the Torah but not the sex trafficking.'

'It was so complicated. It was too much to believe. Mariam died and I feel so responsible. It was all my fault.' She rubs her forehead.

I shake my head. 'Mariam died doing something she wanted to do. You weren't responsible for the earthquake that killed her.'

She wipes her eyes with a tissue. 'So much has happened and I'm so sorry for everything. I wanted to do something to help but everything else has unravelled. It's all such a mess...'

'You sent Ioannis back to the hotel yesterday. You told him to follow me and to keep me safe. You found out about the gulet and that's how he managed to get me away. It's not a mess now. Come with me, Athena. Let's start putting everything right.'

'What do you mean?'

'I'm meeting Mariam's husband Alexandros, and her children outside the Museum. We're returning the Torah.'

The receptionist in my boutique hotel tactfully ignores my bruised face and torn T-shirt. She accompanies me along a narrow corridor to a backroom behind the reception where she opens a large safe.

Like Athena said, it's amazing what you can do with money and a donation. The boutique hotel has kept the parchment safe. Even with his arm in a sling Ioannis insists on carrying it for me. He walks between me and Athena through the streets, dodging tourists and shoppers, past the Martyrs Square in the Jewish Quarter to the Dossiadou and Simiou Streets.

Outside the unimposing building of the Kahal Shalom Alexandros and his children are waiting.

Milos high-fives me but it's Dorika who clutches my hand and my heart leaps at her gentleness.

'What happened to your face?' she asks. She reaches up and her fingers are gentle and soft. The tenderness of her touch and the care in her eyes creates a wistful feeling in the base of my heart and my tummy lurches. Then she looks at the package that Ioannis is holding.

'Is this the Torah? Is this what Mummy went to get in Turkey?'

'Yes.'

'Can I hold it?' ask Milos.

'It's heavy,' Ioannis says handing it to him. 'Can you manage?'

'I'm so sorry, Alexandros,' Athena whispers. They embrace and when they break apart there are tears in their eyes. 'Nikos was wrong. We should have done more to stop him. Perhaps after today we can talk privately?'

She slips her arm through his and I know that after I've left the island she will tell Alexandros the truth and the circumstances of why she became the donor.

'Come on,' I say squeezing Dorika's hand. 'Let's do it! This moment belongs to Mummy.'

A few days later, it's just after eight o'clock in the morning and I yawn loudly, conscious of my blackened eye and swollen

307

face. I'm about to swallow a couple of paracetamols when I change my mind, knowing it won't rid me of the nausea in my stomach that's creeping up my throat. I think back over the past week and the sickness that's followed me, blaming fear and burying the truth that nips at my heels like a nagging puppy.

I toss the small kit I purchased at the airport on the passenger seat then pull out my iPhone wondering what to say.

What's the best way to tell Eduardo the truth?

I type carefully, my hands shaking.

Me: Hola my angel, I miss you. XXX
E: Me too.
Me: I love you XXX
E: Me too.
Me: What time do you finish your shift? XXX
E: I'm leaving now.
Me: Do you miss me? XXX
E: When are you coming home? X
Me: I'm outside XXX

When I look up Eduardo is leaping down the steps of the hospital, two at a time, running and soaring like an angel. I climb out of the car and I can't stop laughing. I run toward him and fly into his arms and he lifts me into the sky and spins me around. His arms are strong and, like his love, reassuring. His smile is constant and I bury my face into his neck inhaling the familiar scent of his skin.

'Oh, madre de dios! Mikky. What happened to your face?'

He puts me down sharply on the pavement and I stagger away slightly off balance until he catches my arm.

308

The smile has drained from his face and his anxious eyes travel over me with all the experience of a trained intensive care nurse.

'It was an accident,' I reply.

He shakes his head and steps away from me pushing his hand through his hair. His dark eyes flash in bewilderment, he looks tired and sounds weary.

'Mikky, not again. This is crazy. I can't live like this–'

'It won't happen again. I promise, cariño.'

'You can't continue like this Mikky. I can't do this any more! How many times does this have to happen?'

I place my finger on his lips and whisper softly.

'I can't continue like this either, my angel, because of something far more important... I'm having our baby.'

THE END.

Janet Pywell's books:

Culture Crime Series:
Golden Icon – *The Prequel*
Masterpiece – book 1
Book of Hours – book 2
Stolen Script – book 3

Other Books by Janet Pywell:
Red Shoes and Other Short Stories
Bedtime Reads
Ellie Bravo

For more information visit:
website: www.janetpywell.com
blog: janetpywellauthor.wordpress.com

Coming Soon

THE FAKING GAME:

Book four in the Culture Crime Series features uncon-ventional heroine Mikky dos Santos, a protagonist who is brilliant, idiosyncratic and who does not always do the right thing.

A rare sculpture goes missing from Glorietta Bareldo's villa and Mikky dos Santos is on hand to investigate. Hot on the heels of the suspects, she's dragged into a labyrinth - an international network, financed by a billionaire who's determined to kill anyone who gets in the way.

But Mikky doesn't have time for games. Pregnant with her first child she fights against greed, jealousy and manipulative behaviour thereby risking the life of her unborn baby.

With a background in travel and a love of and fascination for other cultures Janet Pywell creates a strong sense of time and place, taking the reader to three exciting destinations...

Expertly researched, each book in the series gives a har-rowing glimpse into the hidden world of violence, greed and jealousy within the arts.

About the Author

Hello,

I was Director of a marketing company and I worked in the travel and tourism industry for over thirty years before writing full-time.

I am currently writing my first Culture Crime Series.

Having published two books of short stories and a romance, I am now working on a variety of writing projects including a comedy script, drama for theatre and a film script.

If you'd like to join my mailing list for information on new releases and updates on my work then please subscribe to my newsletter.

You can connect with me on:

🌐 http://www.janetpywell.com

🐦 https://twitter.com/JanPywellAuthor

📘 https://www.facebook.com/JanetPywell7227/

🔗 https://janetpywellauthor.wordpress.com/

Subscribe to my newsletter:

✉ https://www.subscribepage.com/janetpywell

Printed in Great Britain
by Amazon